EARTH TO KAT VESPUCCI

EARTH TO KAT VESPUCCI

Ingrid Anders

iUniverse, Inc.
New York   Bloomington

Earth to Kat Vespucci

Copyright © 2009 by Ingrid Anders

This is a work of fiction. All of the characters, names, incidents, organizations, and dialogue in this novel are either the products of the author's imagination or are used fictitiously.

iUniverse books may be ordered through booksellers or by contacting:

iUniverse
1663 Liberty Drive
Bloomington, IN 47403
www.iuniverse.com
1-800-Authors (1-800-288-4677)

ISBN: 978-1-4401-5263-4 (pbk)
ISBN: 978-1-4401-5265-8 (hc)
ISBN: 978-1-4401-5264-1 (ebk)

Printed in the United States of America

iUniverse rev. date: 7/13/2009

For my parents,
Regine and Richard,
without whom none of this would be possible.

CHAPTER ONE

Ivan

Unfortunately, it is love at first sight. I ignore his lascivious eyes upon me as I fumble to my seat in the crowded economy section of the airplane. I crane my neck in the direction of first class, casting a long, longing glance back to the section I just passed through and then I turn my head in the other direction, casting a longer, longing glance to the rear of the plane, scanning desperately for an open seat—any open seat but mine. In the shuffle, a flight attendant catches my eye and looks at me with a long face; for a moment, she seems as if she is about to tell me there is something she can do.

"I'm sorry," she shrugs. "There is nothing I can do."

Nodding, I heave my bag into the overhead compartment, climb over the nine-year-old in the aisle seat who is too engulfed in his cell phone conversation to notice, and sit down. My seat is smack in the middle of Moscow's delegation to the Little League World Series. Bouncing in the seats all around me are twelve of the cutest, pre-pubescent, Russian Little League baseball players I have ever seen. Bouncing in the seat in front of me is the crudest, post-pubescent, Russian Little League baseball coach I could possibly imagine.

He winks at me. I turn my head and hope that the row of seatbacks might serve as the impenetrable barrier that will hold us apart despite painful longing for each other. I am wrong.

As soon as the flight is in the air, the coach waltzes up to the aisle seat and unseats his player by jerking his thumb over his shoulder and barking, "*Von!*" The child disappears in a flash. The coach puffs out his chest, smiles at me, slides into the empty seat, and leans well into my personal space. He is a commanding figure, over six feet tall, but athletic-looking, with sandy blond hair, bright blue eyes, and deep ruts in his forehead and cheeks. As soon as he plants himself against me, he flags down the flight attendant and orders two glasses of vodka on the rocks.

"*Spasiba!*" he thanks her enthusiastically in Russian. "*Amerikanka,*" he turns to me. "Please. Allow me to treat you to this complimentary beverage."

"No, thanks," I politely respond, leaning away from him. "I had a long night last night."

"I'm Ivan Ivanov," he politely ignores my refusal. "And you?"

"Kat Vespucci." I extend my hand and, instead of shaking it, he slips the vodka into it.

"*Na zdarovye!*"

"What?"

"*Na zdarovye* means 'to your health' in Russian. It's like saying 'cheers.'"

"Oh," I answer. I'm not even going to attempt saying it. "Cheers!"

Ivan seems satisfied. "Kat?" he asks me after a long sip. "What kind of name is it?"

"It's a German name. Short for Katarina."

"German. I see. But Vespucci, that's—"

"Italian."

"Ha! I thought so! She's German and Italian!" Ivan exclaims loudly to the other passengers who are ignoring him. "Someone alert France!"

I roll my eyes and wait for him to laugh it off.

"Is that why you live in America? Because they kicked you out of Europe?" Ivan slaps his knee, really enjoying himself. His face is bright red and scrunched up with laughter.

I look away, hoping to find someone or something that can rescue me.

"I'm sorry," he says when he has finally calmed down. "By the way, I coach baseball."

"That's nice," I reply.

"You know baseball?"

"A little," I reply.

"You are an American genius! You know Little League World Series?"

"Yes."

"No! It is impossible."

"Yes, it is possible."

"How do you know Little League World Series, Katarina Vespucci?" Ivan asks, wide-eyed.

"Williamsport is not far from where I grew up."

"*Bozhe moy!* You are a smart *Amerikanka*. You even know where Little League World Series is played. We drink again."

"No, Ivan, I appreciate it, but I really don't want to drink."

"Nonsense! Who doesn't want to drink?"

"I don't."

"If that's what you want, then I drink two. Okay?"

I agree.

"Stewardess!" Ivan bellows.

The flight attendant in the gangway rolls her eyes to the ceiling and the drink cart back over to our aisle. This time Ivan orders three Bloody Marys.

"*Spasiba!*" he thanks her enthusiastically, and hands one to me.

"I thought you were drinking mine?" I hand the Bloody Mary back to him.

"That's where you are wrong, *Amerikanka*." He hands the Bloody Mary back to me. "I said, I drink two. But you must still drink one. A man cannot drink alone. You are very smart, Katarina Vespucci, but you have much to learn."

"*Spasiba,*" I say, resigning myself to a long flight. Ivan orders drink after drink and hands them to me. I pass them on to the Little Leaguers sitting to my right, who obediently drink them.

Eventually, it is time to eat. I am eager for a respite, hoping that food will occupy Ivan's mouth and allow me to have some peace and quiet. I am not so lucky. Ivan is so drunk by dinnertime that he continues talking, waving his fork in the air, sending missiles of salmon and capers sailing throughout the cabin. Disaster strikes when Ivan tries to open his salad dressing packet. I debate whether to assist him, but I am secretly enjoying watching him struggle with the intentionally well-packaged condiment. The confrontation ends when Ivan brings his fork down squarely in the middle of the packet, launching the oily contents onto his lap. It is a direct hit, and the victorious blob of oil, vinegar, and Italian seasoning seeps gloatingly into his Armani slacks.

"Don't worry," he grabs my arm with a look of serious reassurance. "I've been in this situation before."

"I'm not worried."

"I know how to handle it."

I try to ignore him.

"I bet you think water is the best way to clean up a mess like this, don't you Katarina Vespucci?" Ivan prods.

I scrunch my brow. I have never thought about the best way to clean up salad dressing from the lap of a Russian Little League coach sitting next to me on an airplane to Berlin before.

"Don't you?"

"Yes, Ivan, I suppose I think water is the best way to clean up a mess like that."

"No! It's not. It's not water."

4

"No?"

"It's *salt!*" he bellows. "Salt is the best way." Ivan orders the inebriated outfielders to stumble around the plane collecting salt packets from surrounding passengers. They hold their alcohol surprisingly well for pre-teens and are able to deliver the goods. Once Ivan has a handful of packets, he opens them up and, one by one, pours the white grains onto his lap. When he is done, he has a mini-Matterhorn.

"Just wait, Katarina Vespucci," Ivan says. He pats me on the arm, "There is nothing to worry about." He lets the mound sit for ten determined minutes and then with one glorious swoop, he brushes the pile off into the gangway. Sure enough, there is no stain left. The salt has absorbed the moisture of the salad dressing, and his Armani pants are clean.

"Well, how about that?" I am actually impressed.

"We drink to celebrate!"

I groan.

At some point, when the food is cleared away, the lights have been turned off, and a movie dances silently on multiple screens throughout the plane, I manage to fall into a light sleep. This is not before Ivan suavely offers me his salt-sprinkled lap to use as a pillow and is genuinely hurt when I do not accept.

"American girls!" he comments, shaking his head, "*Ya ne panimayu.*"

Instead of asking what that means, I close my eyes and pretend he isn't there. Five minutes later, I open my eyes and discover that he is indeed there, staring, only inches from my face.

"You awake, *Amerikanka?*"

"I am now."

"You want a drink?"

"You know what, Ivan? Fine. I'll have a drink. Make it a double."

CHAPTER TWO

Mrs. Vespucci

Tired and bleary-eyed, I finally touchdown in Berlin the next morning. My first glimpse of Germany is Tegel Airport, a flashy and modern facility, which stands in sharp contrast to the un-flashy and un-modern Newark Airport I took off from seven hours before. Fighting delirium, I plod my way through the gleaming corridors to the baggage claim area, collect my suitcases, schlep them outside to the taxi stand, and hail a cab, which is not yellow, but off-white.

"*Wo gehen Sie hin?*" asks the taxi driver. I hesitate before answering him. *Where am I going?*

"You know where I am going," I say to my ex-boyfriend over coffee at the diner after sleeping through church. "You don't have to keep asking."

"Okay, you're right. I know that you are going to spend senior year in Berlin," he replies. "I guess the real question I'm asking is, 'Why?'"

"What do you care?" I reply, and feel a little bit bad about my tone. I look down at the spoon I am using to stir my coffee so I don't have to look him in the eye. "I don't want to spend senior year in Berlin," I explain, softening my voice, "I want to spend it in London."

Matt actually looks pretty sexy today. I've always thought he was sexy; he's a big guy with dark hair, almond eyes, and an olive complexion. For some reason, I've found him even sexier since he broke up with me.

"Then why are you going?"

"Because my parents are paying for it, and they say that if I insist on leaving the country for a year, then they insist I go to a place where I at least have some heritage."

"I don't see why you have to study abroad at all. I mean, what do they have over there that we don't have over here? Plus, it's your senior year. You're going to totally miss out on it."

"Well, I would have studied abroad my junior year, like most people, but *somebody* thought that would put too much strain on our relationship. Now, I'm not in that relationship anymore."

Matt flinches at my words. "I know, I know. I'm a jerk. I'm sorry. I can't fix what happened."

"Right."

"Nobody's perfect, you know. I was perfect for five years, Kat. Cut me a little slack."

I roll my eyes. "Oh, you poor thing! I've been so hard on you, getting mad at you for cheating on me and then breaking up with me. You know, I really feel bad for you."

I don't know why I agree to spend time with Matt. It's totally stupid, and it's not helping me move on.

"Look. Just because everything between us went to shit this year, that doesn't mean I'm not going to miss you when you're gone."

I look out the diner window, away from Matt. "Well, at least you've got your new girlfriend to keep you company."

It's been months since Matt and I broke up, but we still hang out all the time. It doesn't help that we grew up three miles from each other and that our families are close friends. We were together for a long time, and some habits—like breakfast at the diner after sleeping through church—are just impossible to break. I need a change.

"You know, if it's too hard over there for you, you can always come back early."

"It's not a war zone, Matt. I'll be fine. I'll be back in May."

"What if you don't come back?" my best friend, Dana, asks me as we shop at the mall for an outfit for my going-away barbecue.

"Don't be ridiculous," I answer her, flipping through a rack of sundresses.

"No, seriously, you could meet the man of your dreams over there, get whisked away to the Bavarian Alps, and we'd never see you again."

"Dana, they don't have twenty-four-hour diners in Germany—and they make you pump your own gas. I'd never survive more than a year there."

"They make you pump your own gas in Pennsylvania," Dana reminds me.

"I'm not moving to Pennsylvania, either."

Dana knows deep down that I mean that. I'm a Jersey girl through and through. Nobody loves the Garden State more than I do. And I firmly believe that anyone who doesn't love it, has never ventured off the Turnpike. They are the same people who write the New Jersey jokes, such as, "Why are New Yorkers so grouchy? Because the light at the end of the tunnel is New Jersey," that I have painfully endured since birth.

Besides the Turnpike, I have determined that Newark Airport is also to blame for the animosity that the rest of the country feels toward my state. Imagine you're flying into New York City for the first time in your life, and you don't know that Newark Airport is actually in New Jersey. You exit the plane and find yourself a little farther west than expected. If it's nighttime, the shock is minimal; but I pity those poor individuals who arrive in broad daylight, press their noses against the taxi window to catch their first glimpse of the Big Apple, and don't see Broadway or Park Avenue, but the simmering swamp some cruel satirist decided to name, "the Meadowlands."

You have to laugh at the name Meadowlands. It's an industrial marsh, neither meadow, nor land, and the only things that flourish there are chain hotels, strip malls, and oil refineries. It's so embarrassing that even the football team—whose home stadium is in the Meadowlands—insists on calling itself the New York Giants, as if people wouldn't figure out where it really plays.

I've always thought it was too bad New Jersey has such a bum rap, because it really does have everything a person needs in life. There's good hiking at the Appalachian Trail and the Delaware Water Gap. There are good beaches at the shore. You can gamble in Atlantic City, and Jersey tomatoes are the juiciest I've ever tasted. Nevertheless, we're known around the country as the "armpit of America," and there isn't anything I, Jon Bon Jovi, Jack Nicholson, Frank Sinatra, John Travolta, nor the E Street Band, can do about it. I'm going to miss New Jersey when I'm gone.

"Your father and I burned you six Springsteen CDs to play at your going-away barbecue today," my mom informs me as we set up tables in the backyard.

"Awesome," I give her the thumbs-up. "You can never have enough Springsteen."

One thing I am especially going to miss when I am in Germany is my family barbecues. My family lives on a nice property with woods and a small in-ground pool. Though technically it is a suburb of New York, my neighborhood feels more rural than anything.

You can barely see the other houses through the trees surrounding the house, and you can't get anywhere without a car.

For the party today, we are expecting a small gathering of family and friends, some already starting to arrive. The last minute preparations are being made, my mom is laying out drinks and condiments, and my dad is firing up the grill. As soon as enough guests arrive, my mom kicks off the festivities by grabbing a hot dog and a packet of rolls, and sauntering up to my dad at the grill. "Wanna roast my weenie and toast my buns?" she teases him, winking at her guests.

My dad clenches his jaw and tries to ignore the crudeness of his wife, while everyone else enjoys a silent chuckle. My mom has been making that joke at family barbecues since I can remember, and it never ceases to catch my father off guard, which only adds to his embarrassment, which, of course, only adds to my mom's amusement. I normally derive great pleasure from watching this exchange, but today, I have other things on my mind.

"I've changed my mind," I announce to my mom as we are clearing the tables between dinner and dessert. "I'm not going to Germany."

"Don't be silly, dear," my mother says. "You will love Germany."

"What if I don't?"

"Just try to focus on the positive—like the good German beer that will be available all around you."

"I can get good beer in London," I whine.

My mom looks at me as if I have just cursed the Pope. Being German, my mom holds certain things to be self-evident, and the superiority of German beer is one of them.

It's hard for me to put my finger on why I'm so nervous about spending senior year in Berlin. I try to help my mother understand. "Do people over there speak English, or am I going to have to speak German all the time?"

My mom shakes her head. "You're going to Germany, Kat. Even if people there can speak English, you should take advantage of this opportunity to practice your German. You speak it very well already."

"Isn't it enough that I'm majoring in German? Why do I have to actually go there?"

An unsettling grin appears on my mom's face. "You're right, dear. Majoring in German is enough. You've read a bunch of books about Germany, written a few papers. You know everything already. You don't have to go."

I know that there's a punch line coming, so I wait for my mom to continue.

"By the way, I borrowed your *Kama Sutra* from your bottom drawer."

"*What?*"

"Now, since you've read all about sex, you don't ever have to bother doing it. You're father will be ecstatic to hear you've chosen a life of celibacy."

"Mom," I roll my eyes. "I'm being serious here."

"Me too, dear. I think you'll find that convents these days are a lot more comfortable than they used to be. They probably even have wireless Internet access."

I look at my mom in frustration. "What if Germany's not what I expect?"

"So what?"

"What if it's ... lonely?"

"Dear," my mom puts down the stack of plates that she is about to carry into the house. "I know why you don't want to leave. It's the same reason you decided to go in the first place. Believe me, you've made the right decision. It's time you put some space between you and Matt, you know, went to a place that has nothing to do with him. You two have been together for so long that you don't know where one of you stops and the other one begins. This experience will give you a chance to start learning who you are, without him."

My mother's wisdom surprises and discomforts me. After all,

this is the woman who bore and raised me. What does she know about life?

"Besides," my mom continues, "maybe, just maybe, you'll find Otto over there."

I raise an eyebrow at my mom. She turns away to avoid looking me in the eye. "Mom? Uncle Otto is—"

"Dead? I know. I know."

"Even if he's not, he was *how old* when he disappeared?"

"Three."

"How would I recognize him?"

"You wouldn't, dear," my mom sighs. "You'd just have to rely on your instincts, I guess."

I give my mother a troubled look.

"Never mind, dear. Forget I said anything. Put on a smile and enjoy the party. By the way, I've got a surprise for you."

My mom is always full of surprises. This one is in the form of a going-away cake. Recently, the local Shop Rite has developed the technology to scan pictures of customers' choosing and digitally reproduce them on cakes. My mom's choosing turns out to be an endearing picture from my infancy, picked specifically to test the thickness of my skin, while at the same time, exposing as much of it as possible. It is of me on the day I had snuck into the bathroom, naked and unsupervised, seized the end of the toilet paper roll, and unraveled it around myself with uninhibited zeal. Of course, the angle of the photograph leaves none of the important parts concealed. Leave it to my mother to take that tender moment and portray it twenty-one years later at my going-away party in exquisite, colored frosting atop two inches of rich, moist, vanilla cake. Though I am mortified, I have to admit, I look delicious.

I hear an "Awwwww!" from the crowd when my mother reveals the cake.

I hear a "Gasp!" from my father, who must have been expecting the picture that he had picked out of me, fully clothed in a tasteful sundress on the day of my first Holy Communion.

Unbeknownst to him, but knownst to my mother, she had switched the pictures without telling him.

Just when he is about to express his disapproval, my mother produces a large knife and begins to cut the cake. The guests line up enthusiastically for my various body parts, wrapped and unwrapped, and my mother dishes them out with relish. Cries of, "Who wants a thigh?" and, "Save me a cheek!" can be heard throughout the crowd. Soon, there is nothing left to dish out except for my infant pelvic region, which no one will touch. I feel rejection rising up inside me.

"It's just cake, for God's sake," I implore my guests. "Doesn't anybody want the last piece?"

Not a chance. In the end, my entire groin area goes to waste. I have the distinct impression that this is going to have psychological consequences for me in the future, including feelings of repression and guilt regarding sex. Those hotshots at Shop Rite will never understand the full impact of their big idea, scanning pictures on cakes.

Once my guests and I have recovered from the excitement of my edible dismemberment, the party continues. The sun tucks itself away behind the rolling Jersey horizon. Fireflies begin twinkling around our heads. Parents and relatives start to head home, and friends linger around the pool, talking and enjoying the last of the wine and beer. We have already decided that we're not going to sleep tonight, with the idea that I'll have plenty of time to sleep tomorrow on the plane.

I look around at my friends. We are all feeling pretty emotional at this point, and Dana looks at me like she's never going to see me again.

"I'll only be gone ten months," I try to reassure her, but it doesn't work. My saying it out loud has the opposite effect that I intend. Ten months suddenly seems like an infinite amount of time in my just-turned-twenty-one-year-old brain. I am infinitely sad and infinitely amazed that I will be gone for that long.

CHAPTER THREE

Herr Stern

The taxi ride to Humboldt University takes forty-five minutes longer than I expect it will, and I have no idea if I'm being ripped off or if that is just how long the drive from Tegel Airport to Humboldt University is. When I finally arrive, an official-looking gentleman with a clipboard and an eager grin on his face greets me at the gate. His nametag reveals him to be Hans Stern, Director of the Humboldt Academic Exchange Program, whose acronym in German is *HAA*.

"Guten Tag Herr Stern," I dust off my German skills.

"Guten Tag. Und wer sind Sie?"

"I'm Katarina Vespucci," I announce.

Herr Stern's head snaps up from the clipboard.

"Kat-a-hhhrrriii-na Vespucci!" he heralds, annunciating every syllable of my name as if he has been looking forward to heralding it since he first came across my application. "I've been looking forward to heralding that name since I first came across your application."

I love the way Germans roll their *r's*, by the way. Not like Spanish or Italian *r's*, made by rolling the tip of the tongue. Germans roll their uvulas, and it took me years of gargling in front of the mirror to learn how to do it.

"Kat-a-hhhrrriii-na Vespucci," repeats Herr Stern, smacking his hands together. "You must explain to me how you, an American, earned this intriguingly mixed European name. I know, I just know, there is a story there, a scandal perhaps, involving defiance, betrayal, banishment, and forbidden love."

Herr Stern is fit and compact, with a kind face, a smooth jaw, and a head of light brown hair sprinkled with strands of white. His translucent gray eyes widen with anticipation of the story he has been waiting to hear.

At first I laugh, because I have never thought of my parents' meeting in this way, but he is actually right. Luckily, I have told this story many times before, so I take a deep breath and tell him how I got my name.

"It is quite an interesting story, starting just after my grandparents came to America from Italy in the early 1930s. My father, Angelo Vespucci, was born and raised in Hoboken, NJ, right across the river from New York City. My dad, growing up in a poor, Italian, immigrant family, had the mind but not the money to go to college. But he had always dreamed of a white-collar life. So, with the help of our influential Uncle Carmine, who made his fortune on rare, imported olive oil, my father contacted our Congressman, who wrote him a glowing recommendation for the Military Academy at West Point. The admissions committee, whose most influential member also happened to be Uncle Carmine, was highly impressed with my dad and accepted him into the Academy.

"After four years of polishing his shoes, marching in formation, and learning how to defend his country, my dad, now Lieutenant Vespucci, was ready to serve, but the only problem was that the

15

United States was in the middle of a war. It was then that my father discovered his life-long passion for medicine, in particular, disorders of the internal glands, and was allowed to postpone the defense of his country in order to spend the next six years at the New Jersey College of Endocrinology, learning how to defend the pancreas, thyroid, and adrenal glands from the onslaught of conditions such as diabetes, metabolic disorders, and pituitary malfunctions.

"When he had finished medical school, the United States was still in the middle of a war, but my dad, now Dr. Vespucci, was ready to pay back his debt to Uncle Sam, and to Uncle Carmine. So he laced up his boots and loaded his syringe. Somebody with some pull at headquarters, however, whose name happened to be Uncle Carmine, saw to it that my dad received orders to join the Medical Corps in Stuttgart, Germany where, instead of taking part in the now highly unpopular war in Vietnam, he could take part in the occupation of a country defeated in a popular war, where he could also drink quality German beer, go skiing in the Alps, and socialize with beautiful German women, like my mom.

"It just so happened that my mom, Angelica Bittner, a lanky, German hospital receptionist whose father had forbidden her from marrying a foreigner, was on the lookout for one. Mom and Dad were attracted to each other immediately, but it wasn't until she found out he was a Catholic, which made him the devil incarnate to her staunch Lutheran family, that they fell madly in love. She married him the first chance she got, and when my dad's tour of duty was finished, they left Germany together with all the fanfare of a full-out Bittner family scorning.

"I was on the way soon after they got themselves settled down in New Jersey. When it came time to pick my name, my dad, who was convinced his first child would be a boy, stood frozen in the delivery room, shocked at having detected none of the signature male parts on my newly emerged undercarriage. In no state of mind to consider female nomenclature, he sat dumbfounded next to my mom's hospital bed, watching his dreams of wrestling trophies and father-son fishing trips off Sandy Hook swirl down the drain. My mom, on the other hand, smacked her hands together and decided she was going to make a political statement.

"You see, Mom was born in East Germany."

"Me too. Where?"

"Dresden."

"How about that? Me too."

"So you're a Saxon, then."

"Yes, I am. Give your mother my greetings."

"I'll tell her. My mom is actually only originally from Dresden, though. The family fled to West Germany right after she was born. Even still, my mom has always maintained a fondness for the GDR, 'the little political engine that couldn't,' as she puts it, because they did have some good ideas but not a can of elbow grease to implement them."

"So that day in the hospital, sweaty and exhausted from labor, my mom, glowing like an Olympic Gold medalist, declared that she would name me after the only admirable thing she could think of, besides the Duraplast automobile, to be produced in the GDR—figure skater Katarina Witt."

"So, Vespucci is the name I got from my father, and Katarina is the name I got from my mother."

Herr Stern takes a moment to absorb the information I have just imparted on him. "Like I said, 'defiance, betrayal, banishment, and forbidden love'—there is no other way you could have gotten that name, Frau Vespucci," Herr Stern beams. "It is very nice to meet you. Please step into the office so we can get you settled."

Together we sit down at Herr Stern's desk and he hands me a large and unwieldy map of Berlin, which, when spread out, looks more like wallpaper than a map. In addition to the map, Herr Stern gives me a schedule for the *S-Bahn*, city train, and the *U-Bahn*, subway, and a book about the bus system, a shopping guide, a pocket-sized copy of Germany's constitution, a slightly bigger book called *Facts About Germany*, a schedule for the first few weeks of the *HAA* program, a coupon for a free dinner that night at a local pizza restaurant, the first installment of my monthly stipend in cash, and the key to my dorm room. I am intrigued to hear that student dormitories here are not set up as long halls of double rooms with communal bathrooms and without kitchens, but rather as three bedroom apartments, much like how normal people live. Foreign students will each have one fellow foreign roommate and one local German roommate.

"Your official student ID will be issued to you next month when your classes begin."

"Thank you," I say, overwhelmed by everything he has just given me.

With a proud smile, Herr Stern shakes my hand again. "I like you, Frau Vespucci. You remind me of my daughter. She is also very far from home, studying abroad in China."

"China!" I say. "Oh, wow. That must take some guts."

"I'm worried to death about her, Frau Vespucci," he says cheerfully.

I laugh. "I can understand that. Hopefully there's someone over there just like you looking out for her."

"Let's hope so. Now off you go!"

I gather the things he has given me, re-attach my luggage to my torso, and hobble out into the city. Once in the city, I realize that I have no clue where I am going. I unload my burden onto the sidewalk and bring out the map. Spread out on the sidewalk, it blocks the path of all potential passersby. The dormitory is located on a street called *Coppistrasse* in the borough of Berlin called *Lichtenberg*, which, as best as I can tell, means "mountain of lights." That sounds pretty nice; I just pray it's not nice in the same sense as the Meadowlands.

One look at the map and I realize that I am in trouble. I don't see numbers and street names; I see a virile mass of buildings, streets, tracks, intersections, waterways, parks, and monuments.

Finding *Coppistrasse* in this maze is going to be like looking for a buoy in a hurricane. There must be a map key on here somewhere. On the back of the map is a listing of street names and their coordinates. Flipping back to the front of the map, I locate the borough of *Lichtenberg* and my *Coppistrasse* way in the eastern part of the city, only inches from the Polish border.

Wondering how I am going to get there, I pull out my transportation guide. It looks to me like both the *S-Bahn* and the *U-Bahn* go to *Coppistrasse*, but how do I get to the *S-Bahn* or *U-Bahn* from here? I turn the map around and consult the index to find the Humboldt University and then flip back to the front to find that I am currently smack in the middle of Berlin, in the borough called *Mitte*. The nearest transportation hub is the *Friedrichstrasse Bahnhof*, so that is where I am headed. It only appears to be a few blocks away, but I am exhausted, so I hail a cab.

When I arrive at the *Friedrichstrasse Bahnhof* and make my way to the *S-Bahn* platform, I am unable to figure out how it works. Strangely, there are no turnstiles demanding tickets, nor employees checking passes. The track appears to be completely unregulated, and people are just getting on and off the trains without paying or displaying evidence that they have paid. The only semblance of regulation that I can see is a sinister sign on the wall that says in sharp black letters, *"Schwarzfahren Verboten!"*

Riding Black Forbidden? What could that mean? I have no idea what to do from here, so I decide to ask somebody.

"Entschuldigung," I approach a man on the platform. "Do I need a ticket for this train?"

"Of course you do, young lady," he snaps.

"Where do I buy it?"

"From the ticket booth. Where else would one buy tickets?"

"Um, if you don't mind me asking, where is the ticket booth?"

"Upstairs on the opposite end of the train station."

"I see. And where do I show the ticket once I've bought it?"

"Where do you show it?"

"Yes."

"Nowhere."

"Nowhere?"

"Yes."

"Isn't somebody going to check my ticket?"

"Not likely."

"You mean I can just get on the train without a ticket?"

"Young lady, if it is your intention to ride the train black, then I must end this conversation. I do not wish to be associated with *Schwarzfahrer.*"

"I'm sorry; I'm just not sure what I'm supposed to do."

"You're *supposed* to go upstairs to the other side of the train station and buy a ticket. Then you're *supposed* to come back down here with the ticket and get on the train. If it's your time, the undercover controllers will come to you in the train and ask you to show your ticket. If you cannot produce one, then you will be issued a very heavy fine," he paused for effect, "for *Schwarzfahren!*"

"Oh, I see, they'll check my ticket once I'm on the train."

"Probably not."

"I beg your pardon?"

"They probably won't check you."

"Why do you say that?"

"Because they hardly ever check anybody."

"They hardly ever check anybody? Then why do you buy a ticket?"

"Who, me? I never buy a ticket."

"Why not?"

"Well, that would be a waste of money, being that the controllers probably aren't going to check me, now wouldn't it?"

"Wow. Have you ever been caught?"

"Everyone gets caught," he answers, looking away.

The man's train pulls into the station and he gets on it without a goodbye. Now I really don't know what to do. I'm tired and not at all prepared to deal with the moral dilemma that is slowly setting in. I consider jumping on the next train without going upstairs and buying a ticket. My hand starts to reach inadvertently for the little golden crucifix that I wear around my neck. Damn it! I hate temptation! I wish there was a turnstile to make me pay. I wish I had never gone to Catholic school where I became addicted to the combination of guilt and exhilaration that results when I don't do the right thing and don't get caught. Not today, I tell myself. Today I will not ride *schwarz*.

I haul my luggage up the escalator and across the train station to the ticket office. Upstairs, the train station is more crowded than church on Christmas. I navigate my way through the swarm to the ticket office, which is sectioned off from the main hall by steel beams and glass. Inside, there are racks of maps, schedules, and travel brochures, and seven shiny ticket counters. Only one of these shiny ticket counters is open. There are two employees fussing about, dusting the racks and arranging the materials into orderly piles. The line of customers is out the door.

Buying a pass is not going to be easy. After releasing a groan of irritation at the sight of the line, I get on at the end. What a drag this is. I let my backpack slide heavily to the floor and set my two suitcases down, creating a mini-fortress around myself. The people in line before me are waiting patiently, reading, staring off into space, whining about the weather, but it is the darnedest thing, nobody is complaining about the line. Nobody seems to wonder why there are six other ticket counters available, but no one working them. Everybody looks perfectly content to be standing here in line at the train station.

One of the dusting ladies passes briskly through the line to get to another rack, bumping me along her way. She does not excuse herself. I look at the man in front of me, who is holding the leash of a black dachshund in a pink sweater. The dachshund is waiting just as patiently as his owner. The line moves up and I notice that a German shepherd accompanies the man, who has just finished at the counter. I calculate that in order for this man to exit, he will have to walk his shepherd right by the black dachshund in the pink sweater. Now I have something to entertain me. Here it comes—the approach. The German shepherd strides austerely behind its owner. The dachshund squats motionless on the glossy floor. Both rivals face each other. Eye contact is made between the two canine adversaries. The shepherd draws nearer. The dachshund scratches its ear with its hind leg. The tension mounts. The shepherd opens its mouth and yawns. The dachshund stops scratching its ear with its hind leg. The deciding moment is nigh. I hold my breath. The shepherd passes the dachshund. The dachshund squats motionless on the glossy floor. The shepherd and its owner exit the ticket office. The dachshund squats motionless on the glossy floor. It is the anti-climax of the century.

How could it be possible? I am incredulous. Not a bark, not a snarl, not a leap of excitement at confronting another member of the canine family. Not a nip at the neck, not a sniff of the groin, not a hump of any kind—only pure obedience and good behavior. What kinds of dogs are these?

I spend the rest of the wait asleep on my feet. When it is time to move up, the little old lady behind me nudges me with her walking stick. Eventually it is my turn. I approach the counter, excited to get down to business.

"*Bitte schön?*" asks the saleswoman.

"One *Bahnpass* please."

"Single ride or monthly pass?"

"A monthly pass would be great."

"Are you a student?"

"Yes."

The saleswoman holds out her hand through the slot in the glass as if to accept my money.

"I'm sorry," I hesitate. "How much does it cost?"

"It costs forty euros."

"Okay, just a minute."

"Documentation first."

"Documentation?"

"You have to submit documentation in order to get a monthly pass."

"What kind of documentation?"

The saleslady gives me an irritated stare. "Passport."

"Okay, one moment, please." I have to dig my passport out from the secret purse I am carrying under my shirt. "There you are."

The saleslady takes it, looks at it for a full thirty seconds, and hands it back to me.

"Resident permit."

"Oh, yes, one moment." I pull out the folder that Herr Stern gave me, shuffle through some papers, and find my resident permit. I hand it to the saleslady. The saleslady takes it, looks at it for a full thirty seconds, and hands it back to me.

"Two passport pictures."

"Pardon?"

"You have to submit two passport pictures," her irritated stare has not changed.

"Why?"

"I need one to put on the *Bahnpass*, and one for us to keep for our records."

"I'm sorry, I don't have two passport pictures with me."

"Then you'll need to get some."

"Where do I get some?"

"In the photo booth on the other side of the train station. You'll see it right next to the main entrance."

"Really, I'm sorry, but I've waited a long time in this line. Do you really need two passport pictures? Here, I have a photocopy of my passport. Will you accept that?"

"No."

I can see it is a losing battle. "Okay, I'll be back. May I leave my luggage here, at least?"

"No."

Irked, I haul my pile o' luggage across the train station and find the photo booth next to the main entrance. The sign on the outside reads, "One euro per two passport pictures." I pull out the envelope of cash that Herr Stern gave me. The smallest bill is fifty euros. The photo booth doesn't take bills. There is no change machine. I decide to do what I do at home when I need change: find a deli. I am pretty hungry. I could go for a calzone or a slice of pizza. Of course, I see nothing that remotely resembles a deli or a pizzeria in my immediate surroundings. What I do see, however, is a *Wurst* stand, and no longer willing to schlep my luggage around the train station, I decide that *Wurst* will do just fine.

I approach the counter and order one *Currywurst mit Ketchup*. The transaction proceeds smoothly, except that the employee rolls his eyes dramatically when I hand him the fifty-euro bill. After accepting my change and consuming my *Wurst*, I return to the photo booth. I climb inside and pull the curtain closed. There are no instructions and no buttons, just a slot for the one-euro coin. I insert the coin and look around for some indication of what I am supposed to do. Nothing happens. I look around. Nothing happens. I lean forward to get up, and the camera flashes. *"Scheisse!"* I exclaim, practicing cursing in German. I wasn't ready for that. I am looking bewildered at the camera when the second flash goes off.

Two minutes later my pictures come sliding out a little chute on the outside of the photo booth. One picture has cut off my entire forehead and the other is the worst picture of me ever taken. But they are two passport photos, so I take them back to the ticket counter. I hover around the front of the line for a minute, hoping that the saleslady will recognize me and allow me to get in front, but she ignores me. After several dirty looks from the other people in line, I return to the back.

When it is finally my turn again, I present the saleswoman with my two passport photos. She takes them, looks at them for a full thirty seconds, and keeps them.

"Student ID."

"Oh, I won't be getting that until classes start next month. Here," I shuffle again through the folder from Herr Stern. "Here's a piece of paper with my course schedule."

"That is not a valid student ID."

"I don't have a valid student ID yet. I told you, I won't be getting that until next month."

"Then you can't have the student discount until next month."

"Look. This is an official document stating that I'm enrolled at the Humboldt University with the school of Social Sciences."

"That is not a valid student ID."

"And here, wait, here is a letter from the President of the Humboldt University, on official letterhead, welcoming me to the school and stating that I am registered as a student for the next academic semester."

"Frau Vespucci, in order to get a *Bahnpass* at the student discount, you need to have a valid student ID."

"How much is the *Bahnpass* without the student discount?"

"Eighty euros."

"Eighty euros! That's a lot of money."

"Of course it is. That's why I need to see your student ID."

"No student ID until classes start."

"Why don't you go to Humboldt and ask them to issue you a temporary ID in advance?"

"I could do that, but I'll need to take the *S-Bahn* to get there," I bluff, "and in order to take the *S-Bahn* I'll need a *Bahnpass*."

"Well, you'll have to buy a *Bahnpass* if you want one."

"Good idea. I'd like one *Bahnpass* please."

"Sure. I'll just need to see your student ID."

I stare at the saleswoman to see if I can break her, but her steely gaze far outmatches mine. I'm the one that breaks. "You know what? Forget it. I'll just pay full price."

"No, you won't."

"I won't?"

"That's correct."

"Why not?"

"You said you were a student."

"That's right."

"Students pay a reduced price."

"Only if they can produce a valid student ID."

"But if I issue you a full-price adult *Bahnpass*, and really you are a student, people might think you are someone other than who you are."

"So?"

"Are you trying to pass yourself off as someone other than who you are?"

"No, I just want a monthly *Bahnpass*."

"Oh, we sell those here."

"You just said you wouldn't sell me one."

"Of course I will."

"So—"

"As long as you're a student."

"Which I am."

"Then all I need to see is proof."

"Proof? Like a piece of paper with my course schedule, an official document stating that I'm enrolled at the Humboldt University with the school of Social Sciences, a letter from the President of the Humboldt University, on university letterhead, welcoming me to the program and stating that I am registered as a student for the next academic semester?"

"No, Frau Vespucci, proof like a valid student ID."

"How about proof that you even sell these damn passes!" I retort. "Forget I asked." I gather up my luggage and try to storm out of the ticket office, but I am too weighed down with luggage to storm anywhere.

"You can try to storm out all you want, but you won't get far without a *Bahnpass*," the saleswoman calls after me.

In complete frustration, I waddle across the station and down the escalator to the *S-Bahn* platform. My decision is made. When the train arrives, I'm just going to get on it. I'm going to become

26

an outlaw, cheat the system, turn to the dark side. I will ride *schwarz*, and I will love it.

The train arrives. With my best *I didn't buy a ticket and I'm proud of it* face, I step up to the halting vehicle. I stare down a passenger on the inside of the train, just for kicks. Adrenaline surges through my veins, and I know that, at this moment, an army could not hold me back from boarding this *S-Bahn*. The train comes to a halt in front of me. I step up to the doors. The doors do not open. I stand there. The doors do not open. I do not just get on. I do not become an outlaw. I do not cheat the system. I do not turn to the dark side, or ride *schwarz*, or love it. Instead, the doors remain closed, I remain standing on the platform, and the train rolls away without me.

What the hell? Exasperated, I look around. An electronic sign above tells me that the next *S-Bahn* is due in exactly two minutes and twenty-six seconds. When it arrives, I step into position in front of the doors, and demand, "Open Sesame." A man comes up behind me, looks impatiently at the train, gives me an irritated glare, and scolds, "This isn't New York, young lady. In Germany you have to open the doors yourself!" With that, he reaches around my waist, pushes a button on the side of the train, and the doors open. He shoves past me. I sheepishly follow him in.

Inside the *S-Bahn*, I find an empty seat and crumble into it, embarrassed and deflated. Around me are a dozen other people with their best *I didn't buy a ticket and I'm proud of it* faces. I huddle into my seat and drop my heavy head into my hands. I feel more unprepared for this experience than anything else in my life. Away the train goes.

CHAPTER FOUR

Pete

The train pulls away from *Friedrichstrasse Bahnhof,* and I barely notice it is moving. Unlike the New York subway, the Berlin *S-Bahn* runs smoothly and silently, as if it is floating on a cushion of air. The fact that it rides suspended above the city only strengthens this effect. At this point, I am too tired to sleep, but too exhausted to be fully awake, so my mind wanders into a state of dreamlike memory.

I find myself back in ninth grade, reliving the first time I felt as unprepared as I do now. I am on a camping trip in the deep woods of West Virginia, and little do I know, I am about to have my first period. I am convinced that I will never go through puberty, despite the reassurances of my endocrinologist father. I have been wearing a training bra for a year and a half with the hopes that it will entice my breasts to start growing, but to no avail. I occasionally shave my armpits with the hopes that it will entice my underarm follicles to start producing hair, but to no avail. My ovaries, however, begin producing ova without any help from me, and without any warning at all.

It is a bright and dewy morning when I wake up in the tent I am sharing with one other girl my age, seven adolescent boys, and Counselor Jared, the first man I have ever loved. Now, I have dreamt many times that Counselor Jared would be involved when I finally became a woman, but this is not exactly what I had in mind.

The moment I notice that something is awry, I shoot up in my sleeping bag, which causes everyone else to notice that something is awry and shoot up in their sleeping bags.

"What is it?" Counselor Jared asks.

"Nothing," I lie. "Just going to the outhouse."

I fumble knock-kneed out of the tent, stepping on several of my fellow campers' ankles in my haste. Naturally, there is no shower or flush toilet within a three-mile radius of the campsite, so I shimmy to the green Port-A-Potty and lock myself inside. Having discovered what is happening, I stare, stunned, at the dark ribbons of blood and uterine lining that lace my underpants. Is it supposed to look like this? I am disgusted. It then dawns on me that I have no feminine products whatsoever at my disposal. What the hell am I going to do?

After wracking my brain for several minutes, I determine that my only option is to sit where I am for the next five to seven days, having Counselor Jared deliver my meals. It seems like a viable plan, that is, until Stevie starts pounding on the door for me to get out. The other campers have woken up and are lining up to use the john. I have to come up with Plan B and fast.

Finally, I undo the latch and poke my head around the door. The whole group is standing in front of the outhouse, looking annoyed. Counselor Jared asks me if everything is all right. My face turns as red as my period as I realize that I have no other choice but to turn to the man of my dreams and ask, "You wouldn't happen to have a Maxi-pad, would you?"

The *S-Bahn* comes to a stop, bringing me back to the present. Passengers get off the train and new ones get on. I keep my eyes on the doors, watching for undercover police officers or *S-Bahn* employees. Nothing out of the ordinary happens. The *S-Bahn* starts moving again.

Reliving the last time I felt as unprepared as I do now, my mind jumps to my junior year of college. The fall semester has just ended, and it is the first morning of Christmas break. I have prepared a surprise for my boyfriend Matt. Matt and I have grown up together, been a couple since high school, and now go to different colleges, I to Rutgers, he to The College of New Jersey. This week, Matt is still in finals. Having already come home for the break, I decide to surprise him by waking up early, making the hour drive, and arriving at his apartment in time to bring him breakfast. I am a sensible girl, however, and I realize that unexpected breakfast during exams is probably not the best idea, so I warn him of the surprise in advance. Matt, however, being immersed in his studies, and the new girlfriend that he has recently started dating, forgets about the announced surprise. I ring his doorbell that fateful morning and the surprise is on me when a bouncy girl, wearing nothing but a pair of socks and Matt's oversized TCNJ sweatshirt, greets me at the door.

"May I help you?" the bouncy girl asks, surprised.

My hands go limp, sending the coffee cups plunging to the floor. Their lids fly off upon impact and the steaming coffee drains rapidly into the welcome mat. Neither I, nor bouncy girl, move a finger to clean up the mess; we just stand there staring at each other, quite surprised, wondering how neither of us had known. The most surprised of all is Matt, when he comes out of the bedroom and discovers both of his girlfriends standing face to face.

"Kat!" he exclaims, stepping toward me, but then stops short. "Jesus, this isn't how I planned to tell you." He pulls at the hair on the back of his head, takes a look at bouncy girl, and takes another look at me. "Kat, Katie, uh, since you're both here, you girls wouldn't be up for a threesome, would you? I'm sorry. I'm sorry. Bad taste. Shit!"

I don't know what I expected him to say after that incident. "I'm sorry," maybe, "Give me another chance?" I was so in love with him that I probably would have forgiven him, but he never asked me to. He just switched girlfriends from one moment to the next, and there was nothing I could do about it except try to move on with my life.

I shake the sleep from my eyes and take a look out the window. What I see looks like nothing I have ever seen before. It's not that anything is completely out of the ordinary, per se, but everything looks completely different. The houses are older and pressed up against each other. There are no yards in between them. The streets are narrower. The cars are smaller. The colors are—different.

It occurs to me that the farthest I've ever been from home, besides the New Jersey shore, is Pennsylvania, which is always strange for me because people call soda, "pop," and submarine sandwiches, "hoagies." That's not to say I don't like going to Pennsylvania every now and then. I love skiing in the Poconos or going shopping at the outlets in Tannersville. But I've always preferred spending the bulk of my time at home. New Jersey really does have everything you need.

That's why I chose to go to Rutgers University. A lot of my friends from high school also went there, so I didn't have to make all new ones. I wonder what the guys in Germany will think of me. I'm not the ugliest girl on the planet. I'm average height. I'm in pretty good shape. My light brown hair and light brown eyes are kind of boring, but Matt always called my hair golden brown and my eyes cappuccino. He has such an imagination. I wonder how he'd describe this place, I ask myself as the *S-Bahn* comes gently to a halt at my stop in *Lichtenberg*.

Exiting the train, I feel like I am in the Land of Oz, only this is no Emerald City. Now, I know that East Germany was supposedly more industrial than West Germany. I also remember learning in one of my classes that much of the current infrastructure of East Germany was built in the 1970s and neglected since the 1970s. What I have not expected, is that what I learned in school would be true.

The scene in front of me is apocalyptic, and I find myself inadvertently fingering my crucifix. The *S-Bahn* platform overlooks a cemetery of factories. There are piles of rubble resembling gravestones scattered around, interspersed with thick patches of weeds. Crumbling smokestacks punctuate the scene, not one of them emitting smoke. Railroad car cadavers sink into the earth. The biggest standing structure I can see is a deceased warehouse that has been embalmed in neon and now serves as a discotheque. A glowing sign on top of the warehouse reads "Dance Factory." What the Dance Factory has, that the other buildings don't have, is windows. The surrounding ground is littered with broken glass.

In an uncomfortably artistic way, everything semi-flat is covered in graffiti. The works that especially catch my eye are several black swastikas and an *"Ausländer raus!"* on a crumbling brick wall just a few feet in front of me. I am *so* not in Kansas anymore.

"Where the hell are we?" I hear a male American voice approaching on the platform behind me.

"We can figure this out. Just look at the map," says another voice behind him. "If you were the German government, where would you stick ninety-two foreign students?"

"Like I can find anything on this map," replies the first guy, drowning in paper.

"Foreigners, get out!" I yell, greeting them. The boys stop dead in their tracks.

"I beg your pardon?"

"Hi. I'm Kat. Fellow *Ausländer*. I'm with *HAA*."

"Yeah, us too," replies the first guy.

"Hope I didn't scare you. I was just reading the welcome mat. Nice, huh?"

The two stop for a minute to look around.

"I've never seen such a wasteland," says the second guy.

"Home, sweet home," replies the first guy, peering over the map.

"Lovely. I'm Billy," says the second guy, stretching out his hand to me.

"I'm Pete."

I take a look at Billy and Pete. Billy looks to me like a hockey player, who quit sports to concentrate on his drinking. He is not much taller than me but about three times as wide, with a muscular frame padded by a healthy layer of fat. He has a friendly face with acne scars on his cheeks and dark brown hair. He is wearing a college sweatshirt and baggy jeans. Pete is two heads taller than Billy and very lean, with a light complexion, blond eyebrows, and shaggy, nearly white hair that sticks out at the ears and teases his eyes. His look is slightly more European, with snugger jeans, a worn leather jacket, and a traveler's backpack that straps around his hips, leaving his hands free to wrestle with the map. His look is casual, but planned; I am intrigued.

"Whaddaya say we find our way home?" Pete suggests.

"Lead the way."

Our way home consists of a few steps down from the platform which takes us by a small market stand, which is closed even though it is one o'clock in the afternoon; around a corner, where a tiny Vietnamese man jumps out of the bushes and offers to sell us illegal cigarettes; under a canopy of large, unsightly green pipes, suspended ten feet in the air through which none of us can guess what flows; and to the entrance of a path that is paved, but overgrown on both sides with weeds that are so tall they are supporting vines, which dangle down like sinister fingers, beckoning us forward. There is a sign on the side of the path that reads, *"Privatweg der Deutschen Bahn – Betreten auf eigene Gefahr!"*

"I guess we're taking the Private Pathway of the German Railroad," says Billy.

"But it says 'Trespass at your own risk,'" I say.

Pete consults the map. "Unless we want to traipse through all of *Lichtenberg*, the Private Pathway is the only way."

"Private Pathway it is," Billy and I agree, and off we go.

The weeds get no less overgrown and the vines no less sinister as we navigate our way down the path. There are some streetlights, but they are not lit because it is day. At night, I will soon find out, they will not be lit because they don't work. Both sides of the path are lined with the large, unsightly green pipes, wide enough in diameter to accommodate a human being. I look forward down the path. The pipes snake horizontally a ways and then disappear into a dark tunnel. Soon, Billy, Pete, and I are standing in front of the same tunnel, not quite so willing to disappear into it. There is a sign at the entrance to the tunnel that reads, *"Privatwegtunnel der Deutschen Bahn – Betreten auf eigene Gefahr!"*

"I guess we're taking the Private Pathway Tunnel of the German Railroad," says Billy.

"It also says, 'Trespass at your own risk,'" I say.

Pete consults the map. "Unless we want to traipse back through the Private Pathway and then through all of *Lichtenberg*, the Private Pathway Tunnel is the only way."

"Private Pathway Tunnel it is," Billy and I agree, and in we go. When the three of us emerge on the other side of the tunnel, we know we are home. Before we even see the street sign that reads, *Coppistrasse,* we know where, if we were the German government, we would stick ninety-two foreign students. We are standing face to face with our first *Plattenbau,* the quintessence of East German architectural innovation. I have never seen a building quite like it.

To me, the *Plattenbau* appears to be a concrete tsunami rising high from the pavement in front of us, a cold, unpitying, quadrilateral swell that will engulf us if we get too close. The *Plattenbau* on *Coppistrasse* is the only building on *Coppistrasse*, as it consumes the entire length of the street. It is a colossal building block, an enormous, opposing, rectangular edifice, ten stories high and one kilometer long, left over from Socialist times when housing tens of thousands of families together in identical apartments under the same roof was thought to be a good idea.

"Have you ever seen anything so enormous, opposing, or rectangular?"

"It looks like Stalin himself dropped it from the sky," I reply.

"At least it's kind of colorful," Pete remarks about the pale, pastel paint that changes color every hundred yards.

"I've read about this building," Billy says. "Have you guys heard the story?"

Pete and I shake our heads no.

"Apparently, after Communism collapsed in East Germany, the council of *Lichtenberg* recognized the heinousness of it and attempted to give it a facelift. There weren't enough funds available for a proper façade, so the council scraped up some money by taxing alcohol and cigarettes, and they bought some paint to throw on the front side. The building had been a dismal gray since the 1970s, but the new color was to be eggshell."

Pete and I listen to Billy, nodding our heads.

"The council hired a painting crew, who had been out of work since the Wall fell, and the job began. The people who lived in the *Plattenbau* came out to watch the refreshing with intense anticipation, whispering to each other, and nodding their approval. Everyone was pleased with the brand new color, until the painting crew ran out of paint with two-thirds of the building left to go. The *Lichtenberg* council had no choice but to fire the painting crew and to declare that the job would remain unfinished. Depression swept over the *Coppistrasse* dwellers."

Pete and I nod, indicating that we sympathize with the *Coppistrasse* dwellers.

"They moped around with hanging heads, chided themselves

for getting their hopes up for a better life, and buried their sorrows in alcohol and cigarettes. After a month or so, the *Lichtenberg* council had generated enough revenue from the additional sales to buy some more paint. Elated, they placed another order, rehired the painting crew, and sent them back to work. The people of *Coppistrasse* nodded and smiled, and tried not to notice that the additional paint going up was pink, instead of eggshell. The price of eggshell had risen since the last purchase, and pink was all the council could afford. The refreshing continued, however, and the city council saw that it was good. People walked around on the street and were nice to each other. Birds came out to sing. Children laughed."

Pete and I now exchange a doubtful glance.

"Until the painting crew ran out of paint again. *Coppistrasse* plunged back into another depression. The painters, who were suddenly out of work, turned to the bottle, and the residents suffocated their sorrows in clouds of nicotine. Sales of alcohol and cigarettes increased, and just like that, there was money in the treasury again. Paint was repurchased. Painters were rehired. The people came out to see if the third part of the building would be the original eggshell or the new pink. Since the last purchase, however, the price of both eggshell and pink had risen, and the borough council could afford neither. What they could afford, however, was brown, and the end result of the grand refurbishing of the *Plattenbau* on *Coppistrasse* was the most enormous slice of Neapolitan ice cream the world has ever known."

"I don't believe that story," I say to Billy.

"Well, that's because it's not true," Billy giggles. "I made it up."

"The building *does* look like Neapolitan ice cream," Pete admits.

"Well, then, *Guten Appetit*," I say, and in we go.

CHAPTER FIVE

Janika

The *Plattenbau* isn't nearly as ugly on the inside as it is on the outside. The apartment consists of a long corridor with three bedrooms and a common kitchen and a bathroom. The walls are painted a sterile white, and the furniture is all the same pastel blue. I walk into my room and set my luggage down on the bed. It feels odd to be given an actual apartment, with my own room all to myself. At Rutgers, I live in a miniscule dorm room with another student and share a communal bathroom with the whole floor.

I meander into the kitchen, which has a tiny refrigerator, half as high as a fridge in the States, and a stove, but no oven. The kitchen grants access to a concrete balcony. I walk out onto it and notice that it is identical to the concrete balconies of all the other apartments.

The view from the balcony is actually pretty good. The centerpiece is the *Berliner Fernsehturm*. It is an eye-catching, smokestack-like television tower, triple the height of any other building in view, with a blinking glass ball three-quarters of the way up, and a large, candy-striped, antenna on top. To me, it looks like a massive, psychedelic, hypodermic needle. It is also the only landmark in the Berlin skyline, making it the polar opposite of the New York skyline, in which hundreds of skyscrapers compete for attention. The simplicity of the Berlin skyline, with the TV tower floating above a vast expanse of human-sized buildings, makes me feel less intimidated by the city than I was this morning.

I actually know a thing or two about the TV tower from school. It was built by the East German government during the Cold War as a "naa naa na-naa naa" to the West. When the city had been divided, the TV tower was one of the only structures in the East that could be seen over the Wall, and East Germans were proud of it. The only problem was that the panes of the glass ball, perched high atop the chimney-like stack, were arranged in such a way that when the sun shines on it, a glare appears in the shape of a cross. This was unacceptable to the East German government, who was trying to run an atheist country, and very acceptable to the West Berliners, who chuckled and called it "the Pope's revenge." No amount of painting or scratching the surface of the TV tower on the part of the East German government would drive the ironic cross away, and the only saving grace for the Communist regime was that it is rarely sunny in Berlin.

The only other thing I notice on this first look at Berlin from my balcony is directly below me, in what I guess would be considered the backyard of the *Plattenbau*. There is another factory, questionably defunct, which serves as a hub for several of the gangly green pipes that I noticed on the walk from the *S-Bahn*. Nine of these tubular serpents emerge from the side of the low, flat building and then slither out into the community to disperse their mysterious contents. I still cannot fathom a guess as to what could be inside these pipes. My imagination runs the gamut from radioactive waste to human fat, though I hope neither is the case.

The thought overwhelms me suddenly, and I notice that I have a pounding headache. The excitement of the day has made me forget that I am utterly and completely exhausted. I totter back in from the balcony, push my bags off of my bed, and collapse with a heavy frump. Ahhh, sleep—the best thing that's happened to me all day.

The next thing I know, I am being roused from my slumber by a loud knock at the door. I lift my head from the pillow, and I don't know where I am. It takes a moment for my surroundings to register. I shake my head to clear the fog and take a look at my watch. It's only eleven o'clock in the morning, but I notice that the sun has almost gone down and the view out the window is splashed with pink, red, and orange light.

"Kat, it's Pete," I hear a voice calling through the door. "Are you in there?"

"Um, yeah. I'm in here," I shout, and the sound of my own voice ricochets painfully inside my skull. "Just a minute." I push myself up off the bed and stumble to the door.

"Open up," he calls again.

I open up to find Pete standing there. He has changed, and his blond locks are damp from a shower. His black leather jacket fits snug around his shoulders, and he wears it unzipped. It contrasts with the whiteness of his hair, eyebrows, and facial stubble. He has a cigarette tucked behind one ear. He looks handsome and a little bit dangerous.

"Hi," I say, blinking my eyes. "I was taking a nap."

"No sleeping yet. Ninety-one of your closest strangers are waiting to meet you at the XII Apostles."

"The XII Apostles?"

Pete looks strangely at me, half staring, half investigating. "Yeah, that pizza restaurant where we're all supposed to meet for dinner."

"Dinner? It's too early for dinner."

"It's almost five o'clock."

"No, it's only eleven," I say, showing him my watch.

"Somebody hasn't reset her watch," Pete teases me.

"Oh, right," I say, smacking myself in the forehead. Pain waves bounce around inside my head. "That whole time difference thing. What time do you claim it is?"

"Quarter to five. Six hours later than EST."

I struggle to wind the hands of my watch into place.

"Thank you so much for telling me." I look at Pete, not sure what to say next.

"So are you coming to dinner?"

"Oh, right! Of course. Wait right there. I need five minutes." I am delirious. I am in no shape to make ninety-one first impressions, but there is no alternative in the matter. I splash some cold water on my face, change my shirt, and pull my Rutgers baseball cap down over my hair. While I am doing that, Pete saunters into the kitchen and opens drawers looking for matches. He doesn't find any. When I emerge from the bathroom, he is bent over the stove, trying to light his cigarette on a burner. It takes him a minute, but it finally works. Though I hate the smell of cigarettes, I am impressed with his ingenuity.

Pete smiles at me through his first puff of smoke. "Ready?"

"Let's go," I reply, and off we go.

In the elevator we run into Billy, who has run into another foreign student, named Janika.

"Janika is from Estonia," says Billy. Meeting Janika makes me gulp. I am embarrassed to admit to myself that not only have I never met anybody from Estonia before, I don't even know where Estonia is. And if that's not bad enough, I'm not even sure if Estonia is a country, like Germany, or part of a country, like say, Bavaria. I realize very quickly that I'm going to have to brush up on my European geography.

"Estonia is the northernmost of the Baltic countries," Janika explains after we have been introduced.

I give Janika an uncomfortable smile while my brain does loops. Okay, so we know that Estonia is a country. Good. But what are the Baltic countries? Wait, the name is ringing a bell. Yes, there are three Baltic countries, okay, but are those the little guys up by Scandinavia or those ex-Yugoslavian loonies down south? Jesus Christ, why didn't I look at a map before coming here?

"Just across the bay from Finland," Janika explains further.

"Yes, of course," I reply. Trying to change the subject, I point to Billy and Pete and announce, "We're all from the United States."

"All three of you?" Janika asks.

"It's the middlemost of the North American countries," I explain.

Janika looks awkwardly at me.

"Just south of Canada," I explain.

There is a prickly second among the four of us before Janika lets out a laugh.

"I'm sorry," she says. "That was quite presumptuous of me to assume that you didn't know where Estonia was. It's not usual that people know it, so I've gotten into the habit of explaining."

I let out a laugh, happy that I have successfully deceived my new friend. "It's perfectly okay. I'm sure Pete and Billy didn't know where Estonia was." I shoot them a wink and breathe a private sigh of relief as the elevator doors open.

The pizza parlor is a few blocks behind the *Plattenbau* on a street called the *Karl Marx Allee*. When we turn the corner onto *Karl Marx Allee*, I am taken aback by the straightness, wideness, and seeming never-endingness of the boulevard. It is a colossal thoroughfare. Unlike the humble roadways that snake through my hometown in New Jersey, this boulevard is broad and protractor straight, proceeding unobstructed to the horizon. It is framed on both sides by wide, imposing, not tall, but grandiose buildings with decorated stone façades.

"Makes you kind of feel like Moses standing between the walls of the Red Sea," I remark to Billy.

"That's funny," he laughs. "Considering Karl Marx was an atheist."

When Billy, Pete, Janika, and I arrive at the XII Apostles, we present our coupons at the door and enter into a room teeming with excited foreign students. Herr Stern catches my attention and waves us over to a table where he is handing out preprinted nametags with people's names and home countries. "Welcome!" Herr Stern beams, smacking his hands together.

After pinning my nametag to my shirt, I look around the room at my fellow foreign students. My heart sinks. The nametags read Russia, Latvia, Bulgaria, Belgium, Czech Republic, Lithuania, Ukraine, Slovak Republic, Albania, Romania, France, Macedonia, Hungary, Slovenia, and Poland. I don't know where three-quarters of these countries are. How embarrassing. On the biggest journey of my life this far, these people are going to be my shipmates, and they may as well be from outer space. A warm feeling flashes through my body, and I can feel my face turning red. The room starts spinning, and I can't focus on anyone or anything. I grasp a chair to steady myself, but my knees buckle under me.

Pete catches me before I hit the floor. "Are you okay?"

I look up at him helplessly.

"Looks like you need some fresh air, my lady."

Pete leads me outside the restaurant. There, I lean on him before trying to stand on my own, which also affords me the opportunity to feel his arms. I can already tell he's not as muscular as Matt. I like the feel of the leather jacket. After a minute, I finally get my bearings.

"Looks like jet lag is hitting you pretty hard," he says.

I look up at him and, in the corner of my eye, catch a glimpse of a bookstore down the *Karl Marx Allee*.

"What time is it?" I ask.

"Five minutes to five, why?"

"You know what? I'm going to take a little walk … you know, get some fresh air … compose myself."

"Okay, I'll join you?"

"No. I don't want to keep you from the party. Go on back inside and I'll meet you in a few minutes."

"Okay, suit yourself," he replies and goes back into the restaurant.

I turn away and walk briskly down the street. On the way I pass a coffin and headstone store, an Internet café, a small travel agency displaying pictures of Russia, China, and Mongolia, and a stand selling *Döner Kebap*, a Turkish, gyro-like fast-food specialty that I have never heard of before. It smells pretty good as I pass, and I realize that I am very hungry. But for now, I have more important things on my mind. I arrive at the bookstore at 4:58 PM, just in time for the clerk to slam and lock the door in my face.

"Feierabend," he announces.

"No! It isn't closing time yet!"

The clerk looks at me through the glass and shrugs his shoulders as if to say *tough break.*

"There's still two minutes left!" I protest.

The clerk shrugs his shoulders again, indicating that it is, indeed, a tough break.

"Don't do this to me," I implore. I knock loudly on the door. "Please, I'm desperate!"

The clerk turns around and gives me an irate stare.

"Bitte," I plead.

The clerk comes hastily to the door and undoes the latch. "Make it quick."

I lope to the travel section and find a mini-map of Europe the size of a paperback novel. Perfect! I buy it and stuff it in my purse. I thank the clerk profusely, who glowers and follows me out the door, locking it this time with zeal and finality.

On my way back to the XII Apostles, I study my mini-map of Europe. When I arrive, I pause at the door and take a deep breath. Bring on these Eastern Europeans!

Inside, people are already seated and waiters have begun

taking orders. I slide into the seat that has been assigned to me, which happens to be at the same table as Pete, Billy, and Janika. The foreign students occupy most of the restaurant, arranged in four groups around four tables. There is a sign in the middle of my table telling me that I am part of Group Number Four.

The waiter comes over to take my order and, not having much time to browse the menu, I pick the first pizza I recognize on the list of specials, *peperoni.*

"I'll have two pieces of this one," I point to the menu.

"I beg your pardon?" the waiter says.

"Slices. I'll have two slices. Of pepperoni."

"I will bring you the whole pizza, and you can eat what you want and leave the rest."

"The whole pizza! My God, I'll never finish it."

The waiter ignores me and moves on to the next person.

"I'll never finish a whole pizza," I turn to Billy, who is laughing. "Why are you laughing?"

"You're obviously from New York."

"New Jersey, but close enough."

"I think these are like personal pizzas," Billy informs me.

"Oh, I see. Well, whatever they are, I can't wait to eat. I'm famished."

Of course, what I think I have ordered is *pepperoni* (two *p's*), which, in my Northern New Jersey world of Italian immigrants, is something of a hard, spicy sausage. What comes to me on my individual-sized pizza is *peperoni* (one *p*), which, in the Germans' German world of native German people, is something of a Jalapeno pepper. When the erroneous entrée is placed before me, I blanch, knowing my intolerance for spicy food, and I hastily order a beer to wash it down. In my haste, however, I confuse the German words *helles,* meaning "light," and *heiliges,* meaning "holy," and only add to my embarrassment by ordering a "holy beer." I notice a few of the Europeans taking notice of my crucifix necklace, and once the waiter is gone, I try to subtly tuck it inside my shirt.

Once the group has been served, Herr Stern stands up and asks us all to raise our glasses. "To the students of the Humboldt Academic Exchange Program. Welcome to Berlin. *Prost!*"

"*Prost!*"

"Now, you will notice that you are sitting in four groups," explains Herr Stern.

"I like Herr Stern," I whisper to Pete. "His daughter is studying abroad in China."

"I know, he told me that too. Apparently, she speaks Mandarin."

"Whoa."

"The German *Bundestag* and Humboldt University have arranged some seminars for you to attend during the first weeks of your stay," Herr Stern continues. "They will be in various locations around Germany, with the idea of exposing you to as many local German beers as possible."

The group laughs.

"The groups you are sitting in now are the groups in which you will be traveling. I wish you much joy in getting to know one another, but more importantly, enjoy your meal here with us. Might I also recommend that you all try the local *Berliner Pilsner. Guten Appetit!*"

"*Guten Appetit!*"

With that, we all begin eating. I have used the distraction of the toast to remove the mini-map of Europe from my handbag and strategically place it on my lap, cloaking it from the others with my napkin and the tablecloth. I am now ready to start up a conversation. First, however, I must think of something to say. The twenty new faces seated around me come from all over Europe, which means that the usual small talk no longer applies. They like different sports than I'm used to, different movies and music; we have all just arrived, so we can't yet complain about the weather. Then, the perfect topic dawns on me. Proud of myself, I pipe up, "Did anyone follow the Little League World Series?"

Everyone shakes their heads no.

"Oh." I am disappointed. But then I realize that I didn't follow the Little League World Series either and am glad that I will not be forced to talk at length on the topic.

Luckily, Svetlana, from the Ukraine, breaks the ice. *"Es ist sehr angenehm, Sie kennenzulernen,"* she says to the group, articulating carefully.

I smile at Svetlana and then scan the mini-map for the Ukraine.

"Yes, yes," bubbles the group in response to Svetlana. "It is very nice to meet you too."

"Svetlana," Evelina from Romania speaks. "What part of the Ukraine are you from?"

"Es ist sehr angenehm, Sie kennenzulernen," Svetlana says to Evelina, articulating carefully.

"Yes," Evelina repeats. "It is very nice to meet you too. The reason I ask is because my mother was born there. In the Ukraine."

For some reason, Evelina's accent sounds very familiar to me. I can't put my finger on it.

"Es ist sehr angenehm, Sie kennenzulernen," Svetlana says to Evelina, articulating carefully.

"In Kiev," Evelina adds.

Kiev, Kiev … I scan the map. I still haven't found the Ukraine. Finally, I find the Ukraine, and then Kiev, which is the capital. "Kiev," I whisper out loud enough for everyone to hear me.

The group looks at me.

"Have you been there?" asks Evelina.

"It's the capital," I say, not knowing what else to say.

"Yes. Exactly!" Evelina is impressed.

I realize that I am in over my head. I also realize that Evelina has the same accent as Count Dracula, which makes me suddenly want to giggle out loud. Better change the subject fast, before I have to explain this one. "I've always wanted to visit the Ukraine," I bluff. "Svetlana, tell us about Kiev."

"Es ist sehr angenehm, Sie kennenzulernen," Svetlana says

to me, articulating carefully. Svetlana turns nervously to Irina, a petite, fine-featured, green-eyed girl with long, wavy, brown hair. Irina's nametag reveals her to be from Russia. Svetlana says something quickly to Irina in Russian.

Irina chuckles. "Of course, Sveta. I don't mind at all." Irina turns to the group. "Svetlana wants me to tell you all that she doesn't speak German yet."

The group absorbs the information, nodding its understanding. Svetlana pokes Irina's arm and says something else to her in Russian.

"But she promises to learn quickly."

The group nods its understanding.

Svetlana says another sentence to Irina in Russian.

"And she wants me to tell you that it is very nice to meet you."

Svetlana nods her approval and repeats, "*Es ist sehr angenehm, Sie kennenzulernen.*"

"Yes, yes," bubbles the group. "*Es ist sehr angenehm, Sie kennenzulernen.*"

"Irina," says Alexander, a sharp, blue-eyed, strong-jawed, sandy-haired countryman of Irina's. "What part of Russia are you from?"

"I don't consider myself from Russia," Irina replies.

"But your nametag says—"

"I'm from Siberia."

"*Ooooooooh!*" a gasp passes through the crowd.

"Off to Siberia!" declares Marek from Poland, raising his index finger high into the air.

Irina makes a scornful face. I recognize that pained expression; it is the same face I make when people make bad New Jersey jokes. I feel an instant bond with Irina.

"Siberia is not as bad as everybody thinks," says the Russian girl defensively.

"Neither is New Jersey," I add.

Billy almost spits out his beer when I say this.

"Irina, how long was the journey from Siberia to Berlin?" asks Janika from Estonia.

"Four days on the train from my hometown, Omsk, to Moscow, and then three hours via airplane to Berlin."

I almost spit out my beer when Irina says this.

"*Four days* on the train!" exclaims Pete. "How is that possible?"

"Oh, easy," contributes Alexander from Russia. "You see, the train tracks in Russia were not all built the same size. Every region built them differently, so what would probably only take two days if the tracks were all of uniform size, takes four days, because the train has to stop so that its wheels can be adjusted to fit the different tracks."

"Unbelievable," I say, not able to imagine a four-day train ride. "I thought my flight from Newark was long, and that only took nine hours."

"How do you possibly keep yourself occupied for that long?" asks Pete.

"Lots of vodka," replies Irina in all seriousness.

"That, I believe," I say, remembering the Russian Little League coach.

"It's not so bad," Irina continues. "You get used to long journeys when you live in Russia."

"My grandparents lived in Siberia for awhile," interjects Istvan from Hungary. "They were sent there to work on the railroads," he pauses for effect, "in a *gulag*."

The group looks at him, confused as to how they should respond.

"That's where they met, actually. My grandfather lost fingers to frostbite because he gave his gloves to my grandmother who didn't have any."

"Yes, it does get cold. We have off from school on those days," she continues with a hint of nostalgia to her voice.

Istvan is annoyed. "And they were forced to work on those days! They almost died. The Russians kept them there for years."

"I'm sorry about your grandmother," replies Irina. "Siberia is still my home and I miss it."

The group blinks at each other, not knowing what to say.

"So, if your grandmother was working on the railroads, Istvan," says Marek from Poland, "she's to blame for the mixed-up track sizes, which is why it took Irina four days to get here."

Istvan blinks at Marek, not knowing what to say.

"You know what, Irina?" interjects Alexander from Russia. "I'm from Kaliningrad, which isn't really part of Russia either."

The group's attention turns to him.

"What do you mean?" asks Evelina from Romania.

I look at the map and see that both Alexander and Irina have a point, sort of. Siberia is separated from the eastern part of Russia by the Ural Mountains. Kaliningrad isn't connected to Russia at all, but is separated from it by Lithuania and Belarus.

"What *is* part of Russia, then?" I ask.

"Moscow," grumbles Irina.

"Just Moscow?" I ask.

"That's right," agrees Alexander. "Moscow has always been the only city of importance to anyone of importance in Russia. It's supposed to be the showcase, you know, and it receives a constant flow of money and resources that are drained from all other cities around the country, especially from Siberia. You won't find another city in Russia like Moscow. It's actually not Russian at all, if you think about it."

The group blinks at him not knowing what to say.

"The only city worth visiting in Russia is St. Petersburg," continues Alexander. "The rest you can forget."

That's kind of a pessimistic thing to say about your country, I think to myself.

"I agree that St. Petersburg is worth visiting," adds Janika. "I was there during the White Nights last year, and it was beautiful. It is only a six-hour bus ride from Tallinn."

Tallinn, Tallinn, Tallinn, I search. Ah ha … the capital of Estonia.

"Forgive me," says Alexander, "but it takes much longer than six hours by bus to get from St. Petersburg to Tallinn."

"Yes, of course," replies Janika. "I wasn't including the Soviet-style border check."

"Ahhh! You must always include the Soviet-style border check."

"Soviet-style border check?" asks Billy. "The Cold War's been over for years now."

"Not at the Estonian-Russian border it hasn't," replies Janika.

"Yes. Only on paper, my friend," says Alexander.

"It takes three hours to cross the Estonian-Russian border?" I ask.

"Yes, welcome to my world. Whenever you want to leave or enter Russia, you must add at least three hours to your trip," explains Alexander.

"What happens at a Soviet-style border check?" Billy asks.

"Allow me to bring you through the process. First, everybody must exit the bus. Armed guards then search every person. This takes about half an hour, if all goes smoothly. Then everybody must take their luggage out of the bus and the guards search each and every bag. This takes about half an hour, if all goes smoothly. Next, the guards search in, around, and under the bus with magnets and mirrors. This takes about half an hour, if all goes smoothly. Then, if they haven't found anything dangerous, illegal, or suspicious, everybody re-boards the bus and it continues on its way."

"That's only an hour and a half," I say.

"Because once you enter Estonia, our border patrol does the same check," explains Janika.

"Are you kidding me?" asks Pete. "The same check twice?"

"Yes," replies Alexander.

"And it takes an hour and a half on each side?" I ask.

"Yes," confirms Janika.

"Isn't one check enough?" asks Billy.

"Not at the Estonian-Russian border," says Janika.

"Don't you trust each other?"

"Old habits die hard."

"Now imagine living in Kaliningrad," adds Alexander, "where everywhere you want to go is out of the country. And if you want to go to another part of Russia, you have to cross the Russian border twice."

"I can't imagine," I say.

"Me neither," says Billy.

"Me neither," says Pete.

The group sits silently for a minute. Nobody knows what to say.

Erald from Albania provides a welcome change of subject. He is looking intently at my nametag, before he bellows, "Kat-a-hhhrrriii-na Vespucci!"

"Yes?" I straighten up as if my name has been called out in class.

"What a name!"

Here we go again.

"Your first name is clearly German. But Vespucci ... that's clearly Italian."

"Yes, it is Italian."

"Ah, ha!" bellows Erald. "I thought so. I can tell by your face."

"Tell what by my face?"

At this point, the group is very intrigued about what Erald is going to say. "That you are Albanian!"

"Italian," I correct.

"One and the same!" declares Erald. "In actuality, the entire population of southern Italy is descended from Albania."

A few group members make skeptical expressions.

"It's true. It can be verified," insists Erald. "The Italians descended from the Albanians, and that explains why Katarina is so beautiful."

The group members look at each other uncomfortably.

"It's true. I mean it seriously."

Pete steps in. "You're right, Erald. Kat's not bad looking."

I am as red as the tomato sauce on my individual-sized pizza. I don't know what to say.

"Yes, Katarina is beautiful," chimes in Marek from Poland, "but her face is not Albanian. It's Polish. Look at her high cheekbones and round chin. Slavic, for sure."

I nervously pull my baseball cap down lower on my face. Marek turns to Svetlana from the Ukraine and translates the conversation into broken Russian, which he had been forced to learn in school. Svetlana, who understands broken Russian because she had been forced to learn it in school, nods enthusiastically, says something back to Marek, and points to me.

Alexander agrees to whatever it was that Svetlana said. "I don't know about Ukrainian," he says, "but Katarina definitely looks Slavic."

"Albanian!" repeats Erald.

"Italian," I insist.

"Polish," declares Marek.

"Slavic," repeats Alexander.

"*Bulgarian!*" trumpets Iosif from Bulgaria, who has been quiet up until now.

"Bulgarian?"

"You see, my friends, if it is a question of beauty, then Katarina is from Bulgaria, because Bulgaria has the most beautiful women in the world."

"Um—"

Looking around for an escape route and seeing none, I begin to gulp my beer.

"Oh!" Iosif brings the back of his hand passionately to his forehead. "To walk down the street in Sophia means to get a sore neck because the head cannot turn as fast as the beauties come walking by. How they strut! How they smile! How they smell! It is too much for one man to bear!"

Sophia, Sophia … Looking down at the map, I find Bulgaria. Of course, the capital. "It sounds like we all need to go to Sophia," I say.

"Katarina is wise," replies Iosif.

"Call me Kat."

"Pardon?"

"My friends call me Kat."

"My friends call me Sasha," adds Alexander from *Kaliningrad*.

"My friends call me Eve."

"If Svetlana could speak German, she would probably want to tell you all that her friends call her Sveta," instructs Marek from Poland.

"Es ist sehr angenehm, Sie kennenzulernen," articulates Sveta carefully to the group.

The next topic of conversation comes from Billy. "Odelia," he says to Odelia from Lithuania, "on my flight over here, I was reading an article about Lithuania in the in-flight magazine. It said that Lithuania is the geographic center of Europe."

"Yes, that's true," replies Odelia proudly.

I search the mini-map for Lithuania and eventually find it. While I never would have guessed it in a game of Trivial Pursuit, Lithuania does kind of look like the geographic center of Europe.

"That's why it was our destiny to join the European Union," expounds Odelia. "I mean, how can you have a Union, whose center isn't even within its borders?"

We all tilt our heads pensively and scrunch our eyebrows. Marek mutters something to Sveta in Russian. Sveta mutters something back to Marek in Russian.

"Sveta says that the Ukraine is also the geographic center of Europe," says Marek.

We all tilt our heads pensively the other way and scrunch our eyebrows. I consult the map. The Ukraine could also be the center of Europe, depending on how you define the borders of Europe.

"You know," interrupts Erald from Albania, "if you include northern Africa, whose populations are actually descended from

Europe, you could argue that the geographic center of Europe is in Albania."

We all tilt our heads pensively back the original way and scrunch our eyebrows.

"Northern Africa is not part of Europe," says Odelia from Lithuania.

"No ... no ... it isn't," we all agree.

"And the geographic center of Europe is in Lithuania," continues Odelia.

"Yes," agrees Marek, "and in the Ukraine."

"Yes," we all agree, "and in the Ukraine," now tilting our heads both ways and scrunching our eyebrows.

It seems like a reasonable compromise to me, of course, what the hell do I know? I've never contemplated the geographic center of Europe before. These people have, and the answer actually makes a difference to them. On the walk home from dinner, my mouth burning from Jalapeno peppers and my head spinning from the good German beer I have imbibed at an accelerated rate, I feel a profoundness descending upon me.

It is suddenly apparent to me that there are going to be many, many new issues for me to contemplate over the coming months. It also becomes apparent to me that, despite my prestigious and expensive education, I am going to be caught off-guard by each new issue to contemplate, which leads me to contemplate the worth of my prestigious and expensive education which, except for my ability to speak German, has prepared me for nothing of what I have experienced today. Then again, it is as part of this prestigious and expensive education that I am participating in *HAA* in the first place.

This new profoundness is confusing and it suddenly makes me feel exhausted. When back in my room, I descend profoundly upon my bed, where I descend profoundly into sleep. But not before reaching into my purse, pulling out the mini-map of Europe, and placing it under my pillow.

CHAPTER SIX

Fritz

The next morning, I wake up and realize that in order to do anything, I have to buy everything: food, cleaning supplies, toothpaste, shampoo. I remember yesterday seeing a supermarket near the entrance to the Private Pathway Tunnel, so I throw on some jeans and make my way over there. When I get there it is closed, though it is already ten o'clock. It is a nice day, so I decide to take a walk down the *Karl Marx Allee*. Four blocks away, I find a small shopping mall. It is also closed. What the hell? Is today a national holiday?

I stop a woman on the street and ask her why all the stores are closed.

"It's Sunday," she replies.

I give her a puzzled look, waiting for more explanation.

"*Ladenschlußgesetz.*"

"What's the *Store Closing Law?*" I ask.

"It's why all of the stores are closed on Sundays."

"I'm sorry, are you telling me that all of the stores in *Lichtenberg* are closed on Sundays?"

"All of the stores in Germany are closed on Sundays."

"What?" I gasp. "But I need food, cleaning supplies, toothpaste, and shampoo. What do I do?"

"You wait until Monday," the woman replies.

All stores in Germany are closed today because it is Sunday, I repeat to myself after she has gone. How could that be possible? How has Germany survived for this long under such conditions? I mean, what better day to shop than Sunday! This doesn't make any sense. This *Ladenschlußgesetz* is going to take some getting used to.

Back in my apartment, I have more time to look around. I meander into the kitchen to see if there is anything at all to eat. Well, there isn't any food in the house, but there are four different garbage cans in which to throw it all away. As far as I can tell, one bin is for paper, one is for plastic, glass, and aluminum, one is for biodegradables, and the fourth is for a mixture of the contents of the first three bins. *Restmüll* it says on the outside.

My eyes wander from the garbage bins to a very large book on the counter next to the kitchen sink. I walk over to it and see that it is *Telefonbuch Berlin*. A thought suddenly occurs to me. I open the book and thumb to the *b* section. I find over three pages of entries for my mother's maiden name, Bittner, and seventy-five entries under her lost brother's name, Otto. I stare at the page for a minute and then I remind myself that I would have no way of knowing him even if he were on this list. Plus he's not even from Berlin.

I close the book and go back into my room to confront my luggage, which is piled in a heap on the floor. I don't want to unpack it until I can wipe down the furniture, which has acquired a layer of dust since the last tenant. Hungry, I dig through my carry-on bag to find the extra packet of airline peanuts that Ivan had given me as a peace offering. In the search, I come across my *Rough Guide to Berlin* and decide to see what it has to say about

my neighborhood. Let's see … *Lichtenberg* … page 186. I leaf to
the page and begin to read. It says:

There's not much to write home about in *Lichtenberg* proper.

Great start. It continues:

Industrial grime and high-density living reassert
themselves here.

Okay, so I'm not the only one who noticed that.

In Berlin, racial violence, though fairly rare in central
parts of the East, is definitely a risk in outlying areas like
Lichtenberg or *Marzahn*, which are perceived as neo-
Nazi/skinhead strongholds. Such thugs are likely to pick
on anyone who might stand out—and not only because
of their skin colour. Simply being "foreign" or looking
unusual is reason enough to be at the rough end of their
attention. Avoid these areas at night.

Great, so *Lichtenberg* is a neo-Nazi/skinhead stronghold.
This is where the German *Bundestag* decided to stick ninety-two
foreign students? Having never lived in a neo-Nazi/skinhead
stronghold before, I suddenly feel very out of my element. I
mean, I don't feel like I look particularly unusual, but there is no
denying the fact that I am foreign, and I certainly don't feel like
being at the rough end of anyone's attention. Not to mention
the fact that, living in this neighborhood for ten months, there
will certainly be an occasion or two when I will find myself here
at night. This guidebook is only scaring me, I decide, and I toss
it aside. Instead, I pull out the Group Four schedule that Herr
Stern gave me yesterday. It tells me that *HAA* has arranged a
tour of the city starting at *Alexanderplatz* at one o'clock in the

afternoon. *Alexanderplatz* is where the TV tower is, I remember from school. I've still got two hours until I need to be there.

For now, a shower is first on my list of priorities. Luckily, I have packed a small travel bag with single-serving bottles of shampoo and shower gel from various hotels in my lifetime. The only problem is that I didn't pack a towel. I had planned on buying one, but that will have to wait until it isn't Sunday anymore. My T-shirt will do for now.

Gingerly, I step into the bathroom and take a look around. At first glance, it looks more like the inside of a space capsule than a facility for washing. There is a sink, a toilet, and a stand-up shower packed into a space that is just large enough for me to stand with my elbows, but not my full arms, extended. I now understand why Germans call their bathrooms "water closets." There isn't even a shower curtain in the bathroom, and given the size of it, it is instantly clear that there is no hope of keeping anything dry once the shower is turned on. I wonder how Billy will even get his wide shoulders into a space like this. I go back into my room and undress there. I return to the water closet, hang my T-shirt-turned-towel on the outside door handle, and climb inside.

I step up to the shower. The controls consist of one knob, with no instructions, save one circular line drawn counter-clockwise around the knob, starting in blue and turning to red. I turn the knob ninety degrees to the left, and hop away, expecting water to surge out. None comes. Interesting. There are no other controls to be seen. I wait. No water comes. I turn the knob 180 degrees to the right and hop away, expecting water to surge out. None comes. Very interesting. I wait. No water comes. Finally, I push on the knob and a few drops trickle out. I give it a harder push, and more water comes. I give the knob a forceful shove and finally water flows out of the faucet. I adjust the temperature, and step under the stream. Warm water rushes over my body, invigorating me. Ahhhhhh, there's nothing like a long, hot shower to make you feel alive.

Six seconds later, my long, hot shower ends. What the—? I look up, blinking at the nozzle. I haven't even had a chance to open the soap. I push the button again, and again, the water flows. This time, I hurry and lather myself up. I scrub speedily, but only get to half of the important parts before the water shuts off. For the love of God! I push the button again. I quickly soap up the rest of my body, and am in mid-shampoo when the water cuts out again. It is, apparently, a water-saving shower, and it only allocates six seconds of water at a time. Damn environmentalists! I seethe, covered in suds.

It doesn't take me long to realize that if I am going to salvage my hygiene experience, I am going to have to find a way to hold the button down while standing under the stream. I try pushing with my elbow, but I am not able to provide enough pressure. I try leaning on the knob with my upper back, but the arch of the stream misses me by several inches. Finally I come up with a strategy to show that water-saving shower who is boss. Standing about a foot away from my target, I bring one knee up to my chest and place the ball of my foot squarely on the knob. I anchor my other foot on the opposite wall of the water closet and lean my body weight into the knob. As long as I hold this position, the water flows steadily. It isn't a comfortable position, but with the proper stretching exercises, over time I believe I can sustain it long enough to actually clean myself. Shaving is going to be interesting.

When I am done with my shower, I instinctively reach for my towel. No towel. Ah yes, it's hanging on the outside of the door. When I open the bathroom door, wearing nothing but a thousand droplets of water, I bump smack into my new roommate, Fritz, who is standing in the hallway, waiting to use the toilet. Fritz is tall and skinny with an angular face, thin hair that looks like it might be blond if it weren't dyed black, and wide-set blue eyes.

"Hallo, Schatz!" he greets me with the most euphoric twinkle I have ever seen in the eyes of a roommate I am meeting for the first time. I give a shriek and slam the door in his face.

"*Schatz,* what's wrong?" he protests. "Is that all you have to say to me on our first meeting?"

"I can't believe it!" I fume from behind the bathroom door.

"What's the problem?"

"We've never even met and you've already seen me naked."

"So what? You look great," Fritz consoles me. I am too embarrassed to respond. "Well, are you coming out? I have to take a whiz."

I crack the door and reach around for my T-shirt. I pull it on and shimmy from the bathroom to my bedroom. In my mortification, I cannot bare to look Fritz in the face.

"How do you like the water-saving shower?" he asks, before I can disappear into my room.

"It's fine."

"You know, *Schatz,* it saves even more water if you shower in pairs," Fritz teases.

I pretend to ignore the comment from behind my bedroom door. The nerve of him! In my room, I seize my German-English dictionary and look up the word *Schatz. Darling* or *treasure,* it says.

CHAPTER SEVEN

Sasha

"The nerve of him!" exclaims Pete, once I have related the story of my first meeting with Fritz to him. We are standing together on the *S-Bahn* platform, waiting for the train to take us to *Alexanderplatz* for our introductory tour of the city.

"I know," I reply.

"That's so rude!" exclaims Pete.

"I know," I reply.

"What's happened to chivalry these days?"

"I have no idea."

"What kind of world do we live in when a guy doesn't even offer to hold down the button in the water-saving shower for his female roommate?"

Pete is teasing me, I realize, and I give him a scolding look.

"If you want me to next time, I'll—"

"Too late. Fritz already made the showering together joke."

Before the *S-Bahn* arrives, Pete and I are joined by ten other

HAA students, who have moseyed their way down the Private Pathway to the platform.

"Beautiful day for a walk down an overgrown path through a dark and dingy tunnel," Billy comments.

As the train arrives, I remember that I still haven't purchased a *Bahnpass*. I look around to see if anyone else still hasn't purchased a *Bahnpass*, and I notice that everyone else is looking around to see if anybody else still hasn't purchased a *Bahnpass*, which, it turns out, nobody has. When the train rolls to a stop in front of us, I push the button on the door, remembering the scolding I got the day before, take a deep breath, and step into the car. Everyone else takes a deep breath and steps into the car after me. The doors close and away we go, a whole herd of *Schwarzfahrer*.

The air is crisp and cool when we emerge from the *S-Bahn* at *Alexanderplatz*. Herr Stern is waiting for us in the middle of the square. As the group comes down the escalator from the *S-Bahn* platform, I look around. I know that *Alexanderplatz* is supposed to have been the town center of the East, but everything here is made of the same drab concrete that reigns in *Lichtenberg*, giving me the feeling that former East Berlin is one giant concrete sandbox.

Herr Stern smacks his hands together and begins the tour. We start at the TV tower, where Herr Stern explains most of the stuff that I already know. I am pleased when he mentions the glare on the ball in the shape of a cross, "the Pope's revenge," which confirms for me that my German teachers were not lying to me the whole time. One can just barely make it out today, because it's not sunny enough for the full effect. Next on the agenda is the *Weltzeituhr*, a tacky bronze clock that tells the time in cities throughout the world, but not New Jersey.

From the World Clock, Herr Stern takes us across the concrete plain to the *Rotes Rathaus*, Red Town Hall, where the city and state governments of Berlin hold their offices. It bores me when he talks about the Venetian architecture and large mural illustrating scenes from the history of Berlin, although,

I do admit, it is a small relief to see a building that is made of brick instead of concrete. I am amused to hear, however, that not long ago, the mayor of Berlin befuddled an audience during a party convention, when, instead of a long-winded campaign speech outlining his policies and promises to improve the city, he took the opportunity to get something personal off his chest and declared, "I am gay, and that is okay." Since that day, the Red Town Hall has been more popularly known as the "Pink Town Hall."

From *Alexanderplatz*, we make our way up the famous boulevard, *Unter den Linden*, which, Herr Stern informs us, had been the great axis of Imperial Berlin. It certainly is an impressive thoroughfare, stretching all the way from *Alexanderplatz* to the Brandenburg Gate, which used to mark the end of East Berlin. As we walk toward the West, Herr Stern points out museums and embassies, as well as the many elegant linden trees we are walking under, giving the street its name. He points out that the trees were uprooted during the 1930s and replaced with Nazi flags, which, given the sheer number of linden trees, must have been a wild sight. Luckily, after the war, the flags were re-replaced with the non-ideological trees that are standing here today. In fact, the walk is quite romantic, which, for some reason, makes me realize that Pete is not paying attention to me at all. Instead, he is talking exclusively with Odelia from Lithuania, who is a strikingly cute girl with a cropped platinum bob, light features, and sea green eyes. I notice that the two of them seem to be really enjoying each other's company.

Suddenly, Sasha from Russia approaches me. "You know," he says as we stroll down *Unter den Linden*, "Berlin is where the Russians and Americans met in the final days of World War II—"

"That's true," I remark. I hadn't thought about it.

"—and then threatened to annihilate each other for half a century."

I look up at Sasha. Unlike the Little League coach, I find

this Russian to be very pleasant. They look quite similar, actually, tall, blond, strong-jawed, but Sasha has much softer features and doesn't reek of vodka.

"Thank goodness American-Russian relations have improved since then," I say.

Sasha nods in agreement.

Continuing on our walk, we approach the Humboldt University on the right-hand side of the street, and I recognize the sidewalk where I spread out the map the day before. How much I have learned since just yesterday! Herr Stern lists off a group of distinguished Humboldt alumni, whose ranks we will soon be joining, including Karl Marx, Friedrich Engels, the Brothers Grimm, and Albert Einstein. What footsteps to follow! I wonder how I'll fit in. Then I take another look at Sasha. It dawns on me that he was raised on Marx and Engels. He must have been in his early teens when Communism fell. I wonder what he thinks of them now. I want to ask him, but I am afraid to.

"You want to ask me something?" Sasha asks me, sensing my unspoken question.

"How do you say 'hello' in Russian?"

"*Priviet.*"

"Oh, that's right," I reply excitedly. "I just learned that. And 'thank you' is … don't tell me … *spasiba!*"

"Very good, *Amerikanka!*" Sasha is impressed.

"If you don't mind, never call me that again."

Rather than taking the group inside the university, Herr Stern bears left, and brings us into the middle of a broad square across from the Humboldt University. *Bebelplatz,* he informs us, was built by Frederick the Great and was supposed to emulate an ancient Roman piazza. I have never seen an ancient Roman piazza before, but I can imagine that it might look something like this. It is a wide square surrounded by large, impressive, Roman-looking buildings, with large, impressive, Roman-looking façades featuring columns and large, impressive Roman-looking sculptures. I have the feeling that I am in a very significant place.

"This is a very significant place," Herr Stern tells the group that has gathered around him at the center of the square. "This is where the infamous *Bücherverbrennung* of 1933 took place. Hundreds of students sympathetic to the Nazi cause brought thousands of 'degenerate' literary works from the library and burned them in the center of this square. The fire burned for four days."

Wow. I am astonished. My mind immediately flashes to the scene in *Indiana Jones and the Last Crusade*, where the book burning is portrayed in frightening detail. That's what that was. And it happened right here! Standing in the square, my imagination produces the sounds of shouting and crackling and the smell of burning paper as the students throw hundreds of works of literature into the flames.

"Among the so-called degenerate authors whose books were burned here are Erich Maria Remarque, Thomas Mann, Heinrich Mann, Stefan Zweig, Erich Kästner, H.G. Wells, and Ernest Hemingway."

"Ernest Hemingway?" I say out loud. It is the only name in the list that I recognize. "What is degenerate about Ernest Hemingway?"

Herr Stern explains that books depicting warfare as anything but glorious went against the Nazi ideal of militarism.

"I see."

"Isn't it funny?" Sasha says to me, "This very militarism is what brought the Nazis to their demise. If they hadn't been so power hungry, they might have actually stayed in power."

"Hmm," I reply, trying to think of something to add. "World domination is so cliché."

Before leaving *Bebelplatz*, Herr Stern instructs us to peer one by one into a pane of glass that is implanted into the center of the square. The window offers a view down into a small white room lined with empty bookshelves. The room is lit up, which casts an eerie glow reminiscent of fire. Next to the piece of glass is a plaque with the quote: "Where they start burning books, they'll end burning people—Heinrich Heine 1820." I shudder, daunted by this foreshadowing.

On from *Bebelplatz*, the group heads West toward the Brandenburg Gate, and Herr Stern informs us that we are walking on what used to be "No Man's Land," or "Death Strip," a barren patch of earth, one hundred yards wide, that separated the East German citizens from the Berlin Wall. The reason it was called Death Strip was because anyone that set foot onto it was to be shot on sight "like rabbits" as the official order decreed. I thumb my crucifix as Herr Stern says this. I suddenly feel guilty walking here, knowing that people have died here.

We continue up to the Brandenburg Gate, which, to our chagrin, is undergoing renovations and is completely obstructed by scaffolding and canvas. Lucky for us, the construction company has painted a huge picture of the Brandenburg Gate on the canvas shrouding the Brandenburg Gate. I wondered if anybody is fooled.

"It's almost like looking at the real thing," I say to Sasha.

"No, it isn't."

"You're right, it isn't," I admit.

Once on the other side of the Brandenburg Gate, I notice a narrow, cobblestone strip traversing the street that marks the path where the Berlin Wall had stood, and I notice a handful of crosses displayed on a nearby fence in memory of those that were killed trying to flee East Berlin. I am very conscious of the fact that, in recent history, the walk I have just taken would have earned me a hail of bullets to the back of the head.

The final destination on the introductory tour of Berlin is the *Reichstag*, the parliament building, which housed Germany's first democratic congress during the Weimar Republic, the building that had burned down in 1933 allowing Hitler to become chancellor, the building that was captured and ransacked by the Russians in the final battle of World War II, the building that stood empty and obsolete for fifty-four years during the Cold War, the building that had been reinstated as Germany's capitol nine years after reunification, and the building that will be my office in a few weeks when my internship begins.

From the outside, the *Reichstag* is an impressive neo-classical building, evoking old-fashioned power with a modern twist. Herr Stern tells us how the original marble dome roof had been destroyed during the war and replaced by the flashy, glass dome in order to symbolize the transparency of the new, united German democracy.

From the inside, the *Reichstag* Building is a modern German office complex, decorated with a futuristic motif of glass and steel. The building has an entirely open feel. Herr Stern tells us how, in the daytime, the building is lit primarily with natural light, and vents in the ceiling collect rainwater, which is used to humidify the inside air.

Herr Stern takes us into the plenary chamber where the *Bundestag*, the lower house of Parliament, holds its sessions. It is an impressive room, furnished with the bright blue stadium seating. Herr Stern informs us that, after years of arguing about whether this color is royal blue or navy blue, the designers decided to compromise and name it *"Bundestag* blue."

The thing that impresses me most about the plenary hall is the giant, steel eagle that hangs above the main podium. It is a massive piece of art weighing one metric ton, and it is suspended by thin cables that look entirely too weak to support such a colossal hunk of metal. I imagine it breaking free and crashing down onto the Speaker of the House. I wonder if anybody else is imagining the same thing.

"Leave it to the Germans to dangle a colossal piece of steel over everybody's head," jokes Billy, behind me. "Would mounting it on the wall have been too easy?"

"Maybe it's to keep everyone on their toes," adds Pete, admiring the precarious art piece.

"It sure does look like it could just fly away," remarks Odelia from Lithuania.

"I guess that's the point."

Next, Herr Stern takes us behind closed doors into a special corridor that the German parliamentarians use to mill back and forth between their offices and the plenary hall. The walls are covered in Russian writing, and we are told that these are stones from the original *Reichstag* Building that remained standing after the Russians had invaded. It is astounding to me that the German government decided to preserve the graffiti, hard evidence of the destruction and humiliation that Germany suffered at the hands of the Russians, and not only that, but to leave it in view of present-day lawmakers on their way to work. That is some self-reflection, I remark to myself. When I mention the thought to Sasha, he reminds me that the destruction and humiliation that Germany suffered was at the hands of Hitler, not the hands of the Russians. The Russians had been the liberators, he explains, and I admit that I had never thought of it that way.

"What does it say?"

"This one says, 'This is the day of victory over Fascism.'"

"What about this one?" I ask.

"This one says, 'I came from Vladivostok to obliterate Berlin.'"

"That's cheerful. And this one?"

"This one says, 'Igor was here, 1945.'"

"It does not say that."

"It does."

The final stop on our sightseeing tour of Berlin is the roof of the *Reichstag* Building. From here, we enjoy a breathtaking view of the city, despite gray clouds and a light drizzle. Over a dozen German flags flap softly in the breeze, and Herr Stern points out that government buildings are the only buildings in Germany where Germans display the flag.

"And at soccer games," says Sasha.

"You know a lot about Germany," I say.

"Really? I don't think I know much more than the next guy."

"You definitely do. I am the next guy, and you know a hell of a lot more than me."

Sasha laughs.

"Why don't Germans display the flag?" I ask Herr Stern, realizing that I haven't seen any of the black, red, and gold banners anywhere else since I arrived in Germany.

"Because of World War II," he replies.

"But that was so long ago."

"Not in our minds."

The history I have seen today suddenly overwhelms me. When preparing to come to Berlin, I hadn't thought much about the fact that I was going to a place that has shaped the modern world. Berlin had been the Nazi headquarters. Berlin had been entirely destroyed in World War II. Berlin had been divided by the Russians and the Americans, who then pointed all sorts of deadly weapons at each other for almost half a century. With the death and destruction that this city has seen, I can't believe it's even still standing. It's hard to understand how so many people still live here and can manage to lead normal lives.

I think about New Jersey. My own hometown hasn't known a war since the American Revolution. We have tragedy, sure, two girls a few classes ahead of me in high school died in a car accident, and my great aunt died of cancer, but those are on an individual scale. How would we react if the whole town were leveled by air raids? Would we rebuild it afterward, like Berlin has rebuilt itself, stone for stone? I shake my head in disbelief.

To commemorate the new Russian-American relations, I ask Janika to take a picture of Sasha and me standing together in front of the *Reichstag's* glass dome.

Herr Stern takes us on a loop around the roof and points out significant buildings on all sides. After that, we are worn out and ready to wrap things up.

"How you feeling?" Pete asks me as we ride the elevator back down to ground level.

"I could use a beer."

"And how!" agrees Pete.

"And how!" agrees the group.

CHAPTER EIGHT

Odelia

The next week is a period of adjustment for me and my fellow foreign students. We decorate our sparse apartments, become friends with the clerks at the grocery store across the street, sample Internet cafés around town, and find the movie theatre that plays undubbed American movies. We also take our turns meeting with Herr Stern to get out student IDs, register for our courses, and learn where we will be placed during the internship portion of the program. I will be working in the office of *Bundestag* Representative, Wilbur Kaufmann.

At the end of the meeting, Herr Stern smacks his hands together and says, "You seem to be getting along just fine, Frau Vespucci. Keep up the good work!"

"Thank you Herr Stern."

"And if there is anything you need, young lady, please don't hesitate to ask."

"Okay, thank you, sir. That's good to know."

"If you have any problems adjusting to life in Berlin, or with your job or your classes or your classmates or co-workers, you just let me know."

"I will, Herr Stern. Thank you."

"Unless you want my permission to elope with a German to the Bavarian Alps. In that case, you're on your own."

"Good to know," I laugh. We shake hands and I begin to leave his office. But then I stop.

"What is it, Frau Vespucci?"

"Oh, nothing, I say," feeling my forehead crinkle.

"You've got something to say. What is it?"

"This is going to sound silly, but you wouldn't happen to know anyone named Otto Bittner, would you?"

Herr Stern thinks for a minute. "Hmmm, I know of an actress in Berlin named Anna Bittner, but offhand, I don't know any Otto Bittner's. Why, who is he?"

"Oh, a family member of mine. My mother, um, lost touch with him some years ago, and asked me to ask around a bit about him."

"Well, if he lives in Berlin, he'll be in the *Telefonbuch Berlin*."

"Thanks, I'll try that," I lie.

"Do that, Frau Vespucci. And if I run into any Otto Bittners, you will be the first to know."

"Thank you, Herr Stern. *Auf wiedersehen*."

"*Auf wiedersehen.*"

With my student ID, I attempt to buy a monthly *Bahnpass again*, but fail *again,* because the allotted time at the beginning of the semester for issuing student *Bahn* passes has elapsed. My biggest triumph this week is discovering the weekly magazine *Zitty*, which prints a comprehensive listing of every entertainment event taking place in Berlin. From *Zitty*, I learn that Wednesday night is live music night in Berlin and all the premiere clubs offer jam sessions with minimal cover charges. It just so happens that it is Wednesday night when I discover this tidbit of information, and I start making immediate plans to hit the town.

The first person I think to invite is Fritz, figuring he knows a thing or two about the music scene in Berlin. I knock on his door, but there is no answer. A tall, fashionably dressed woman had come over earlier, but now I'm not sure if they are in his room or not. I can see at the bottom of the door that his light is on, so I knock again. No answer. I am pretty sure I hear Fritz's voice on the other side of the door and the voice of the woman.

"Fritz," I call through the door.

"Come back later, *Schatz*," he answers.

"Okay." I leave to go find another music-listening companion.

Skipping down one flight of stairs, I knock on the door to Pete's apartment. Another American named Nat answers the door. Nat is in Group Three.

"Hi, Kat," says Nat as he opens the door.

"Hi, Nat," I say as Nat opens the door. I always get a kick out of guys with names that rhyme with mine. After breaking up with Matt, I have been missing the fun. "Is Pete around?"

"Yeah, he's in his room."

I hear two voices coming from Pete's room, one is Pete's and one is a girl's. I think about leaving them alone, but then decide to knock anyway.

"Come in," calls Pete.

I open the door and poke my head into Pete's room.

"Kat!" exclaims Pete, when he sees who it is. "So nice of you to come by." Pete pats the bed next to him, inviting me to have a seat. Sitting on the bed on the other side of Pete is Odelia from Lithuania.

"Odelia and I were just discussing what we were going to do tonight. Any ideas?"

"That's why I stopped by," I reply, not sure if I am invited. "Tonight's live music night in Berlin. I was wondering if you guys wanted to check out a few clubs with me."

"Sure," says Pete.

"Love to," says Odelia.

"Do you have a particular place in mind?"

"I was thinking about this one club, Quasimodo. *Zitty* says it's the best place to hear live jazz in Berlin. They have a free jam session tonight."

"What time does it start?"

"Ten o'clock."

"Great! We'll meet you downstairs in half an hour. Is that okay with you, Odelia?"

"Sure."

"Great."

"Great."

It takes us an hour by *S-Bahn* to get to Quasimodo, and we walk in after the jam session has already started. It is a small club in the heart of West Berlin, smoky and intimate, crowded with beautiful people in swanky outfits. The group on stage is rocking out to "Mustang Sally." They sound awesome. Pete and Odelia push through the crowd to the bar where they find one free bar stool and counter space enough for the three of us to rest our drinks. Pete offers the stool to Odelia, and she sits down. We order three *Hefeweizen*, a wheat beer served in a curvy glass with a fresh slice of lemon. When we receive our drinks, the three of us give a toast to our first night out in Berlin. I turn to face the band. After one glance at the lead guitarist, I fall madly in love with him.

For a few unexpected seconds, I am paralyzed. I cannot think, feel, speak, move, breathe, nor behold anything else in the room except for the man on the stage with the guitar. What I see is a disarmingly handsome and mischievous-looking musician. He is wiry, but athletic. He has rich brown hair styled to look messy, bright blue eyes that sparkle in the stage lights, a straight nose, a solid jaw, and a wide grin that reveals teeth just crooked enough to be adorable. In both cheeks he has long dimples that frame his smile like parentheses. Around the back and sides of his neck is the upturned collar of a beige suede jacket. The guitarist is perched on a stool on the right side of the stage, his right arm cradling the body of a blood red guitar while the fingers of his left hand dance over the fret board. My face feels hot and my heart is pumping overtime. It makes me want to drive a steak knife into my chest.

"All you wanna' do is ride around Sally," croons the lead singer.

"Riiiiide, Sally, riiiiide," sings the guitarist after him. They are both grinning like schoolboys, basking in the attention around them.

When I finally regain my motor skills, I turn and ask the bartender, "Who is that?"

"Who?"

"The guitar player."

"Um … I can't really see." He cranes his neck. "Oh, that's Thor."

"Thor?" I take another long look at him.

"Yeah, Thor."

My heart quivers at the sound of his name. I place my hand on my chest to calm my heart. It works for a minute; but then I look at Thor again, and my stomach drops to my knees. I gulp and turn again to the bartender. "Where did he come from?" I ask.

"Sweden. Are you okay?"

I realize that I haven't exhaled in a while, so I let out a slow breath. "I think so. How often does … um … Thor … play here?" I ask. My heart does the quiver thing again when I say his name.

"From time to time."

"I see," I say, turning back around to face the band.

"Mustang Sally now baby," belts the lead singer.

"Guess you better slow that Mustang down," sings Thor, grinning at the audience.

"Did you see that?" I exclaim to Pete and Odelia.

"See what?" ask Pete and Odelia.

"Thor just smiled at me!"

"Who's Thor?"

"The guitarist."

"He just smiled at everyone."

"What difference does that make?"

"You been runnin' all over town," croons the lead singer.

"Oow! I got to put your flat feet on the ground," sings Thor.

Thor and his band play three songs, and then it is time to turn the jam session over to someone else. In the meantime, Pete has grown tired of standing and is now sitting on the bar stool with Odelia on his lap. He is clearly enjoying this. I can't take my eyes off of Thor. I haven't been this attracted to someone since Matt, and even that wasn't quite like *this*. The problem is, having been in a relationship for the past five years, I have no idea how to talk to men. Pete, Odelia, and I order another round of *Hefeweizen*.

The next band on stage features a female guitarist who makes the guys in the audience go wild. She has a killer body, wild black hair, and she is just wailing away on the guitar. This group opens with "Stand by Me," and her guitar solo has everybody whooping and hollering. My attention is still focused on Thor, who is now mingling his way through the crowd talking to people. I can't hear what he is saying, but I like the way he is saying it. He is holding a beer in the air as he pushes through the crowd, and I catch a glimpse of his hands. They are muscular and lean, and I can make out veins springing up on the backs of his hands and forearms. I can tell that Thor has well-trained hands. I have to meet this guy to find out more, and I have no idea how to do it. Am I supposed to just go up and talk to him?

"Why don't you just go up and talk to him?" says Pete, tiring of my gawking.

"To whom?"

"To Mr. Social Butterfly over there."

"Yeah, right," I respond. "I think he's got enough admirers right now."

"Tell him you like his music. You can't go wrong with that."

"Yeah, right."

"Suit yourself."

The third band that night moves the music into the soul realm. The lead singer is a German woman, on the heavy side, with huge breasts and a plunging neckline. She is teasing the crowd with a German-accent rendition of "Giving Him Something He Can Feel." Odelia is starting to yawn. Thor has settled into a booth behind us and is surrounded on all sides by friends and admirers, who occasionally slap him on the shoulder and give him high fives. Pete is getting bored with the music. It is getting late. Pete offers us a cigarette, but we both decline. A few minutes later, Odelia announces that she is ready to go home.

"Let's go."

I hesitate. They put their coats on and start making their way to the door. It is less crowded now than earlier. I glance over at Thor, who is between me and the door, reclining with his beer, looking absolutely content. Oh well, I guess. Maybe next time. I follow Pete and Odelia across the bar to the exit, trying not to stare too obviously at Thor as I pass him. We exit the club and start walking to the *S-Bahn*.

"Wait!" I stop.

"What?"

"Did you forget something?"

"Yeah."

"What?"

"My wallet."

"You better run back in and get it."

"Okay, I'll be right back."

Running back into Quasimodo, I lope up to the bar and snatch a pack of matches and a pen. On the inside of the pack, I scribble my phone number and *I like your music. —Kat.* I take a deep breath, turn toward Thor, pretend he is sitting there alone, and walk up to him. Gulp!

"Hello." I can barely eke out the word and have to clear my throat and say it again, *"Hello."*

Thor looks to his left and then to his right to make sure I am talking to him.

"Hello?" he asks.

I hold out the pack of matches for him to take. Thor straightens up in the booth, reaches out to accept the matches, and gives me a curious stare. "Have we met?" he asks.

When he speaks to me, I lose the sense of having a body and forget to let go of the matches. I begin to say something, but my voice box is empty.

"I'm sorry it's so loud in here," Thor says. "Have we met?"

"I hope so," I reply.

Thor chuckles. "What's this?" he tugs on the matches.

"That's, um," I pause, suddenly realizing my death grip on the matchbook and release it. "I hope you enjoy them." Oh, God, I am stupid. I give a bashful smile to the group that is now all staring at me. "Sorry, I'm in a rush. It was nice to meet you all," I say, turn around, and scurry out of the club.

"That's so cool!" I hear someone say as I disappear out the door. "Thor, you're a rock star!"

Outside again, my hands are shaking. I can't believe I did that!

"I can't believe you did that!" exclaims Pete as I relate the story to him and Odelia out on the street.

"Wow!"

"You know you made his night," continues Pete.

"I don't know. I feel stupid."

"He'll definitely call."

"Whatever." I give a shrug.

"You made him look really cool in front of his friends. That's no small thing for a guy."

"Let's just get home."

"Okay, but you gotta tell me when he calls."

"Okay."

"What about your wallet?" asks Odelia.

I pull it out of my pocket with a mischievous grin.

"I can't believe you lied to us," teases Pete.

"Let's go home."

The three of us take the *S-Bahn* back home. We don't buy tickets, and we aren't controlled. Pete and I walk Odelia to her door, at which point I feel like I should probably disappear. But Odelia disappears first into her apartment, with nothing more than a quick wave to us both.

"You know, you could have walked me home first," I say as the two of us are suddenly standing there alone.

"Why?" asks Pete.

"So you and Odelia could have had a more romantic good-bye or kept hanging out or something."

"Odelia has a boyfriend."

"She does?"

"Yeah."

"Oh."

" ... "

"Where is he?"

"Lithuania."

"Oh."

"They're pretty serious."

"Too bad."

"It's okay."

" ... "

"Shall I walk you to your door?"

"Sure."

Pete walks me to my door and gives me a big hug.

"Goodnight, my lady," he says, giving me a tender squeeze. Then he turns around and walks down the hall. I shake my head, turn my back, and put the key into the lock.

"Hey!" Pete calls from down the hall. "Maybe tomorrow night you and I can catch some music by ourselves."

"Maybe," I laugh as I push the door open. "But tomorrow night's not cheap live music night," I inform him. Pete shoots me a wink and then disappears into the stairwell.

When I get inside my apartment, Fritz and a male friend are smoking homemade cigarettes in the kitchen.

"Hallo Schatz!" He greets me the same way he has been greeting me ever since I stepped out of the shower naked that first day and into his life. *"Schatz,* I want you to meet Thorsten. He's a friend of mine."

"Nice to meet you."

"A pleasure," says Thorsten, unenthusiastically. Instead of making conversation, Thorsten snuffs out his cigarette, gets up from the table, and leaves the kitchen.

"Time for bed," responds Fritz, taking a long drag on his cigarette before snuffing it out, getting up from the table, and leaving the kitchen. *"Gute Nacht, Schatz,"* he whispers, and pinches my cheek on his way out.

"Gute Nacht, Fritz," I reply, shaking my head.

CHAPTER NINE

Jenny

You would think that five years of dating a guy would make me somehow knowledgeable about men. You would think that in the million plus conversations I had with my ex-boyfriend, I might have learned a thing or two about how the male mind works. You might also think that meeting some new men, and spending some time with them, would further increase my understanding of the male sex. Instead, I am finding that the more men I meet, the less I understand them. It's been a week since I've seen Pete, Thor hasn't called at all, and Fritz has just invited me to go shoe shopping with him in the premier shopping district of West Berlin. Go figure.

I try to put men out of my mind as Fritz and I bounce from shop to shop along the *Kurfürstendam*, the wide, bustling avenue near West Berlin's main train station, the *Zoologischer Garten*. I had been under the impression that *Friedrichstrasse Bahnhof* was the main train station in Berlin, but I'm starting to realize that Berlin has two of everything. In its divided state, the city planners on both sides had engaged in such a rigorous policy of keeping up with the Jones, that the result was two TV towers, two airports, two zoos, two central parks, two theatre districts, two opera houses, two concert halls, two lake resorts, and most importantly for Fritz, two premiere shopping districts.

Today is a nice day, and Fritz is enjoying himself immensely as he tries on fourteen plus pairs of shoes. Every now and then he stops, purses his lips, and stares thoughtfully into nothing. When I ask him what he is thinking about, he answers with a ridiculous question like, "How do Yoga instructors relax after work?"

Before I can even begin to fathom an answer, he asks me, "What do you think of this pair, *Schatz?*"

Each one looks great, I tell him, and it isn't a lie. Fritz's fashion sense is intimidating, to say the least, and hanging around him I'm starting to get the feeling that I need a complete makeover. In the end, Fritz buys nothing but two cappuccinos, which we drink together at a sidewalk café overlooking an eerily bombed-out church that stands out like a sore thumb among the Ritz and glitz of the *Kurfürstendam*. As we drink, Fritz sits properly on his chair with his legs crossed, rolling cigarettes in between sips from his cup.

"What's the deal with that church?" I ask Fritz.

"You mean the Kaiser Wilhelm Memorial Church?" he answers, not looking up from his cigarette.

"It was destroyed in the war, I assume?"

"The church and everything else, *Schatz*. The church and everything else."

The church looks like someone took a massive mallet and smashed it on one side. The original frame is still there, but its steeple is half-crumbled and blackened by fire. A chill runs up my spine.

"You mean, after the war, the entire city looked like that church!"

Fritz looks up from his cigarette at the church, blinks, and looks back down at his cigarette.

"Yep."

"Why didn't they rebuild the church, like they rebuilt the rest of the city?" I ask.

"So we don't forget. That's why it's called the Kaiser Wilhelm *Memorial* Church."

His comment makes me again aware of the tragic history of Berlin. It's easy to forget as you are going about your daily business, shopping, talking, going to class, having coffee with friends, but then you stumble across a bombed out church here or a cluster of crosses there. I am looking hard at the church and I notice some strange nicks in the stones on one side.

"Those aren't ... bullet holes, are they?" I ask Fritz.

Fritz nods without looking up again.

The rest of the week consists of more exploring for me. Thursday night I go to an East German dance party with Janika from Estonia in another factory-turned-music venue, the *Kulturbrauerei*. This place had been an East German beer brewery and now plays nothing but East German rock music to the delight of nostalgic former East Germans throughout the city. I am surprised to see several signs up outside the club that say, "*Ossies* Only."

"What are *Ossies?*" I ask Janika as we wait in the line.

"That's what the *Wessies* called the East Germans."

"And the *Wessies* are—"

"The West Germans."

"I see. How do you know that?"

"I don't know. I've always known that."

"Are *Wessies* really not allowed in here?" I ask the doorman on our way in.

"Of course they are allowed in."

"Then why does the sign say, '*Ossies* Only.'"

"We just want them to know they're not welcome here."

"I see."

"It's true," says Janika as we get inside. "I read in *Zitty* that this is an *Ossie* hangout."

"You would think that after all this time, East and West Germans would have blended."

"Ha! You have much to learn, *Amerikanka*."

"Why does everyone keep calling me that?"

Friday afternoon, Billy and I go to *Potsdamerplatz* to the big Cineplex movie house where Hollywood movies are shown in both dubbed and original versions. *Spiderman* is playing. Billy and I watch it twice, first in English and then dubbed over in German. In between films, we go to the gelato parlor where we eat multiple scoops of sweet, gooey Italian-style ice cream, and Billy complains that he can barely squeeze his "wide-American ass," as he calls it, into the narrow seat. After the second film, Billy and I feast on *Döner Kebaps* at the Turkish snack stand.

"So your roommate Fritz is an interesting character," Billy observes.

"You can say that again."

"Have you figured out yet, you know …"

"What?"

"His sexuality?"

I laugh. Fritz continues to be an enigma to me. He dresses to kill, rolls his own cigarettes, and wields more sex appeal than *GQ Magazine*. He's so damn suave, that I feel inarticulate, outmoded, and awkward in his presence. But after observing an assortment of female, male, and miscellaneous companions romping into, out of, and around his room, I still have no idea whether he himself is straight, gay, or miscellaneous.

"The jury's still out, but right now I'd put my money on miscellaneous."

"Get back to me when you have a final verdict," Billy teases.

"Okay, I will."

"In other guy news, have you seen Pete lately?"

"No, you?"

"Yeah, he said he was looking for you this morning but wasn't able to find you."

"He was?"

"He wanted to make sure you knew about the soccer game this Saturday."

"Soccer game? Who's playing?"

"We are."

I finally see Pete again at the pick-up soccer game on Saturday. Jenny, an American in Group Two, has bought a soccer ball and organized a *HAA* soccer face-off on the field a few blocks from the *Plattenbau*. Eight of us show up, half girls and half guys. When I arrive at the field, I see Pete stretching out.

"Where have you been?" I ask him.

"Oh, I've been away visiting family."

"Where?"

"Potsdam."

"Oh."

When we are all stretched out and warmed up, Jenny suggests that she and Pete be the captains, and that they start picking teams. Erald from Albania is incredulous.

"You don't mean to tell me that you girls are going to play with us?"

"Ah, yup, that's what I mean to tell you," Jenny responds.

"Oh, right, I forgot, American girls are so strong and independent," Erald mocks.

Istvan from Hungary butts in, "Wait, Erald. We should let them play. After all, it's Jenny's ball."

Erald shrugs his shoulders.

Istvan continues, "How about we play the first game with the girls and the second game just guys. It will be a good warm-up."

Pete watches our reactions with keen curiosity.

Anne from France gives a chuckle, "If you guys are ready to

start 'warming up,' maybe we could get around to picking teams so we can get things going."

"I just want it to be fair," says Erald.

"It should be two men as captains, though," adds Marek.

"Why should it be two men as captains?" says Anne.

"I have an idea," says Jenny. "Let's play the first game guys versus girls. If the guys win, I'll leave the ball for you and we'll go home. If the girls win, then the second game will be mixed teams with the girls as captains. Deal?"

"Suit yourselves," the Eastern European men agree.

"First team to score three goals wins," adds Jenny.

"It's really not going to be a fair game," comments Erald. "Maybe we should make it three goals to win for the girls, and five goals to win for the guys."

"Yeah, just to even things out," adds Istvan.

"First team to score three goals wins," repeats Jenny. "Let's go, girls."

What the guys don't know is that Jenny from America, Anne from France, and Milena from the Czech Republic, have all played in semi-pro women's leagues in their home countries. I played soccer in high school and am no stranger on the field. After ten minutes of play, we girls have won three to two. While we are gutting it out, a small crowd of locals gathers to watch the action. When the game is finally won, we take a break to catch our breath and to pick teams for the second game. While standing there, I notice some hecklers starting to get vocal.

"Hey Baby," someone calls out.

"Oooooh, you're so sexy when you sweat like men!"

And then a girl's voice calls, "Dykes!"

We four female soccer players turn around and stare, not believing what we are hearing.

"It's like they've never seen women play soccer before," I say.

"Ignore them," says Jenny.

"They're just jealous," says Anne. "Look at them in their

make-up and heels. I'm sure they've never broken a sweat in their lives."

"What do you expect?" asks Erald. "You girls come out here and you play like boars and then you want to be treated like ladies?"

"Shut it, Erald!" Jenny snaps.

"Look," intervenes Pete. "These people *haven't* seen women play soccer before. Women weren't exactly known for being athletic in East Germany."

"What about the East German swim team?" I ask.

"Yeah," says Erald. "What about those dykes?"

"They were drugged with testosterone, Erald," Jenny explains. "They can hardly be blamed."

"I'm not blaming them. I am just saying that they were very, very dykey."

Pete continues, "Look guys, you obviously aren't used to girls playing sports like this. Or else you wouldn't have let them win. Am I right?" he says to help his teammates save face.

The guys nod.

"But these women can play. I'm not surprised they kicked our asses. So let's just get over it, ignore the 'fan club,' and get on with the game before I need another cigarette."

Jenny and Anne square off as captains, pick teams, and the second game is a more even contest. I am exhilarated to be stretching my legs, and I have a blast running, kicking, and dribbling around the field. We are sweaty and exhausted by the end of the game, and the 'fan club' is still getting a big kick out of it. Unfortunately, when it is all over, we have to pass through them to exit the field. The guys go first, hoping that the crowd will back off.

"Lesbians!" snarls a girl with bright red lipstick.

"Go take a shower!" orders her friend, who is having a hard time seeing through her hair-sprayed bangs.

"Soooo sexy, soooo sexy," coos one of the guys, rubbing his

hands all over his chest. I bite my tongue. The other girls stare straight ahead.

Suddenly, one of the guys reaches out and pinches Jenny's ass. She lets out a growl and turns around to punch him. Pete also turns around to punch him. The guy backs off and so do his friends. We exit the field and head home.

Pete knocks on my door a little while later when I have just finished showering. I am standing in the water closet in my towel, trying to figure out how to remove the piece of dental floss that is stuck between my teeth. The dental floss that I bought at the supermarket across the street is not the same quality that I am used to, and it shreds as I am flossing between my upper left canine and bicuspid. Now the stubborn piece of floss is lodged in there and I can't get it out.

"Why don't you try flossing it out, *Schatz?*" says Fritz.

I roll my eyes.

A knock on the door startles me. Fritz goes to answer it while I debate whether or not I want the guest to see me in my towel. I am too slow, and Pete walks in while I am standing in the hallway.

"Nice," he says, lifting a platinum eyebrow.

"This is how I keep her when no one else is around," Fritz explains to Pete.

Pete laughs.

"Well, gotta get back to my room!" says Fritz. "Those CDs aren't going to alphabetize themselves!"

"Did I interrupt something?" Pete asks, after Fritz is gone.

"Never mind Fritz," I say. "What's up?"

"I was just coming to tell you that Istvan is organizing an evening out tonight. He's trying to get everybody together to go to this Hungarian bar around the corner."

"That sounds like it could be fun." I smile at Pete.

"You have something stuck between your teeth," says Pete.

"Yeah, I know. Thanks for pointing that out."

"Do you want to borrow some dental floss?" he asks me.

"It is dental floss."

"Bummer."

"You're telling me."

"So anyway, you don't have plans for tonight already, do you?"

"No."

"Good. Everybody's leaving at nine. Meet us in front of the house?"

"Sure. I'll be there."

"Great."

Chapter Ten

Istvan

The bar that Istvan has found is a smoky nook on the *Karl Marx Allee* called Café Avalon. It is decorated on the inside with yellowed bamboo stalks and plastic palm trees. There is one pool table in the middle of the bar surrounded by smaller tables along the walls. Tonight, Café Avalon is having a special on tequila, one shot for one euro, along with 1980s pop music. When the group arrives, I sit down at a table with Pete, Janika, Odelia, Billy, and Erald. The waitress comes over, and Pete orders a round of beers and shots for everyone. A few students get up and begin a game of pool. Others are at the bar, helping the bartender select songs from a grand collection of 80s CDs. At my table, Erald is asking Pete about his family history—how it is that an American found himself with the name Peter Bittner, a name as German as they come.

Pete explains that his father was born in Potsdam, a city that was to become part of East Germany after the war. He had been going to college at the Humboldt University in the early 1970s when his mother, an American student from Virginia, was completing a year abroad in West Berlin. Pete's father lived in an apartment that was very close to the border between East and West Berlin. In fact, the Berlin Wall stood only a few meters from his house.

Over on the democratic side of things, the West German government had erected platforms where tourists could come, look over the Wall, and observe, firsthand, the tragic state of affairs on the other side. There was no Death Strip at that point, so onlookers could watch the East Berliners going about their daily lives, much like at the zoo. Over the years, Pete's father had learned to ignore the platform observers, that is, until one day he saw Pete's mother blinking at him from above.

Pete's mother was startled when she first caught sight of the handsome, young man that had stopped to take a better look at her before disappearing into his *Plattenbau*. He was unfashionably dressed, but confident, and through the shaggy, sandy blond hair that hung in his eyes, Pete's mother saw an adventurous twinkle that was absent from the eyes of his East Berlin neighbors.

What Pete's father saw in Pete's mother was a vision of beauty the likes of which he had only seen on scrambled Western television that his family was able to receive because they lived so close to the Wall. Her clothes were bright and new, her hair was a rich, shiny auburn color, and her smile was so straight and so white that he thought he might be looking at a live toothpaste advertisement. The young couple stood there staring at each other until the chaperone of the class trip that Pete's mother was on turned and directed the students off the platform. Before Pete's mother turned away, she promised herself that it would not be the last time she laid eyes on this East Berliner.

The next day, Pete's mother skipped class, marched herself to the East German Visa Office, and applied for a twenty-four-hour visa that was typically issued for shopping excursions. Two months later, visa in hand, Pete's mother crossed through

Checkpoint Charlie and went straight to the door where she had seen Pete's father. She knocked, but there was no answer, so she sat down on the step and waited. Later that afternoon, Pete's father came home from class.

After getting to know one another better that night, Pete's mom returned to West Berlin, determined that no amount of concrete, barbed wire, machine gunnery, or land mining would keep her apart from Pete's father. Now back on her side of the Berlin Wall, Pete's mom began a quest to smuggle him over to her side of civilization. She began to assemble large women's clothing.

When the time was right, Pete's mother packed a wig, a scarf, a dress, stockings, and the largest pair of high-heeled shoes she could find into a suitcase and snuck it through the checkpoint. Over on the East side, she made Pete's father shave, plastered his face with make-up, and dressed him in the clothes she had brought. She made him practice walking in the heels, and when he could do it without limping, it was time to go. The two women then walked out of East Germany together through Checkpoint Charlie. If anyone had asked Pete's father a question, his voice would have betrayed him and he would have been shot.

"A picture of my mom and my smuggled dad in drag now hangs in the Museum at Checkpoint Charlie," Pete finishes.

"It does not," says Erald.

"It does."

"There is a picture of your father in the museum at Checkpoint Charlie?" I ask.

"Yes. In drag. And my mother."

"And we'll see it if we go there?"

"You sure will."

"That's pretty amazing!" remarks Billy.

I suddenly freeze. "Pete," I exclaim. "What was your father's name?"

"Otto Bittner. Why?"

"My mother's maiden name was Bittner. And she had a brother named Otto."

"She did?"

"Yeah. I don't know much about him. Only that they lost him in the war. He got separated from the family. My grandparents tried to find him after, but with no luck. His chances of survival were slim. My mom wants me to try to find him, but I think he's gone."

"Are you suggesting that your Uncle Otto, whose last name is Bittner, and my dad, Otto, whose last name is also Bittner, are the same Otto Bittner?"

I look wide-eyed at Pete.

"Are you suggesting that we might be ... cousins?" Pete eyes me suspiciously.

"No!" I gasp. "I'm not suggesting that ... I mean ... that would be kind of ... weird ... wouldn't it?"

"Why?"

"Um ... I don't know why. Wouldn't that make you feel weird?"

"Well, hold on," interrupts Janika. "Pete, you said your father was born and raised in Potsdam, right?"

"Yes."

"And Kat, where was your uncle born?"

"Dresden."

"So that's it. Not the same guy. You're not cousins."

"Actually," continues Pete, "my father is not sure where he was born. His birth certificate was lost in the war. His family did a lot of moving around in the years after, but he thinks he was born in Potsdam. That's what his new birth certificate says."

"Huh."

"Pete, your grandfather on the Bittners' side, lives in Potsdam, right?"

"Yes."

"And Kat, where does your grandfather on the Bittners' side live?"

"Actually, my Grandfather Bittner died."

"Then there it is. You have different grandfathers. You're not cousins."

"Actually, my father was adopted by my grandfather in Potsdam," says Pete.

"Uh-oh," giggles Billy.

"Well, wait a minute," Janika persists. "Pete, if your father was adopted by your Grandfather Bittner, and only became Otto Bittner after the adoption, and Kat's uncle was always Otto Bittner, then it's not very likely that they are the same person."

The whole table is watching the conversation with acute attention.

Pete downs his beer and orders another round of shots from the waitress. I am trying to figure it out in my head. Could it be possible that my mother's lost brother is alive today, and living in …?

"Pete, where does your father live now?"

"Virginia."

My mom's lost brother living in Virginia? It couldn't be possible. "Pete," I begin again. "How old was your father when he was adopted by your Grandfather Bittner?"

"Well, with the lost birth certificate, we can't know for sure, but he was still a toddler."

"Well, I know my Uncle Otto was born sometime in 1942, which would have made him about three years old at the end of the war."

"Okay, that's a little older than my father was when my Grandfather Bittner adopted him."

"You know, when children go through traumatic experiences early in life," says Erald, "their growth is sometimes stunted, making them seem much younger than they really are."

"That's not true!" argues Billy.

"You're right," Erald admits. "I made that up. But you two are too funny. Imagine the idea of you being cousins. That would be a disaster!"

"Why? Why would that be a disaster?" I ask, pretending I'm not weirded out by the idea.

"Oh, come on," says Erald. "Everyone can see it. You two can't wait to jump in the sack together. And, why shouldn't you? You'd be great together … well, depending on your DNA, of course." Erald smirks.

"Erald," says Pete, ovals of color emerging in his pale cheeks, "shut up and take your shot." We all take a shot. Pete slams his glass down on the table. "Kat and I are not cousins."

The group is looking at the two of us, trying to form an opinion.

"Kat's uncle was born in 1942," Pete reiterates. "My father was born in 1944."

"According to his fake birth certificate," says Billy.

"I'm not hopeful that my uncle is alive," I remind everyone.

Pete runs his forefinger pensively along the rim of his empty shot glass. "Waitress! Would you please bring us another round?"

The waitress brings us another round. I sit thinking about the possibility that I might be related to Pete. It really seems impossible. After all, if Pete were my cousin, it would be kind of disgusting for me to be attracted to him. I would definitely not be attracted to him. Then I remember something.

"Pete, is your father left-handed?"

"Ambidextrous."

"Oh no," I gasp. "My uncle was left-handed."

"Ambidextrous and left-handed are not the same thing, Kat."

"That's true," I admit. "They're not the same thing. It's just that so many left-handed people train themselves to—"

"You and I are not related, Kat," Pete assures me. "Kat and I are not related."

"You know," jests Erald, "when children go through traumatic experiences early in life, they often become ambidextrous."

"That's not true!" argues Billy.

"You're right. I made that up," admits Erald.

"Knock it off, Erald," says Pete. "Take your shot." We all take our shot.

The group lets the conversation drop and turns its attention to the jukebox. I feel like I might want to play a game of pool. I get up and a few people follow me to the pool table.

"Who thinks they can take me?" I begin trash-talking my potential adversaries. No one volunteers. I persist, certain that someone will relent. No one volunteers. I ask again, "Who thinks they can take me?" Istvan volunteers. "Okay, you're on."

I begin racking the balls, but I can't make out the numbers or distinguish between stripes and solids. Man, I've had too many shots of cheap tequila. As I am leaning over the rack, I slip and fall to the floor.

"Someone's had a little too much to drink," says Erald.

"Erald, we've all had a little too much to drink," says Odelia.

On the floor, I realize that I am actually pretty tired. The floor is way more comfortable than floors usually are, and I decide to take a quick nap.

"Whoa," says Pete, coming to my side. "Up, up, up. You are not spending the night on the floor of Café Avalon."

"I just wanna take a lil' nap."

"Not here," says Pete, picking me up from the floor.

"A Kat nap?" I crack and cackle my face off.

"That's very funny."

"Please, just a little one?" I begin purring.

"C'mon, Kat. You've got to get up."

Pete helps me to my feet. I feel dizzy and sick. The room, the pool table, and what seems like a hundred faces are spinning around me.

"I'll walk you home," promises Pete.

"That's what family's for," jibes Erald.

"Cut it out, Erald," says Odelia. "The horse is dead."

"It's just a joke! Can't anybody take a joke around here?"

Pete drops some money on the bar and walks me out. On the walk home, I feel like saying things out loud that I know I shouldn't.

"Pete!" I call out.

"I'm right here."

"I wanna tell ya somethin'."

"Whoa, New Jersey. Where'd that accent come from?"

"I wanna tell ya I'm really, really, really, really, reeeeaaaally, wait stop—"

"What?"

"Stop, I wanna si'down."

"No, no, no," instructs Pete. "You've got to keep walking. You'll feel better once we walk a little bit."

"Okay."

"Now, as you were saying ..."

"What was I saying?"

"I don't know. You're the one that was saying it."

"I can't remember."

"You were saying you are really, really, really, really, reeeeaaaally—"

"Attracted to you."

"Attracted to me?"

"Yeah, but you're not."

"Not what?"

"Attracted to you."

"Attracted to me?"

"Yes. Attracted to me."

"What are you talking about?"

"I mean, I thought you might like me, but then I thought you liked Odelia, but, I think you like me too, and I don't know what to think."

"I don't like Odelia."

"Men are so confyooooooosing."

"Well, Kat, I gotta tell you, you never seemed like you liked me."

97

"That's cause I dunno how to talk to guys. I wuzina layshunship … withu guy for … five years and so … I dunno anything about men."

"You were in a relationship for five years?"

"Yeah."

"That's a really long time."

"Yeah."

"I'm sorry. That must be pretty hard."

"Yeah."

Pete and I continue walking. He has his arm around my shoulder.

"Can we si'down?"

"No, we're almost home. So, do you miss him?"

"Who?"

"Your boyfriend."

"He's *Katie's* boyfriend." I make a sour face when I say *Katie*.

"Katie, huh?"

"Katie," I repeat with disgust.

"Sounds like you do miss him."

"Yeah."

"Still love him?"

"Yeah."

We have finally reached the entrance to the *Plattenbau*. Pete can tell that I am going to have a hard time with the stairs. He scoops me up, carries me into the elevator, and pushes the button for the seventh floor. By the time we get upstairs, I am almost asleep in his arms. Pete rings the doorbell and Fritz answers it. He is in the kitchen with the tall, fashionably dressed woman listening to jazz and smoking homemade cigarettes. Pete carries me down the hall and pushes the door to my room open. He lays me down on the bed and goes into the kitchen for a minute.

"Kat had a little too much to drink tonight," I hear him say to Fritz.

"I see that."

Pete comes back into my room with a glass of water. I open

my eyes and prop myself up when he sits down on the bed next
to me.

"Here, drink this."

I take the glass and take a sip. I put it down on the floor.
"Thanks for bringin' me home."

"Sure, no problem." Pete smiles at me.

I look up at him. I notice his pretty, pale blue eyes.

"You have pretty blue eyes," I say to him.

"Thank you," whispers Pete.

"Why you whisperin'?" I whisper.

Pete laughs. A piece of hair has fallen onto my face. Pete
brushes it away and lets his hand linger on my cheek. "You have
pretty brown eyes," he tells me, "the color of milk chocolate."

"Cappuccino," I correct him.

"Uh, okay. Whatever."

Pete leans in for a kiss but before our lips meet, the unthinkable
happens.

"Pete!" I yell at point-blank range.

"What?" he jerks his head back. "What's wrong?"

"Garbage can! *Now!*"

"Oh, shit."

Pete springs out into the kitchen, disrupting Fritz and his
guest.

"Shit, shit!" I hear him yell. "Fritz! Which garbage bin do I
use for vomit?"

"*Restmüll.*"

"Thanks!" Pete returns to my room with the *Restmüll* bin.
He positions it in front of me just in time for the floodgates to
open. I sink my head into the garbage can and release alcohol and
stomach acid. Pete sits next to me and does his best to bundle my
hair together so that it won't get splashed. He pats my back with
his free hand. When I am finished, he hands me a tissue and then
pushes the bin aside. I don't notice the tissue in my hand and
instead, wipe my mouth with my forearm. Pete hands me the
glass of water. I take another sip and then lie back down. I close

my eyes. Pete climbs onto the bed next to me and props himself up on his elbow.

"Do you feel better?" he asks me.

"Yes, much," I answer without opening my eyes.

Pete contemplates his next move. "You'll probably feel even better if you brush your teeth."

"Yes, much," I agree without opening my eyes.

"Guess I'll let sleeping Kat's lie," Pete says and rests his head on the pillow next to me. A few minutes later, I sit up.

"What is it?" asks Pete.

"I need the garbage can again!"

And on it goes.

CHAPTER ELEVEN

Carmelita

When I wake up the next morning, I feel like death incarnate. Pete is gone, and I notice a few light, blond hairs on the pillow next to my head. Focusing on them hurts my eyes. I hear Fritz milling around in the kitchen. Each clink of a dish and clank of a utensil pierces my brain like a dart. I make a deal with God that if he makes the pain go away, I will never take another sip of alcohol in my life. I close my eyes and try to will my pounding headache into submission.

When I wake up a few minutes later, I feel a little better, though I cannot figure out why it is dark outside. Fritz is still milling around in the kitchen.

"Guten Abend, Schatz!" he announces cheerfully as I emerge from my bedroom. "Want a *Wurst mit Sauerkraut?* I've got some left over from dinner."

"Ugh!" I feel my stomach turn. "No, thanks. I think I'll start with some bread." I sit down and help myself to a buttered roll from a plate that Fritz has prepared in the middle of the table. Fritz is making tea.

"Should I make you some too?" he offers.

"That would be great." Then something occurs to me. "Fritz?" I ask.

"Yes?"

"Aren't we supposed to have a third roommate?"

"We do."

"We do?"

"Yes."

"What's his or her name?"

"Her name is Carmelita."

"Carmelita?"

"Yes."

"Well, where is she?"

"Oh, she doesn't live here."

"She doesn't live here?"

"No."

"But she's our roommate."

"Yes."

"So … where does she live?"

"She lives in San Diego."

"San Diego. Interesting. Another American girl."

"Yes."

"When do I get to meet her?"

"You don't."

"Why not?"

"Because she doesn't live here."

"But she's our roommate."

"Yes. She's in Group Two."

"Our roommate, in Group Two, who I don't get to meet."

"That's correct."

"Because …"

"I didn't get to meet her either."

"Why not?"

"She was only here for one day. The same day you arrived. Remember? I was out that day."

"So how do you know that her name is Carmelita?"

"Just by living with her, you know, you learn things about a person."

"Oh ... what else do you know about her?"

"She's about twenty-two years old, medium height, olive complexion, dark brown hair. I think her parents are Mexican. Back in San Diego she has a boyfriend, a dog, and she lives in a small house with palm trees in the backyard. She went to UCSD and studied Spanish, German, and International Business. She likes to drink margaritas."

"Margaritas! Good choice."

"I prefer mojitos."

"And you learned all this from living with her?"

"Yes."

"But she lives in San Diego."

"Yes."

"And you've never met her."

"That's correct. She left before I had the chance."

"When did she leave?"

"When she found out she was pregnant."

"Oh. Who's the father?"

"Her boyfriend in San Diego."

"Now I understand why she moved back home."

"She didn't move back home."

"She didn't?"

"No, all of her stuff is still in her room."

"What stuff?"

"All her stuff ... books, clothes, pictures on the wall, pregnancy test in the trash can."

"I see. So that's how you know so much about her?"

"Like I said, when you live with someone, you learn things about them."

"Although she doesn't actually live here."

"That's correct. She lives in San Diego."

"Right."

I munch on my roll quietly for a few minutes. Fritz pours out two cups of tea.

"Janika came by looking for you earlier today, but I told her you were in a coma."

"Thanks. Did she say what she wanted?"

"Yes, she wanted to remind you that the group is going all together to the bus station tomorrow morning."

"Oh, right. I almost forgot. We're leaving for our first seminar tomorrow."

"How long will you be gone?"

"Just a few days."

"Wow. I'll miss you."

"Don't worry. You've got Carmelita to keep you company."

"That's true."

Monday morning begins with all of Group Four congregating in front of the *Plattenbau* on *Coppistrasse*. We wave good-bye to the gangly, green pipes, soldier through the Private Pathway Tunnel, march down the Private Pathway, and board the *S-Bahn* without buying passes. We ride to the bus station, where Herr Stern greets us and herds us onto a large bus with cushy seats that will take us up to a little town called Wohlde in the northwest of Germany on the North Sea. We are to discuss environmental issues with the Green Party and spend some time appreciating Germany's nature. We arrive in Wohlde a little after dark.

Unlike Berlin, which has two of everything, the town of Wohlde has only one of everything ... one convenient store, serving also as the town department store, liquor store, and pharmacy; one doctor, serving also as the town dentist, veterinarian, and barber; and one inn, serving also as the town youth hostel, restaurant, and pub.

Hosting our group is a jolly old German man named Uwe, who wears only one outfit ... black leather pants with red suspenders and a blue and green-checkered shirt. By day, Uwe holds political seminars about the Green Party, which groups of students are forced to attend. By night, he runs the town convenient store, department store, liquor store, and pharmacy. He also happens to be a doctor and serves when needed as the town dentist, veterinarian, and barber. He makes most of his income running the town inn, youth hostel, restaurant, and pub. In his spare time, Uwe enjoys eating organic cheese that is manufactured in Wohlde's organic cheese factory and admiring the pigs and cows that are raised on Wohlde's free-range cow and pig farm. The person who runs the organic cheese factory and free-range cow and pig farm is Uwe.

That first night, jolly old Uwe welcomes us to Wohlde and cooks us a warm supper of split pea soup sprinkled with organic Edamer from his factory. After dinner, he invites us into the pub and opens a few bottles of wine from Wohlde's vineyard, which he runs as a hobby. We sit on wooden chairs at wooden tables in front of a wood-burning fireplace and enjoy the coziness of the inn, youth hostel, restaurant, and pub. This evening, we are in a lively mood.

The liveliest of the bunch this evening is Istvan, who graces the group with a verbal reenactment of Hungary's courageous uprising against the Austrian Empire in 1848.

"It should have been a shining moment in our history," Istvan trumpets, "but unfortunately, the courageous uprising was defeated by the occupying Austrian army. To insure maximum humiliation of the defeated, yet courageous Hungarian rebels, the Austrians executed fifteen of our top generals in a public square in Budapest. During the execution, a rowdy crowd of Austrians cheered and clinked beer mugs with one another. And that is why," Istvan proclaims, "Hungarians, never clink their glasses when toasting with beer. They just raise them and say *'Egészségedre!'*"

"They say what?" Billy asked.

"Egészségedre!"

"Hmmm."

Istvan's uplifting account is followed by a spirited disagreement between Milena, from the Czech Republic, and Marika, from the Slovak Republic, over whose country's slaves had built Budapest. Istvan solves the debate by explaining that Budapest was not built by slaves but by hard-working and courageous Hungarians. Marika then corrects Istvan by explaining that everybody knows that Budapest was built by Slovakian slaves. Milena then clears up Marika's misconception by explaining that Slovakian slaves had built Prague, not Budapest, and that it had been, in fact, Czech slaves that had built Budapest. Marika then solves the dispute once and for all by informing her fellow exchange students that Slovakian slaves had built both Prague and Budapest and done a good job of it too.

"Who built Bratislava?" I want to know.

"Romanian slaves," responds Eve, to which Marika replies that Brataslava had not been built by slaves at all but by hard-working Slovakians.

"Well, that clears that up!" I say.

After an hour or so of debating, Uwe sends us to bed, warning us that we have a busy day ahead of us. He tells us to show up for breakfast wearing smiles and warm clothes that can get dirty. We comply, finish our wine, and mosey off to our bedrooms in the youth hostel in Wohlde. On our way up the stairs, I catch Pete's eye.

"Thanks for taking care of me the other night," I speak to him for the first time since the other night.

"No problem."

"So, I'll see you tomorrow?"

"Bright and early."

We turn awkwardly away from each other and go into our rooms.

In my room, I gather my toothbrush and towel to take with me to the bathroom. I shake my head as I dig through my bag. I have no idea what is supposed to happen next between Pete and me. We almost kissed the other night, but I was so wasted. And then I ruined everything by getting sick. What an idiot! He probably wants nothing to do with me now.

As I walk to the bathroom, I overhear Pete in the other room talking to Istvan. I can't help but listen.

"I have no idea what is supposed to happen next between Kat and me. We almost kissed the other night, but she was so wasted. And then I ruined everything by trying to hook up with her even though she was sick. What an idiot! She probably wants nothing to do with me now."

"I've never felt anything like this before," I confess to Janika the next day.

"I know what you mean," Janika replies.

"It's so …" I fish for the right word, "indescribable!"

"Yes, it certainly is."

"I mean, it's just so …"

"Dirty!" says Pete.

"Sticky!" says Marek.

"Squishy!" says Odelia.

"Slimy!" says Iosif.

"Sinister!" says Irina.

"Murky!" says Sasha.

"It's sucking me in!" cries Sveta.

"It's so much fun!" I swoon, plunging my hands into the black sea of muck where we find ourselves standing knee deep.

"Welcome to the *Wattenmeer*, my curious fledglings," gleams Uwe like a bear in a pool of honey. "These flats of mud stretch for miles when the tide of the North Sea goes out. You could search the globe and never find mud so rich with life or an ecosystem so perfect!"

I squish my hands further into the black glop. It feels cold and velvety between my fingers.

"In one handful of this glorious, black ambrosia you will find thousands of species of plant and animal organisms," says Uwe.

107

In my handful of *Watt*, I don't find thousands of species of plant and animal organisms, but I do find six twigs, a leaf, and a snail shell. I am picking them out of the perfect ecosystem when it hits me; a large, clammy, sopping shot-put of *Watt* lands squarely on my lower back; it explodes upon impact into thousands of globules, spotting me from head to toe and ruining my hopes of remaining clean and dry. I snap up, letting the thousands of species of plant and animal organisms slide down the backs of my legs into the oxygen-rich abyss.

I survey the battleground for my assailant, who will incur my wrath in the form of a gunky projectile of my own. I set my sights on Erald, who is attempting to make a slick getaway, but is finding himself hampered by the sucking, quick sandy *Watt*. I scoop up an armful of gooey retaliation and make my way toward the unlucky fugitive. My progress is hampered by the sucking, quick sandy *Watt*. I can't pick my feet up out of the mud, but can only plod in his direction. Erald lumbers away from me. I slog after him. The only direction either of us go is down. I launch the mud missile. Istvan calls out a warning to Erald. Erald lunges out of the way, grabbing onto Istvan for stability. Istvan is also lunging out of the way, and the two of them come crashing down under Erald's weight with a loud *slap!* Their double belly flop sends a wave of *Watt* in all directions.

"Ugh!" shrieks Sveta in disgust.

"Ewww!" cries Irina.

"Don't worry!" booms Uwe. "It's good for your skin."

"It's gross!"

"No! It's healthy. Watch!" Uwe scoops up a finger full of *Watt* and plunges it into his mouth.

We curious fledglings freeze and stare at Uwe in horror.

"Perhaps I went a little too far just then," Uwe admits, noticing our facial expressions.

"Yes. Yes, you did," we all agree.

"Help!" calls Istvan, who is still submerged beneath Erald. "I can't get up."

Billy barrels over to Istvan and offers him a hand.

Istvan lets out a gloating laugh and pulls Billy down into the muck with him and Erald.

"You bastard!" shouts Billy.

"You idiot!" laughs Istvan. "You deserve it if you fall for that trick."

"Children," announces Uwe suddenly. "I'm being paged. There must be an emergency at the cheese factory. We lost a whole batch of Camembert to bacteriophage last week, and I hope it hasn't happened again. Stay here and continue to enjoy the wonders of the *Watt* until I return." Uwe makes his way as fast as he can toward the shore.

Meanwhile, we students go back to inspecting organisms. Marek captures worms, snails, slugs, and beetles and tries to make them race. Janika, Eve, Irina, and I lie on our backs and make *Watt* angels. Sasha and Istvan do surface dives until every inch of them is plastered with sticky, black paste. Erald climbs up on Pete's back and springs off of him, landing in a cannon ball, which sends another wave of *Watt* in all directions.

A half an hour later, we see Uwe appear on the shore. We know immediately that something is very wrong. He is frenzied and panicked, running along the edge of the *Watt* like a maniac. No one can understand what Uwe is trying to say, but we can tell that he is calling us in. We curious fledglings make our way to the shore. When we get there, Uwe informs us that the American Embassy in Berlin is under attack.

CHAPTER TWELVE

Uwe

While we had been laughing, splashing, and having the time of our lives in the *Wattenmeer*, three cars packed with explosives had busted through the barricades surrounding the American Embassy, run over the guards, who had opened fire on them, and detonated their bombs within feet of the building. The radio on the bus back to the youth hostel in Wohlde is reporting a gaping hole in the side of the embassy, hundreds wounded, too soon to tell how many dead.

"Children," says Uwe, "once we return, please do not leave the youth hostel. It could be dangerous, especially for the Americans, to be walking around outside. We will stay at home and wait for instructions from the German *Bundestag*."

We are all silent as we pull up to the youth hostel and make our way inside. Most of the students go into the TV room to watch the news coverage of the attack. Uwe invites Pete, Billy, and me to call home using his office phone.

"Your families will want to know you are safe. Make as many calls as you must and don't worry about the cost."

I peer into the TV room while Pete and Billy use the phone. The German news is showing footage of the scene: the smoking building, bodies being pulled from piles of rubble, and survivors standing around bloody, bruised, and confused. An anchorwoman comes on and reports that the terrorist group, Defenders of Islam, has claimed responsibility for the attack on several Arabic websites. I shake my head in disbelief.

When it is my turn to use the phone, I call my parents. My mom, usually boisterous and babbling, is very somber.

"I just can't believe this news, Kat. I would have never forgiven myself if you had been hurt. Thank the Good Lord above that you are in ... that you aren't in Berlin. Where are you again?"

"Wohlde."

"Um ..."

Uwe soon comes out and informs us that dinner is ready. We all shuffle into the dining room and sit down to a meal of organic bread, cheese, free-range sausage, and pea soup. No one is saying a word. After a few minutes, Marika from the Slovak Republic reaches out and touches my arm. She looks at me with big, sympathetic eyes and says, "Words fail me, Kat. I wish there was something I could say."

After dinner, we all head into the bar area and gently sip some of Uwe's homemade beer. None of us is in the mood to party.

"Unfortunately," Uwe informs us, "the environmental seminar will not continue as planned. We do not know if more attacks are coming. I have just spoken with Herr Stern, and he insists that you all return to Berlin tomorrow. We need to have you all together, just in case."

"Just in case, what?" asks Pete.

"Just in case we have to send you home."

"Send us home!" I gasp. "Why?"

"It might be too dangerous for you here, Frau Vespucci."

I think about going home, and it surprises me that I don't

want to go. I mean, of course I want to go home, but this year abroad has only just begun. Going home now would be like turning the ship around before it's even gotten out of the harbor. It is getting late, and now I am really not in the mood to party, so I go upstairs to bed. The other students soon follow. Some hours later, Uwe awakens me from sleep.

"You have a phone call downstairs, Frau Vespucci," he says. He is wearing a red thermal pajama suit with a buttoned flap in the back.

Not wanting to wake anyone up, I feel my way downstairs in the dark, using the wall to guide me. In Uwe's office, I see the phone off the hook.

"Hello?" I croak into the receiver.

"Kat?"

"Yes?"

"Thank God you're alive!"

"Matt. Oh my God! Hi! How did you know to call me here?"

"I got the number from my parents, who got it from your parents. Where are you again?"

"Wohlde. It's a tiny little village on the North Sea."

"What are you doing up there?"

"Well, there's this sea of mud called the *Wattenmeer* and we—"

"The what?"

"The *Wattenmeer* … it's like the Jersey shore, just black and sticky."

"Uh … so, are you okay?"

"Well, I'm a little shocked, but otherwise I'm fine."

"I'm just so relieved you're alive."

"Thank you. That's nice to hear. I am too. By the way, do you know it's—" I look at the clock on Uwe's desk, "—one o'clock in the morning here?"

"It is?"

"Yes."

"Why?"

"Because we're six hours ahead of you guys."

"That's weird."

"Well, I don't know if it's weird. It's just a different time zone."

"Aren't you proud of me that I figured out the country code and how to dial and all of that?"

"Congratulations."

"There are a lot of extra ones and zeros. Not as easy as you might think."

"So what are you doing now?"

"Just waiting for Katie to get home from class so we can go to dinner."

The sound of the name Katie cuts through me like a knife. I suddenly don't feel like talking to Matt anymore.

"So ... you're okay then, right Kat?" he asks.

"Yeah, I'm fine. I'd better go. It's late."

"Okay. Well, I'll be praying for you over there."

"Thanks."

"I can't even tell you how good it is to hear your voice. I was so worried about you."

"Well, thanks for thinking of me. You can rest assured now."

"Thanks for talking to me."

"You're welcome."

"I love you."

I stop. I don't know if he really means it or if he's just saying it out of habit. "Thanks," I reply.

When I hang up the receiver, I drop my head in my hands. It's been awhile since I've cried over Matt, but the tears begin to flow. Talking to him has reminded me just how much a part of my life he has been. When he first broke up with me nine months ago, I said that living without him felt like trying to breathe with only one lung. You can still breathe, but it's a lot harder than it used to be. I pick up my head, wipe my eyes, and walk out of the office.

On my way down the hall, I hear that the TV is on, so I tiptoe into the TV room to turn it off. There, I find Pete watching the news by himself in one of the reclining chairs; he is clutching a glass of Jim Beam in his right hand and a bottle of Jim Beam in his left hand.

He is watching the BBC, and they are showing pictures of Arabs celebrating in the streets over today's attack. Then they cover a speech by the German Foreign Minister, in which he declares that Germany will stand in solidarity with the United States.

"Hey," I say to Pete as I slide onto the couch next to his chair.

"Want some?" he asks, offering me some of his whiskey.

"Sure." I have actually never tasted whiskey before. Pete hands me the glass while taking a swig straight from the bottle. I take a sip from the glass and nearly choke. It tastes like gasoline going down my throat. Once down, however, it feels warm and kind of comforting. I take another swig and nearly choke again.

"What are you going to do if they send us home?" Pete asks me.

"God, I have no idea."

"…"

"Maybe try to finish out the year in London, like I originally wanted to."

"Why London?"

I laugh. "This is going to sound kind of stupid now, but I didn't want to have to speak a foreign language."

"Ha."

"I'd probably just do senior year at Rutgers, like everybody else."

"You probably won't be able to start until the spring semester."

"Good point."

"…"

"I wonder what I'd do until then."

"You should come traveling with me."

"Are you going traveling?"

"Thinkin' about it."

"Where?"

"Don't know. I've always wanted to go to France, Italy, Greece …"

"We can't go to France, Italy, Greece …"

"Why not?"

"Well … do you speak French, Italian, or Greek?"

"There's a lot more to communication than words, Kat. You're a smart girl. You'd get around. Have a little more faith in yourself."

I sigh. "If we get sent home because it's too dangerous for us here, I'm going straight back to New Jersey and never leaving again."

"Well, then," says Pete. He takes a swig of whiskey and transitions to the couch next to me. "I'd better enjoy the time I have with you now, because, if we get sent home, I'm sure as hell not going to visit you in New Jersey."

"Hey!" I rap him on the arm. "What do you have against New Jersey?"

We are very close together now, on the couch, facing each other. A hint of his aftershave drifts to my nose and the skin tightens on my scalp. He looks at me with a look that both startles and excites me.

"Say you're sorry!"

"I'm sorry," he says and kisses me.

It is a soft kiss at first. He is only the second guy I have ever kissed in my life, and kissing him feels remarkably different than kissing Matt. I pull away suddenly. I look at Pete's face for a moment and kind of giggle. He kisses me again, more forcefully this time. Then he pulls away. He scrunches his brow and looks at me. I scrunch my brow and look at him. We try kissing a third time. After only a moment, we both pull away from each other and slump back onto the couch, shoulder to shoulder.

"Have you ever not felt anything like this before?" Pete asks, confused.

"No," I reply, confused.

"Me neither," he confesses, confused.

"I've never not felt so much chemistry in my whole life," I add, confused.

"Me neither," he replies, confused.

"What didn't it feel like to you?" I ask, confused.

"It didn't feel like I was kissing someone I should be kissing," he says, confused.

"That's exactly what it didn't feel like to me," I reply, confused.

"It felt like I was kissing my cousin," he confesses.

"I don't really know what that feels like," I confess.

"Do you think we're cousins?"

"Um ..."

"..."

"That's *disgusting!*" I exclaim. We are both silent for a moment.

"Though it is possible," he admits. We both take a swig of whiskey.

"It's so gross, I don't even want to think about it," I add.

We take a few more swigs of whiskey.

Chapter Thirteen

Nat

When we arrive back in Berlin, we students are greeted by a large demonstration at the Brandenburg Gate. It is officially a solidarity rally in support of the United States, but many in the crowd are treating it as an anti-revenge rally. Signs read, "Peace," and "No Retaliation."

When I arrive back to the *Plattenbau* on *Coppistrasse*, I am relieved to find this letter:

Dear American Friends,

I express to you my condolences on behalf of the entire German *Bundestag*. You have our deepest sympathy. Yesterday's attack on your embassy was cowardly and inexcusable. We will stand up for you, like America has stood up for Germany in the past.

We know you wish to be with your families and friends back home in these difficult times. However, we also hope that you will see how important it is for you to continue your work over here.

Your participation in *HAA* puts you in the unique position to break down the kinds of barriers that create terrorists in the first place. You are helping to improve understanding in this world. You are promoting tolerance and building a global climate of synergy. You are paving the way toward peace on our planet. It is the mission of all of the foreign students in this program, but it now applies especially to you, the Americans.

With deepest sympathy,

Hans Stern

I clutch the letter and am so thankful that *HAA* will not be cancelled. I am also moved. Never before have I been called to build a global climate of synergy and pave the way toward peace on our planet. I guess I am up for the challenge, though I don't quite know how to go about it. First, I decide to check my e-mail.

A few people and I go together to an Internet café on the *Karl Marx Allee*. When we arrive, all of the computers are in use. A girl hears me say something to Billy in English and walks up to me and asks, "Are you American?"

"Yes," I reply.

"Please, take my computer."

Later that evening, a few of us go out to Café Avalon to get a few drinks. The owner of the bar comes out and sits with us. When we try to pay our bill at the end of the evening, he insists that it is on the house.

Life in Berlin suddenly feels different. The attack is felt throughout the city. Streets surrounding the American embassy are guarded with tanks, and snipers now perch on the roof, but a fence surrounding the area is decorated with candles, wreathes, flowers, and signs. One day, as I am walking along *Unter den Linden*, I notice skid marks on the road leading to the American Embassy. They must have been left by one of the cars. I'm not in a hurry, so I follow the skid marks. They are all over the road, as if the driver of the car had been drunk or crazy. Three blocks away from the Embassy, I reach the police barrier and can go no further. From there, I can see part of the building. It reminds me of the bombed out Kaiser Wilhelm Memorial Church in West Berlin, only the wounds are fresh. There is a big hole in one side of the building and the rest of it is black and surrounded by rubble. The clean-up crew is still excavating to find people. I see long bags lined up on the pavement. *Are those … body bags?* I close my eyes and cover my face with both hands.

When I open my eyes, I notice a young German man standing next to me, staring at me. I give him an embarrassed smile.

"Are you American?" he asks.

I nod.

"Hurts, doesn't it?" he says.

"I'm sorry?"

"When it's your people getting killed."

"Um … what do you mean?"

"Well, maybe you'll think twice the next time you supply fanatics with arms."

"What? Who did I supply with arms?"

"The Defenders of Islam."

"The Defenders of Islam?"

"You'd never even heard of them before this attack, had you?"

"Uh …"

"Try looking into your own history a little bit. You won't have to look very far to see that this attack was America's fault," he says and walks away.

I am too shocked to respond. What a cruel, horrible, hurtful thing to say!

"I don't care what you say!" I hear someone bellowing from within Pete's apartment when he opens the door to let me in. *"This terrorist attack was not America's fault!"*

"I didn't say it was America's fault. I said that America deserves the wake-up call that it is getting," argues a second, calmer voice with a French accent.

"What's going on in there?" I ask Pete, worried.

"Oh, Nat and Lambert are having a 'friendly discussion' about the embassy bombing. Want to come in and spectate?"

"Okay." Pete and I walk into the kitchen where several of the students from Group Three are seated around the kitchen table. Nat, a short, plump-faced American with a close-cropped haircut and thick, black-rimmed glasses, has launched himself halfway out of his chair and is pounding his fist into the table to drive his point home to Lambert, a wiry Belgian, who is sitting across from him in a relaxed posture with his legs crossed, smoking a cigarette.

"Don't make America out to be the bad guy in this!" bellows Nat, his face straining like an overburdened weightlifter. "This conflict is not relative. The Defenders of Islam deserve no pity. They chose to commit this heinous act, and we will make them pay."

"Oh, you will?" defends Lambert. "Very interesting. How does America plan, exactly, to make them pay?"

"We're going to hunt down every so-called 'Defender of Islam,' and all those who helped them, until every last son of a bitch of 'em is dead."

"Oh, putain! Violence to end violence. An excellent plan."

"Oh, I'm sorry. You're right. We should probably just let them continue to get away with it. We'll just do nothing, while they attack us again and again. That sounds like the best fucking idea I've ever heard, Lambert."

"Maybe you should focus on why the terrorists behave the way they do in the first place. Ever think of that? Like maybe they're tired of seeing their countries used by Western powers in petty, political, power struggles and then abandoned to poverty, hunger, and hopelessness when they are no longer of use."

"It is not America's fault that those countries can't feed and educate their own people."

"You can't deny that the United States has been interfering in the Middle East for decades. Great Britain even longer."

"Let those countries take a look at themselves and stop blaming other people for their poverty! It's not us that shuts off their women, preaches religious fanaticism, and wastes their money supporting tyrannical and ineffective governments. Let them fix their own countries, rather than trying to ruin ours."

"They can't when Western powers continue to interfere, supporting illegitimate leaders, groups, and regimes according to their preferences of the moment."

"Give me one example, Lambert, of the United States supporting an illegitimate leader or regime."

"Reinstating the Shah of Iran, there's one. Your unconditional financing of Israel, while they murder thousands upon thousands of Palestinians in front of all the world to see, there's two."

"Israel is our ally. Don't change the subject here."

"Your rosy relations with the Saudis, who grant you cheap access to oil, never mind their abysmal human rights record, there's three. Arming the Defenders of Islam when they were helping you fight the Communists, there's four."

"They were helping us fight the Communists! Of course we supported them!"

"You can't just throw your wealth and power around at your own convenience without regard to long-term consequences or who you might harm in the process."

"We have every right to support our allies."

"You leave mangled communities! Artificially imposed power vacuums! You can't just go into a country, decide to support one

121

group of people over the other and then turn your back when it no longer serves your interest. You leave chaos in your wake. The people left behind are powerless to—"

"We didn't create these terrorists! They created themselves! Why are they powerless? Because they can't compete with us. Because their religious dictatorships stifle all creativity and freedom. Because they've shut half of their work force away in their homes. Yes, we support Israel. It's the only democracy in the Middle East! And yes, we supported the Defenders of Islam during the Cold War when they were on our side against the fucking Russians."

When Nat says "fucking Russians," I look around to make sure Sasha and Irina aren't there. Luckily, they aren't.

"And, they beat the fucking Russians!" Nat yells. "They should be thanking us. Instead they're using us as a scapegoat. The terrorists need to take responsibility for their own failures. They need to wake up and smell the democracy."

"And I suppose you believe that America is just the one to bring it to them?"

"Damn straight."

"And what about the innocent people you will kill when you impose your democracy on them by force? Civilians? Why should they die?" Lambert flicks his cigarette.

Nat is now standing up with his full weight on the table. "America does not kill civilians!"

"Oh, no? Your little retaliations have already killed ten times as many civilians as the terrorists have killed."

"It's not on purpose."

"What difference does that make?"

"Look. Nobody messes with America and gets away with it," Nat punches the table.

"That's a nice idea, but your military, with all its might, is powerless against suicide bombers. They will continue to strike unless you put down your weapons long enough to listen to them."

"The terrorists will not get away with this! We will rebuild the embassy," Nat slams his fist onto the table again, "*bigger* than before! And we will show the Defenders of Islam the true strength of America. We will destroy every last terrorist and the whole world will thank us."

"*Ça va pas, non?* Destroy, destroy, destroy! Is that all America is good for?"

Nat huffs, his face borscht red. "That's great, coming from you, Lambert, you French surrender clown!"

"I'm not French, I'm Belgian, you idiot."

"Let me ask you something. Do your parents speak German?"

"No."

"You're welcome!" With that, Nat storms out of the kitchen, ending the discussion.

"*Quel connard,*" Lambert mutters, shaking his head. He puts out his cigarette.

Chapter Fourteen

Frau Tintenpinkler

Later in the evening, I am alone in my room feeling pretty discouraged about the prospects of paving world peace when Janika knocks on my door. She invites me up to her tenth floor apartment for tea. From the tenth floor balcony, you can see even farther than from the seventh floor, and I find Sveta from the Ukraine and Marek from Poland out there enjoying a colorful sunset over Berlin.

After taking in the view for a few minutes, we come back inside and join Janika at the table. She pours us each a cup of peppermint tea, and we help ourselves to the stack of Russian-style crepes that she has prepared. I'm not sure how to eat Russian-style crepes, so I watch Sveta and Marek, who drizzle them with condensed milk and roll them into thin tubes before gobbling them up. They are delicious.

In a pause between sipping tea and eating crepes, Janika asks me, "How are you doing, Kat?"

The question startles me a little bit. "Oh, you know," I reply, bracing myself for an anti-American onslaught, "fine."

"It's okay, Kat. You can tell us," says Sveta, who has already learned quite a bit of German.

"Tell you what?"

"Are you scared?"

"Scared?"

"Yes, scared?"

"Um, I guess so. Although, I was scared before the embassy bombing too."

"Of what?" asks Marek.

"I don't know. Being so far away from home, I guess."

"We admire your courage for staying," says Janika.

"You do?"

"Yes. We think we probably would have gone straight home if we were you." The other two nod in agreement.

"Well, Herr Stern has called us all to build a global climate of synergy and pave the way toward peace on our planet," I say. "He says it's best that we stay."

"Ya ne panimayu," says Sveta to Marek in Russian.

"There's nothing really to understand, Sveta. It's just the *Bundestag* setting unachievable goals." He turns to me. "So how's it going so far?"

"Not so good. I've met a lot of angry people since the embassy bombing. Some actually blame us … they say it's our fault … that we deserved the attack. It seems that some people really hate America. I had no idea."

"Sounds like you've been talking to Lambert," says Marek. "Don't listen to that Walloon. He's just jealous."

"Not everybody hates America," says Sveta. "Those of us who know what it's like to live under repressive regimes … we don't hate America. And we don't blame you for the attack."

I look uncertainly at the three Eastern Europeans. "Thanks, you guys. I really appreciate the encouragement."

"We could tell you needed some cheering up. As for Lambert,

did you know that on Christmas day in Belgium, it is legal for police to throw bananas at children?"

"What?"

"It's true. They have a law on the books that says that."

"Wow. Do they enforce it?"

"Yes, I think so."

"Do you know what Belgium produces more than anyone else in the world?"

"Waffles?"

"Comics."

"Is that true?"

"Yes. So you see, you can't take them seriously."

I giggle. Sveta and Janika suppress smiles, while shaking their heads at Marek.

"Have you heard the joke about the Belgian king, the German Chancellor, and the U.S. President all having sex?"

"Marek!" interrupts Sveta. "Not that one!"

"Yes, maybe save that one for another time," I add, thankfully.

"And the Belgian king turns to the German Chancellor and says, would you—"

"*Marek!*" yells Sveta. "Shut it."

"Okay, okay."

I have another good laugh the next morning when I check the mail. There is a letter for Carmelita Rodriguez from the Berlin Transportation Authority. It looks official and urgent, so I decide to open it. It is a forty euro fine for *Schwarzfahren* issued a week ago. That's weird. I bring the bill inside and call the number on the back.

A scratchy, female voice answers, *"Berlinerverkehrsgesellschaft, Guten Morgen, Frau Tintenpinkler hier."*

"Guten Morgen," I reply. "I'm calling about a fine that was issued to Carmelita Rodriguez."

"What was the fine for?"

"*Schwarzfahren.*"

There is silence on the other end of the line. I can feel a steely, bureaucratic stare of hatred forming on the face of Frau Tintenpinkler.

"I suppose you're calling to say that you're sorry and you'll never do it again."

"No, actually."

"Well, I didn't expect you'd be sorry, but at least you're honest."

"Actually it wasn't me."

"Here we go. *Schwarzfahrer* are never who they say they are. Let me guess, it was your sister, or your friend, or maybe it was your roommate."

"It was my roommate."

"Of course it was."

"Let me explain. The fine was issued to Carmelita Rodriguez, who is, or was, my roommate. But she doesn't live here anymore."

"Yes, she does."

"What do you mean, yes, she does?"

"I mean, yes, she does."

"With all due respect, Frau Tintenpinkler, Carmelita lives in San Diego."

"Carmelita Rodriguez lives at 1 *Coppistrasse*, 7th Floor, Apartment B, Berlin, Germany 10365."

"There is a mistake. She left as soon as she got here and we haven't seen her since. That's why it's impossible that she could have been caught last week for *Schwarzfahren.*"

"It is documented here in the Official Berlin Resident Directory that Carmelita Rodriguez lives at 1 *Coppistrasse*, 7th Floor, Apartment B, Berlin, Germany 10365."

"That explains it, Frau Tintenpinkler. She left without telling anyone, so the Official Berlin Resident Directory doesn't reflect the change."

Frau Tintenpinkler inhales sharply. There is silence for a moment and then an explosion.

"*Frau Rodriguez*, I beg your pardon!"

"It's Frau Vespucci."

"How dare you challenge the accuracy of the Official Berlin Resident Directory? Are you prepared to offer proof to support your accusation?"

"What do you mean, proof?"

"I mean some kind of documentation."

"What kind of documentation?"

"All Berlin residents must register with the Official Berlin Resident Office when moving in or out of a residence. It is clearly stated here that Frau Rodriguez moved into 1 *Coppistrasse*, 7th Floor, Apartment B, Berlin, Germany 10365 on the first of the month. There is no documentation stating a change of address since that date. Therefore, she still lives there."

"But Carmelita never officially moved out. She just left."

"Excuse me?"

"She just left. Without registering."

"Left without registering?"

"Yes."

"Impossible."

"No, it's true. All her stuff is still in her room, but she's back in San Diego."

"Frau Rodriguez!"

"It's Frau Vespucci."

"Are you trying to make a fool out of me?"

"No, Frau Tintenpinkler, I'm trying to tell you the truth."

"Why is it that *Schwarzfahrer* always become so honest directly after they've been caught?"

"I'm trying to tell you that if you want Carmelita to pay the fine, it's best to contact her at her new address in San Diego."

"Thank you, Frau Rodriguez—"

"It's Frau Vespucci."

"—for telling me how to do my job. I'm sure you have many

years of experience working at the *Berlinerverkehrsgesellschaft*. With all due respect to you and your expertise, I'm going to follow the official procedure that has worked most effectively for us over the past forty years, which states that in order to make a *Schwarzfahrer* pay his or her fine, you contact him or her at his or her current address, which is to say, the one at which he or she currently lives. In the case of Carmelita Rodriguez, that address is 1 *Coppistrasse*, 7th Floor, Apartment B, Berlin, Germany 10365. It says it right here. Unlike you, I have documentation to prove it."

"As you wish, Frau Tintenpinkler, but I assure you, she doesn't live here."

"I assure you, Frau Rodriguez—"

"It's Frau Vespucci."

"—she does."

"Fritz," I ask, puzzled, when I get off the phone with Frau Tintenpinkler at the *Berlinerverkehrsgesellschaft*. "Did you see this letter that arrived for Carmelita?"

"No."

"It's a fine for *Schwarzfahren*."

"Oh, yeah. I forgot."

"You know about it?"

"Yes."

"But Carmelita wasn't even in Berlin when the fine was issued."

"Of course not. Carmelita lives in San Diego."

"Right. So how could she have gotten a fine for *Schwarzfahren?*"

"Maybe someone else got caught and gave her name to the *Berlinerverkehrsgesellschaft* instead of their own."

"Who would do such a thing?"

"Someone who didn't want to pay the fine, I guess."

"But who?"

"Well … me, most likely."

129

"What do you mean, you, most likely?"

"I mean most likely I was caught for *Schwarzfahren* and gave Carmelita's name to the *Berlinerverkehrsgesellschaft* instead of my own."

"Why would you do such a thing?"

"I didn't want to pay the fine, obviously."

"No, of course not."

"So, you see? It all makes sense."

"I can't believe you got caught for *Schwarzfahren*—"

"Everybody gets caught eventually."

"—and you gave the controllers Carmelita's name and address."

"Believe it."

"Why would they believe that your name was Carmelita?"

"They don't really care whose name and address you give. All they care about is that they issue the fine to someone, who will pay it. It doesn't matter who."

"But you're not even female."

"That day I was."

"That day you were?"

"Yes."

"What do you mean?"

"I mean that day I was dressed as a woman."

"What are you talking about?" I eye Fritz suspiciously to make sure I am not being mocked.

"It's just something I do from time to time."

"Being a transvestite is something you do from time to time?"

"I beg your pardon!"

"What?"

"I am *not* a transvestite—"

"But—"

"—and I'll thank you not to go around spreading baseless rumors that I am."

"But you just said that you dress as a woman from time to time."

"I only do it when Thorsten asks me to."

"Who's Thorsten?"

"You remember him. You met him the night you came home from Quasimodo."

"Oh, yes, I don't think he liked me very much."

"Don't take it personally. He doesn't like women very much. He views them as competition."

"Competition … because he's …"

"Yes, gay … and very jealous."

"So you dress as a woman when your gay friend Thorsten asks you to, but you're not a transvestite?"

"No. It's just to make Thorsten feel more comfortable when he's dressed as a woman."

"I see," I lie.

"It's never any fun by yourself."

"Of course not. Well, anyway, are you going to pay the fine?"

"Why would *I* pay the fine? The ticket clearly states that it's Carmelita's fine. If I pay a fine that wasn't issued to me, people might think I am trying to pose as somebody other than who I am."

"So who will pay it?"

"Carmelita has to pay it."

"But Carmelita doesn't live here anymore."

"According to the Official Berlin Resident Directory she does."

"So? We both know it's not true."

"The Official Berlin Resident Directory is truer than reality itself."

"I see."

The next day, I am on my way to meet Group Four at the bus station to finish our tour of political seminars around Germany, the tour that was truncated by the embassy bombing. Security is much tighter now than it was before, and two undercover controllers from the *Berlinerverkehrsgesellschaft* approach me and ask me to show my ticket. I cannot produce one.

"*Schwarzfahren,* are you?" they ask with glee.

"I'm afraid so," I admit. "This is my first time."

The controllers look at me disbelievingly.

"First time getting caught."

"Yes, that's more like it. As you can see, everyone gets caught eventually."

"I can see."

"We'll need to take down your name and address, young lady."

"Okay."

"Go ahead."

"That's Carmelita Rodriguez. 1 *Coppistrasse*, 7th Floor, Apartment B, Berlin Germany 10365."

"Thank you, ma'am. You enjoy the rest of your day."

"You too."

They exit the train.

Chapter Fifteen

The Masturbating Flasher

When we return from our journey to the other four political seminars, the weather in Berlin has begun to turn nasty. It has been a long and monotonous two weeks of hauling around from one uneventful town in Germany to the next where we foreign students had been forced to don suits, sit behind tables with our names typed professionally on paper name tents, and discuss the current political issues of the day, such as Germany's role in the U.S. attacks against the Defenders of Islam and expansion of the European Union.

It is dark and glossy as we students exit the bus and return to our neo-Communist ex-worker's paradise on *Coppistrasse*. There is a frosty feeling in the night air and a prickly wind is snaking its way under my collar and up my sleeves and pant legs. I shiver and wish I had brought a warmer jacket.

On the walk home from the *S-Bahn*, the pipes glisten in the precipitation, welcoming us down the Private Pathway to our *Plattenbau*. Also preparing to welcome us down the Private Pathway to our *Plattenbau* is a dirty old man in a trench coat hiding in the brush at the entrance to the Private Pathway Tunnel. As soon as I am in his line of vision, he opens his coat, bearing an ashen white torso and pink, semi-erect penis, which he pumps in his palm, causing his saggy gray testicles to oscillate betwixt his translucent, gray thighs. He has his right leg perched on a stump, exposing his nether-regions to the dim floodlight that flickers half-heartedly. Besides the trench coat, the man is wearing knee-high athletic socks and blue Velcro sneakers, the kind that were popular when I was in the fifth grade. I shriek and stagger backward, grabbing hold of Odelia, who is engrossed in conversation with Irina, and by the time the two of them look to where I am pointing, the man is gone.

"What is it?" the two girls want to know.

"Did you guys see that?"

"See what?"

"That man!"

"What man?"

"That … masturbating flasher?"

"Masturbating flasher?"

"Yes, the one that was just there a second ago?"

"What was he doing?"

"Masturbating."

"Besides that?"

"Flashing."

"Uh …"

"What was he wearing?"

"Nothing."

"Hmm …"

"Well, an overcoat … and some sneakers."

"Weird."

"Yeah, weird."

"We didn't see him."

"You didn't?"

"No."

"I swear he was there just a second ago."

"Weird."

"Yeah, weird."

"We didn't see him."

"That's so weird."

"What kind of sneakers were they?" asks Fritz over a cup of tea as I relate the story to him.

"Pumas, I think."

"I used to have blue, Velcro Pumas."

"Me too."

"When I was in fifth grade."

"Yeah, me too."

We sip our tea in silence for a while.

"So did you miss me while I was gone?" I ask.

"No." Fritz doesn't bat an eye.

"Well, tell me what I missed, then."

"Your fine for *Schwarzfahren* arrived while you were gone."

"Oh?"

"Yes, I put it on Carmelita's bed with all of the others."

"Good. Good."

"Are you going to buy a *Bahnpass* now?"

"I've tried a few times, but they just refuse to issue me one. I never have the correct documentation."

"So it goes."

"Fritz, why won't they issue me a *Bahnpass*?"

"Oh, *Schatz!* You've only hit the tip of the iceberg. If you think getting something issued is hard, you should try getting something registered."

"I can't even imagine."

"Or verified."

"Hmmm …" I ponder.

"Or certified."

"Wow."

"Or authorized."

"W—"

"Or notarized."

"…"

"Or mummified."

"Now you're just being ridiculous."

"I'm serious. Don't even try to get something mummified. You'll just be wasting your time."

"I'll remember that."

We are both silent for a few seconds.

"Anything else go on while I was gone?"

"Oh yes, some Viking called for you."

"I'm sorry?"

"Some Viking guy."

"A Viking guy … did he have a name?"

"Yes."

"And it was …"

"Thor."

"Thor?" I half gasp, half whisper.

"Yes, Thor."

"I can't believe Thor called! What did he say?"

"He said, *'Ich bin Thor.'*"

"And what did you say?"

"I said, *'Hallo Thor. Ich bin Fritz.'*"

"And then what did he say?"

"He said he wanted to talk to you."

"Fritz, this is amazing! Do you realize what this means?"

"No, I really don't know what this means, besides that some guy named Thor knows how to use a telephone."

"It means, he wants to talk to me."

"Okay, well, yes, if that's all it means, I got that part."

"So, what did you tell him?"

"I told him you were away."

"What else?"

"That's all."

"How did he sound? What did he say?"

"You already asked me what he said."

"Oh, sorry, then, how did he sound? Did he sound interested? Or confused, like maybe he called here by mistake?"

"It's hard to tell with Swedes. They're generally not very emotional. Doesn't go with the whole Viking image."

"Oh."

"I took down his number and put it under your door."

"Thanks! Fritz, this is a miracle!"

Fritz is unimpressed. "There was a piece of mail for you too. It's under your door as well."

"Thanks."

"You're welcome, *Schatz.*"

"What did he say?" Pete wants to know later in the evening as he and I share a few *Berliner Pilsner* beers on my balcony while admiring the pipe factory below.

"He said, '*Ich bin Thor.*'"

"*Ich bin Thor?*"

"Yeah."

"He sounds like a Viking."

"That's what Fritz said."

"What else did he say?"

"He left his number for me to call him."

"Are you going to call?"

"Do you think I should?"

"Yes, I think you should."

"Hmm …"

"I told you he would call."

We take a few silent sips of beer and gaze downward at the backyard of green pipes. Pete takes out a cigarette and lights it, cupping his hand around it to block the Berlin breeze. His blond locks ruffle in the wind. Pete takes a deep drag and exhales slowly.

"My co-worker tells me that these pipes are the ventilation

system for a city built under the city for use in the event of nuclear holocaust," he says.

"Wow, that's a good one. Fritz told me they were used for smuggling pornography and bananas from West to East before the Wall fell."

"That's a good one too."

"Indeed."

"So, Kat, tell me, you know your grandfather on your mother's side? The one that might … maybe … potentially be, but probably isn't, my grandfather too."

"Hmm."

"Tell me what he was like."

"Grandpa Bittner?"

"Yeah."

"Well, he died when I was only seven, so I never had a chance to really get to know him."

Pete exhales a lungful of smoke, which stands out sharply against the crisp night air. The scent tickles my nose.

"I really liked him. He always had Haribo gummy coke bottles for me when I saw him."

"I love Haribo gummy coke bottles."

"Me too."

Pete flicks his cigarette and ashes flutter from its tip down into the pipe yard. We sip our beers. The bottle numbs my fingers.

"Funny thing, though. None of the other family members seemed to like him very much."

"Oh?"

"Yeah, not really. He didn't spend much time with his family. By that time, World War II was going on. But my grandfather didn't have to go to the front because they were able to use the factory in the war effort."

"What did the factory make?"

"Normally, stained glass. Just regular glass for the war."

"Huh."

"But even though he hadn't been drafted, Grandma Bittner

remembers him taking off to go 'fight' every couple of weeks. She never questioned this, but other family members told rumors of him having girlfriends in Austria and Czechoslovakia. We assume he had other children too."

"Huh."

"In fact, he was away in some undisclosed location when the factory was bombed and Uncle Otto, the one who might be … you know …"

"My father."

"was lost."

"What do you know about that day?"

"The way my Grandma describes it, it was a nightmare. The factory had a bomb shelter in the basement. When the air raid sirens went off, she hurried her two children into the basement along with as many other mothers and children as could make it. They all survived the bombing, but when they emerged the next morning, they discovered that the factory, and most of the other surrounding buildings, had been hit. She describes the scene as an endless landscape of rubble, bodies, and broken stained glass."

"Wow. Surreal. A landscape of death and destruction, sparkling in brilliant color."

I pause for a moment; it does seem surreal.

"Well, no one that survived the night had slept very well, so Grandma gathered some blankets from the house and made a bed for my mom and Otto. But Otto, probably shell-shocked, wandered away. A friend told her later that she had seen Otto asleep on a pile of debris. The woman saw another man approach and shake him to see if he was alive. When Otto opened his eyes, the man gasped and scooped him up. 'I've got a child here!' the man shouted. 'It's alive! Does anybody want a child?' My grandmother's friend ran up to the man and told him she knew whose child it was and that she would take him to his mother. The man glared at her and told her that his mother was probably dead. My Grandma's friend tried to reassure the man that the child's mother had survived and that she would bring him back to her. The man held Otto tighter. He said there were other mothers whose children were dead, and that they deserved the child more. He took off down the street with Otto. 'I've got a child,' he screamed. 'It's alive! Does anybody want a child?' My Grandma's friend ran after him and grabbed him by the arm, demanding the boy. The man punched her in the face and knocked her unconscious. That was the last time anybody in my family ever heard of Otto."

"Jesus Christ!" exclaims Pete, shaking his head.

"Soon after the Soviets took over, my grandparents took my mother and fled to West Germany, and they had to cut off all ties with the East. They would have been arrested if they had gone back. My grandfather sent letters to remaining family members, but he never got an answer. My grandmother never forgave my grandfather for being away the day the factory was bombed."

"It's all so hard to imagine," says Pete. He drags on his cigarette for a few silent moments.

I finish my beer and chuck the bottle off the balcony down into the pipe yard. It thuds and clangs as it hits the pipes. Pete chases it with his cigarette butt and then his bottle. We take a few more silent moments, leaning against the railing, looking westward into the night. The TV tower blinks at us.

"My mom just sent me a picture actually. It's the only family picture we have of Otto."

"Oh?"

"I didn't even know she had it. It's of my grandparents standing with my mom and Otto in front of the factory not long before it was bombed."

"Can I see it?"

"Sure." I go inside and get the envelope that came while we were gone. I remove the black and white picture and hold it out for Pete to inspect. "The younger one is my mom and the older one is Otto."

Pete squints at the picture.

"What do you think?" I ask. "Does he resemble your father at all?"

Pete cocks his head to the side. "Actually yes … they both do."

"Yeah, I didn't think this picture would help much. I don't know why my mother keeps pushing this issue. The chances he's still alive are—"

"What are they wearing around their necks?"

"Those are necklaces my grandfather made." Both children and parents in the picture are wearing necklaces with diamond-shaped stained-glass pendants.

"How many of them did he make?"

"Just the four you see here, as far as I know."

"Huh. Does your mom still have hers?"

"Yes."

"Were they wearing them the day of the air raids?"

"We don't know."

"Well, I'll ask my father if he has one."

" … "

"If we can find that necklace, we've found your Uncle Otto."

Pete and I are silent until we hear a knock on the door. It is Jenny.

"Want to go play soccer?" she asks Pete and me.

"It's ten o'clock at night."

"I know. There won't be any hecklers this late."

"Isn't it too dark?"

"Nah, the ball is white. Your eyes will adjust."

We think it over for a minute. "Okay. Let's go see if anybody else is up for it."

We go and see and a couple of other students are up for it. We get together and slink to the soccer field like amateur ninjas. We climb the chain-link-fence and take our positions on the field. With pupils wide and our breath hovering around our heads, we get quite a game going. We run, tackle, slide, and jump. We play out of bounds, we use our hands, we score up and down and no one keeps score. After several minutes of hard playing, we stop to catch our breath. That's when we hear a familiar voice yelling at us.

"Are you kids crazy? You all have to work tomorrow!"

It is Herr Stern; he is walking toward us rapidly. We all stop moving and watch him approach.

"Herr Stern, hi!" calls Pete. "We know it's late, but, we just needed to blow off some steam. Were we making too much noise?"

Herr Stern is jogging toward us now. He comes through the gate of the chain link fence. "The whole neighborhood can hear you!" he yells. "I was paying a visit to one of your colleagues, and I could hear you all the way inside the *Plattenbau*."

We all look nervously at each other.

"Sorry!" calls Jenny.

Herr Stern comes right up to the edge of the soccer field and then stops and takes off his jacket. "And that's why I came out here." He smacks his hands together and runs onto the field. "What are you all gaping at? Let's play!"

Herr Stern lopes up to Jenny, steals the ball from her, and dribbles down the field. Everybody chases after him, but we can't catch him, and he shoots a goal.

"C'mon, young people!" he taunts. "You can do better than this!"

Pete throws his head back and laughs. My team absorbs Herr Stern, and we resume our game. Everyone is laughing, scoring, high-fiving, and trash-talking. Our voices resonate in the damp night air. After another good run, I bend over and put both hands on my knees. I observe the crew of people on the dark field. Steam rises from our heads and chests. I look at my hands and notice that they are steaming too. I am alive and among friends, and it feels pretty good.

CHAPTER SIXTEEN

Greta Schindler

That night game of soccer is over too soon, as far as I am concerned. I would have played all night if the others had wanted to, and the others might have wanted to if we didn't have to get up early this morning, put on suits, and go to the *Bundestag* for the first day of our internships. Last night, I had set my alarm for 7:00 AM, though it was in vain. The telephone wakes me up at six o'clock this morning.

"*Hallo. Hier ist Kat,*" I croak into the receiver.

"Hi, may I please speak to Kat?" asks a familiar voice.

"This is Kat."

"Hi, Kat. It's Matt."

"Matt?"

"Hi."

"It's 6:00 AM?"

"What? I thought it was … oh, never mind. Did I wake you?"

"Yes. Is everything okay?"

"For the most part. I'm okay. It's just …"

"What?"

"My birthday's coming up."

"Oh. That's right. Next month. 'Happy birthday' coming up."

"Thanks …"

"So, what about it?"

"Well … I was wondering if you were planning on coming home for it?"

" … "

"Because I was planning on buying Bare Naked Ladies tickets."

" … "

"I was wondering if you would like to go to the concert with me."

" … "

"Kat, do you remember last year we went to their concert for my birthday? That was one of the best concerts of my life."

"Yes, I remember."

"Remember the thunderstorm at the end?"

"Yes."

"And how they played the last song with the thunder and lightning exploding in the background!"

" … "

"We were soaking wet and we all thought we would be electrocuted."

"Yes, I remember."

"Your clothes were clinging to you and your hair was all wet."

The memory jolts me. "And I got a chill and you had to hug me for the whole end of the show because I was shivering. I remember." My eyes moisten.

"That was so awesome!"

"Matt, um, you're not serious about me coming home for your birthday, are you?"

"Well … kind of … yeah."

"I can't do that."

"Why not?"

"Well, first of all, aren't you going to be spending it with Katie?"

"Oh, she hates the Bare Naked Ladies."

"Hates the Bare Naked Ladies? What kind of … never mind."

Matt laughs. "I know this is probably inappropriate to ask, but maybe you don't have to come home for my birthday."

" … "

"Maybe you could just come home."

"Come what?"

"Life's really not the same without you."

"Matt, are you and Katie breaking up?" My heart quivers.

"No. Well, maybe. I don't know. I'm just thinking too much."

"Well, maybe you should figure that out first, before you ask me to come home." I want to hang up on him.

"I'm sorry, Kat. I'm sorry. You're right. Please don't be mad. I shouldn't have called. I'll leave you alone."

" … "

"It's good to hear your voice, Kat, even if you are mad at me."

" … "

"I'm sorry I put you through all of this. I should go. I'll get back to you when I figure stuff out."

"Okay."

"Alright, I'm going now."

"Okay, bye. I'll talk to you later."

"Bye."

I start to hang up the receiver.

"I love—"

Click.

"You hung up on him?" asks Janika as I relate the story to her on the *S-Bahn* ride to our first day of work at the *Bundestag*.

"Yeah. Well, not exactly on purpose."

"And you didn't call him back?"

"No."

"Why not?"

"Why would I call him back?"

"Don't you want to know if he really still loves you?"

"What's the use? He's so confused, he doesn't know himself who he loves."

"Maybe he has figured it out, but he feels too much like a jerk to admit it."

"Janika, we were together for five years. I'm sure he just said it out of habit."

"What if he didn't?"

"What does it matter? He's with Katie now."

"But don't you still love him too?"

"Yes, in a way."

"So you should tell him how you feel."

"What if I'm not sure how I feel anymore?"

I feel like a guppy in a piranha tank when I first set foot into my office in the German *Bundestag*. My representative's quarters are located in a building called the *Jakob-Kaiser Haus*, which is attached to the *Reichstag* building by a series of underground tunnels. The *Jakob-Kaiser Haus* is a seven-story building held together by a skeletal structure of steel and glass. Each individual office inside the *Jakob-Kaiser Haus* has large windows, some facing outside, and some facing a spacious atrium that allows natural light to flow into the building's interior. Though it looks like a solid structure from the outside, *the Jakob-Kaiser Haus* is a spacious edifice of I-beams, cables, suspended bridges, staircases, and glass elevators. From the suspended bridges one can see everything going on in the hallways of all seven floors of the *Jakob-Kaiser Haus* and even into some offices. How excellent for spying! As I tread from the glass elevator across one of the bridges to knock on the door of my representative's office, I wonder if anyone is spying up my skirt.

At my knock, Frau Greta Schindler, a slight woman in her late thirties with bobbed, black hair, greets me enthusiastically through a thick cloud of cigarette smoke. Frau Schindler is Herr Kaufmann's office assistant.

"Frau Vespucci, darling! *Bitte, kommen Sie herein.*"

I accept her invitation and walk through the door.

"Welcome! Welcome! Please have a seat."

"Es ist sehr nett, Sie kennenzulernen," I say, feeling rather like Sveta, but less practiced.

"We're delighted to have you with us," Frau Schindler continues. "We apply for a foreign student every year. It's just so nice to have a cute, little American running around the office, do you know what I mean? It really cheers up Herr Kaufmann. And I'm so glad you're a girl. Julia and I want to keep it a female office, if you know what I mean. Except for Herr Kaufmann, and his staff of lawyers and researchers, it's all women around here. Oh yes, you'll fit in well with us. I'll take you to meet Julia in just a moment. Julia is Herr Kaufmann's intern. She works for us the first and third weeks of every month and spends the second and fourth weeks studying political science at the University of Bonn … kind of like how you will work for us Mondays, Wednesdays, and Fridays and spend Tuesdays and Thursdays studying at Humboldt. You're both part-time, but since she's been here longer than you, she gets the big desk in the interns' office and you will have your very own end table to work from. Plus, Julia is twenty-nine and you're only twenty-one, so naturally she's higher in the pecking order, if you know what I mean. But don't you worry, when Julia is here, you will have your own laptop to use and we will position it so that you can reach the telephone if you need to make calls. When she is not here, then you may have the big desk all to yourself. Oh, we are going to have a lovely time together, do you know what I mean?"

I have no idea what Frau Schindler means.

"I'll show you all around the office and give you all kinds of fun tasks to do. Of course, you don't want to work too hard when you're here. You're here to learn, you know what I mean? I'll make sure you get to explore lots of places and maybe even accompany Herr Kaufmann to some meetings and sessions and all of that jazz. In fact, I'll call the ticket office right now and reserve you a seat for the next *Bundestag* session. Won't that be wonderful? By the way, Herr Kaufmann sends his regards. He is away this week campaigning in his home district, but he wants me to tell you that he looks forward to meeting you next week."

"That's very nice of him," I reply. "Please tell him that I look forward to meeting him next week."

"I will, darling. Now, Frau Vespucci, before we get down to business, tell me a little bit about yourself."

"Okay."

"In fact, this kind of introduction is best done over coffee, you know what I mean?" Frau Schindler walks over to the closet and opens the door to reveal a hidden mini-kitchen, complete with a sink, a small refrigerator, a microwave oven, and a built-in coffee maker. She pours two cups of fresh coffee and adds condensed milk and sugar. She gives one cup to me. It is rich coffee, very strong.

"Now then, as you were saying?"

I tell Frau Schindler about my family back in New Jersey, and my time in Berlin thus far.

"Where are you living?" Frau Schindler wants to know.

"*Coppistrasse.*"

Frau Schindler gasps. "*Coppistrasse!* In *Lichtenberg?*"

"Yes."

"*Um Gottes Willen!*"

"What's wrong?" I ask.

"You poor child, Frau Vespucci. It's an absolute disgrace!"

"What is?"

"There, among the Neo-Nazis and Communists!"

"Actually, I haven't noticed any Neo-Nazis or Communists, to be honest … just some graffiti."

"Just you wait, Frau Vespucci. It's an absolute scandal that the *Bundestag* puts you foreign students there just to save money."

"It's not so bad," I console Frau Schindler. "I've gotten used to it."

"What about that masturbating flasher? Is he still there?"

"Oh yes," I tell her. "I saw him the other day."

"A disgrace!"

"How do you know about him?"

"Our last foreign student bumped into him a few times. What an awful, awful man."

"Yes, he is rather unpleasant."

"Did you call the police?"

"No, my other friends didn't see him. I thought maybe I was just seeing things."

"Well, it probably won't do much good anyway. The police in *Lichtenberg* have a lot more to worry about than that masturbating flasher with all those Neo-Nazis and Communists running about."

"I really haven't noticed any."

"Just you wait, Frau Vespucci. Just you wait, if you know what I mean."

I don't know what Frau Schindler means, nor do I want to.

"To be honest, I'm more scared of those large, green pipes."

"Oh, those? Don't worry about them. They haven't functioned for years. I forget what was in them. It must have been steam. Or was it waste water? Oh, I don't know. Regardless, they can't take them down because they are full of asbestos. Safer just to leave them alone than deal with them, if you know what I mean."

"Asbestos?"

"Either way, I know what you mean. It would be interesting to know what *had been* in them, wouldn't it, darling?"

"I don't know."

"Have you had a chance to do any traveling since you've been in Germany?" Frau Schindler continues.

"Yes, as a matter of fact." I explain to Frau Schindler all about the seminars around Germany.

"Very interesting, Frau Vespucci. Very interesting indeed. Would you like some more coffee?"

"No, thank you."

Frau Schindler pours herself another cup and then sits back down at her desk. She lights a cigarette. Swiveling her chair to partly face the window, Frau Schindler takes a long drag and exclaims, "Can you believe this ridiculous weather we're having?"

I haven't noticed that the weather is particularly ridiculous today, but I look out the window anyway. Frau Schindler's view faces West, offering a clear line of sight to the Chancellor's office and the *Tiergarten*, the large park in the center of Berlin. Over the *Tiergarten* one can make out dark clouds rolling in over the horizon. From her sixth-floor view of incoming weather patterns, Frau Schindler has a leg up on her fellow Berliners when it comes to complaining about the weather.

"I tell you Frau Vespucci, darling, it's never just right, is it? It's either too cold or too hot, too humid or too dry, too rainy or too sunny, too quickly-changing or too not-quickly-changing-enough, if you know what I mean."

"Of course I know what you mean," I lie.

"But at least from up here, we are able to prepare our climate criticisms at least a full half-hour before everybody else in the office even knows what is happening outside. It's a real advantage, Frau Vespucci. It really is!"

"It's nice today, though, isn't it?" I finally add.

"Oh, just you wait, Frau Vespucci. Look at those clouds!"

I look at those clouds.

"Just this morning it was clear and pleasant. Now it's cloudy. In a few minutes it will be raining like buckets. And I bet by this afternoon it will be clear and pleasant again."

"I see," I say.

"You'll see, Frau Vespucci. Most places have four seasons a year. Berlin has four seasons a day."

"Four seasons a day?"

"That's right."

I squint to see better out the window, but from where I am sitting I can't see so well because Frau Schindler is puffing away on her cigarette and there are more clouds inside the office than outside. Frau Schindler's ashtray, full with extinguished butts, also doubles as a paperweight for a stack of invitations that she is filling out for Herr Kaufmann's upcoming sixtieth birthday celebration. Frau Schindler follows my gaze to the invitations.

"I write and write and write these invitations all day long and I never get through them all. It's a miserable, miserable task to perform, do you know what I mean, Frau Vespucci?"

I haven't filled out any of the invitations, so I do not know what Frau Schindler means.

"I would be glad to help you with them," I volunteer.

"Nonsense, darling! You will do no such thing. I can handle the task just fine. You needn't worry your little head about these, Frau Vespucci. They will soon be finished."

"If you say so," I say. "I'm willing to help if you need it."

"What a darling you are, Frau Vespucci!"

"Feel free to call me Kat," I say.

"Oh! How lovely, darling. I was hoping we could skip the formalities. It makes it so much more relaxed in the office. Please, it would be my honor if you would call me Greta."

"Thank you, Greta. It is my pleasure."

"You're welcome, Kat, darling. Oh, we're going to have a lovely time together. But you have worked hard enough for one day, if you know what I mean. Take the rest of the day off. Explore Berlin."

"I'm sorry?"

"Take the rest of the day off, darling. You don't want to be hanging around here in the office when you could be out accomplishing something!"

"Are you sure?" I ask.

"Absolutely. You've been an absolute dream today! Thank you so much for all of your hard work. Now run along and I will see you on Wednesday."

"Alright," I say, standing up and starting to put on my coat.

"Oh, one more thing, darling!" continues Greta, rummaging through her purse. "Do you have plans for tonight?"

"No. Why do you ask?"

"I've got two tickets for a play tonight. *Der Stellvertreter*. It's won lots of awards. It's showing at nine o'clock at *Alexanderplatz*. If you don't already have plans, you are welcome to take the tickets. It's a wonderful play, darling, it really is."

"Well, thank you," I reply. "I would love to take the tickets. I've been seeing posters for *The Deputy* on my *S-Bahn* ride in the mornings. It's just … don't you want them?"

"Oh no, darling, don't be silly."

"Have you already seen the play?"

"No, no. Maybe some other time. It's getting rave reviews."

"I don't understand."

Greta shifts uncomfortably and holds the tickets out for me to take.

"Thank you for the generous offer, but I really cannot accept these."

"If you don't take them, they will go to waste."

"Why?"

"It's at *Alexanderplatz*, darling."

"I know."

"That's in the East."

"Yes?"

"I don't go *over there* at night."

"Oh," I say, scrunching my brow.

"Be a treasure, darling, take the tickets," Greta insists.

I hesitate, not sure if I am overstepping my bounds, but decide to press the issue anyway. "You know, I live *over there*. I'm always there at night. It's really not that bad."

"Of course it's not, darling." She slides the tickets into my hand. "Bye now. Enjoy the show and tell me *all* about it on Wednesday."

"If you insist," I say. I accept the tickets and walk out of her office.

In the hallway, I bump into Billy, who has also been let out early. "Want to join me for a play tonight?"

"Sure."

CHAPTER SEVENTEEN

Herr Fromme

When I come back into the office on Wednesday morning, Greta doesn't ask me about the play. She immediately begins introducing me to the rest of the team. "First I will introduce you to Julia," she says as we walk across the steel bridge to the other side of the floor.

"Julia, darling," whispers Greta as she taps on the heavy, wooden door across the atrium. Julia's office is one of the only offices not made entirely of glass. Because it is connected to the storage closet, she actually has the luxury of opaque walls.

"Come in," calls Julia. Greta and I enter the room. Julia is a young woman in her late twenties with stylish clothes and the *Friends* haircut.

"I want you to meet Kat. She's our new, little American," beams Greta.

"It's nice to meet you, Kat."

"Nice to meet you too, Julia."

154

"Kat is going to be helping us with a little of this and a little of that around the office for a few months, if you know what I mean."

"That's wonderful!" exclaims Julia.

"She'll be sitting at the little end table there in the corner as soon as we get her settled."

"I will be overjoyed to have her company," says Julia.

"That's wonderful, darling," says Greta. "I'm sure you two will get along like old school pals."

"I'm sure we will," says Julia.

"Julia, darling, would you like to join us for a cup of coffee?"

"I would love to!"

The three of us go to Greta's office where we start the morning with several cups of strong coffee and Julia and Greta complain about the clouds coming in over the *Tiergarten*.

"Can you believe the temperature change from yesterday to today?" exclaims Julia. "How can one be expected to dress properly under these conditions?"

"It's insanity, Julia darling. Pure insanity!"

When we are finished with our coffee, Julia goes back to her office and Greta takes me to meet Herr Fromme, whose office is next to Greta's on the same side of the atrium. Herr Fromme is Herr Kaufmann's legal analyst and research coordinator. Greta knocks on his heavy wooden door.

"Come in," calls Herr Fromme. Herr Fromme is a large, calm-looking man, who stands about six feet four inches tall and sits about four feet six. He has an oblong belly, thinning hair, and a calm, patriarchal smile.

"*Hallo, Herr Fromme,*" replies Greta, entering the office. "I hope I am not interrupting you."

"No, no. Please, come in, Frau Schindler. Please come in."

"I would like to introduce you to Frau Vespucci, our new American worker bee. She'll be buzzing around the office for the next few months and she'll be happy to help you with any projects you might have for her, if you know what I mean."

"How absolutely wonderful!" exclaims Herr Fromme, getting up from his chair. He approaches me and pumps my hand aggressively. "It is an extreme pleasure to meet you, Frau Vespucci. I mean that seriously."

"Thank you," I reply. "The pleasure is mine."

"Now that I think of it, Frau Vespucci, Herr Fromme might know the answer to your question about those awful green pipes all over *Lichtenberg*. Herr Fromme, do you happen to know what they were used for when they were still, you know, in use?"

"You mean those gangly green things just about large enough for a medium-sized man to fit inside?"

"Yes, that's them."

"Those were aboveground surveillance tunnels."

"Aboveground surveillance tunnels?"

"Used by the *Stasi* whose headquarters were also *over there*. Everybody knows that, Frau Schindler."

"Does everybody know that, Herr Fromme?"

"They most certainly do."

Greta shoots me a doubtful glance to indicate that everybody does not know that.

"Well, we've got a busy day ahead of us," says Greta. "We'll be on our way now."

"Yes, Frau Schindler. Thank you."

"Thank you."

"Thank you."

The office next to Herr Fromme's office belongs to Herr Bourne. Herr Bourne is Herr Kaufmann's assistant legal analyst and research coordinator, who is directly subordinate to Herr Fromme. Greta knocks on his heavy wooden door. There is no answer. Through the window we can see that he is on the telephone. Greta knocks again.

"Come in!" snaps Herr Bourne.

"Hallo, Herr Bourne," Greta pokes her head into the office. "I hope I am not interrupting you."

"Can't you see that you are interrupting me?" scolds Herr Bourne.

"I'm sorry, Herr Bourne. I thought I heard you say 'come in'."

"No, not you!" yells Herr Bourne into the phone. "You are not the one that is interrupting me, *you* are the person I am having a conversation with. Please hold for one moment. Yes, I did say 'come in,' so that I could ask you not to interrupt me."

"My apologies, Herr Bourne. Is this a bad time?"

"Yes, this is a bad time. I will talk to you later." Herr Bourne puts the phone back to his ear. "No, not *you*. I said I wasn't talking to you. I mean, I *am* talking to you. You are the one I was talking to when I was interrupted by … yes … continue with what you were saying."

"I was saying," Greta continues, "I want to introduce you to Frau Vespucci, our new foreign student."

"No, not you," Herr Bourne says to Greta. "Yes, you," Herr Bourne says into the phone. "No, you're not the one that's interrupting me. You're the one that I am having a conversation with … no, don't hang up! I said don't … she hung up. *Verdammt!*"

"Never mind, Herr Bourne. We'll come back later."

"Yes, please come back when I'm off the phone."

"Actually sir, you are off the phone now."

"That is beside the point, Frau Schindler!" Herr Bourne scolds Greta. "I was having a perfectly good conversation with the person I was having a conversation with, when you interrupted me."

"You're right, sir. I'm sorry. We'll come back later when you're not in the middle of something else."

Herr Bourne looks around the office and notices that he is suddenly not in the middle of something else. "Well, you may as well interrupt me now. Now that I'm not doing anything!"

Suddenly, I notice Billy's barrel frame, three floors down, being led from office to office by his office manager. I give him a sympathy wave. He spies me and waves back. Greta and I enter Herr Bourne's office. He is a slight man with straight brown hair parted rigidly down the left side of his head. He has a pointy, little nose and sharp, little eyes and wears thin, steel-framed glasses that adjust their darkness depending on the light.

"I just wanted to introduce you to Frau Vespucci, Herr Bourne."

Herr Bourne doesn't get up but shakes my hand across his desk. "Yes, nice to meet you. Who are you?"

"Frau Vespucci is our new foreign student, Herr Bourne."

"Ah, yes, you're one of those high schoolers, right?"

"No, Herr Bourne, Frau Vespucci is in her last year of college."

"Impossible."

"It's true," I reply. "I go to Rutgers."

"You are too young to be in college," he informs me.

"Frau Vespucci is a very talented young lady, Herr Bourne. And doesn't she speak excellent German?"

Herr Bourne eyes me suspiciously. "Not bad, for a high school student."

"Thank you," I say. "I'm not in high school."

"And what exactly will you be doing here, Frau Vespucci?"

"Whatever Frau Schindler asks me to, Herr Bourne."

"Well, well, I'm sure I'll have a project or two for you! But as you can see, for the moment, I am very, very busy. Frau Schindler, thank you for bringing her by."

"You're welcome, Herr Bourne. We'll be on our way now."

"It was a pleasure to meet you, Frau Vespucci. Come by my office as soon as you get settled. Now that you mention it, there is something urgent that I will need your help with."

"Certainly," I say.

"Good-bye."

"Good-bye."

"Good-bye."

When Herr Bourne is safely closed away behind his heavy wooden door, Greta makes a face as if she has just sucked on a lemon.

"He makes me want to puke, if you know what I mean."

"Yes," I agree. "I know what you mean."

Back in Greta's office, Greta pours us two more cups of coffee. I am starting to feel loopy from the caffeine.

"Now," announces Greta, "I've got to get to work writing out these birthday invitations.

"What kind of task can I give to you to start you off? I know! Here is a newspaper. Go over to Julia's office and familiarize yourself with German culture."

"Familiarize myself with German culture?"

"Yes, it will be very important for you to know about life in Germany while working for Herr Kaufmann. Make yourself comfortable in Julia's office and let me know when you're through with the paper. Of course, I don't expect you to read the whole thing. Pick a few articles, read them slowly, the Arts and Leisure section is always good, and look up the words you don't understand. There should be a dictionary over there. If not, you may use the Internet. Julia will help you set up the laptop."

I am not sure if Greta is pulling my leg or not. "You know, I'm actually taking a course on German politics and culture at Humboldt. Isn't there something more helpful that I can do?"

Greta looks at me, very surprised. "Hmmmm," she thinks. "Besides the newspaper, I think everything else I have to read will be too difficult. We have some copies of *Der Spiegel* magazine lying around the office, but I'm afraid that might take you forever."

Reading magazines still isn't my idea of productive work, so I ask again for a more *Bundestag* related assignment.

"Okay then." Greta fishes around in her purse and pulls out a pocket-sized version of Germany's constitution. "Here, read this and let me know if you have any questions."

I don't have the heart to tell her that it is the same pocket-sized version of Germany's constitution that Herr Stern gave me on the first day I arrived in Berlin. Though I haven't read that one either, it still isn't what I have in mind. Instead of arguing further, I thank Greta, take the book, the newspaper, and the magazine and head across the atrium to Julia's office. Julia is busy typing and doesn't open the door at first. I wait patiently, not quite sure what to do.

While I am standing in the hall, I see Billy emerge from another office on the third floor. I smile and wave. He takes his hands and wraps them around his throat, pretending to choke himself. Then he disappears into another office. I knock again on Julia's door. She answers it.

"Yes, can I help you?"

"I'm just here to get started."

"In here?"

"Yes, Greta said we would both be working in this office. Remember?"

"Yes, I didn't realize she meant right away. Fine. Come in if you must."

I go in and sit down at the small end table. "Greta also said you would help me set up the laptop. Would you mind?"

Julia looks annoyed. "We keep it in the locked cabinet over here." Julia sets up the laptop for me. "I trust that you'll be able to set it up yourself next time?"

"Probably," I say. "Thanks for your help."

Julia does not respond but sits immediately back down at her desk and turns her computer screen away so that I cannot see what she is doing. Julia sees me scrunch my brow at this move.

"What? A person has to have *some* privacy!"

"That's true," I say and turn my computer screen away from Julia. But I have nothing to hide on my computer screen, because I have no work to do on the computer, so I open the mini-constitution, or Basic Law, as it is known in Germany. But I don't feel like reading the Basic Law, so I skim a few parts and then close it. I open the newspaper and read some articles. Then

I check my e-mail. I read an article in *Der Spiegel.* Then my eyes begin to hurt. I think I might try to strike up a conversation with Julia.

"What are you working on?" I ask.

"Nothing that would interest you," Julia says. "Some of us actually have to work around here, instead of reading the paper and magazines."

I see how it is. I get up and go back over to Greta's office. It is about noon now, and Greta is getting ready to go out for lunch.

"I've finished reading the Basic Law and today's paper," I announce to my supervisor.

"My Goodness, darling!" explains Greta. "Are you trying to work yourself to death?"

"No, I just—"

"Run along, now darling, before someone accuses me of abusing you, if you know what I mean."

"Are you sure?"

"Absolutely, darling. Go home. Get some rest. I will see you on Friday."

"Okay," I say. "I will just gather my things."

Back on the other side of the atrium, Julia is working through lunch. I try to pack up as quietly as possible. Suddenly the phone rings. Julia answers.

"*Hallo, Kaufmann Büro, Julia am Apparat* ... Excuse me? You want to speak with whom? Yes, she is here. No, you may not speak with her. Call back when you know how to introduce yourself properly on the telephone. Goodbye." Julia hangs up the phone.

"Who was that?" I ask.

"Well, that's the question, now, isn't it? Tell your friends they're supposed to announce themselves properly when calling an office."

"That call was for me and you hung up on the person?"

"Well, maybe he'll introduce himself properly next time."

"It's not your job to teach my friends phone etiquette."

"Oh no? I thought you were here to learn."

The phone rings again. Julia answers it. "*Hallo, Kaufmann Büro, Julia am Apparat* … Oh, hello, Herr Thompson. Yes, she's right here. One moment please." Julia hands the phone to me.

"Who the hell is *that?*" Billy asks when I get on the line.

"Billy, you have just met my officemate, Julia."

"What's she got up her ass?"

"Good question. I'll get back to you on that. What's up?"

"Listen, my office is letting me go early again today. How late do you have to work?"

"I'm on my way out right now."

"Awesome! Want to meet me for a beer and trade first-week war stories?'

"I would love to!"

Billy and I go to a beer garden around the corner from the *Jakob-Kaiser Haus*. There, we run into Jenny, Pete, Istvan, and Lambert who have also been let out early. They are trading first-week war stories. Lambert is wearing a T-shirt that says "America Sucks." I sigh and shake my head when I see it.

"How were your first two days?" Pete asks, snuffing out a cigarette.

"I get the feeling," I confess, "that no one in my office takes me seriously."

"Me neither," exclaims Billy. "I can see I'm going to serve the purpose of a highly-educated garnish in my office. I spent the entire morning reading magazines and then my boss thanked me for my hard work and told me to take the rest of the day off."

"Same here," replies Istvan.

Jenny has had an equally humiliating day. "My supervisor actually took the time this morning to explain to me that Berlin was not always like it is today. Believe it or not, there was once a wall that ran right down the middle of the city, and you weren't allowed to cross from one side to the other. The wall was called 'the Berlin Wall.'"

Our first day of classes at Humboldt goes a lot more smoothly than our first two days of work, considering that every single one of our classes ends up being cancelled.

"Can you believe that?" I ask Fritz while we prepare dinner together later on.

"Believe what, *Schatz?*" he says, while stirring some meat sauce.

"That all of my classes were just cancelled—without any notice. When I arrived, there were notes on the doors saying 'No Class Today' and no mention of when the classes would be rescheduled."

"Why should they give you notice?"

"Well, because we students pay a lot of money to take these classes, and we deserve some notice if the class is going to be cancelled or rescheduled."

"Higher education in Germany is free, *Schatz*. And you're getting paid a stipend to attend this program."

"Oh. You're right. Good point."

"The professors can do anything they want, and that includes not having class if they don't feel like it."

On Thursday, the class I attend is overcrowded and students are standing in the back and sitting on the floor and in the windowsills. The professor does not take attendance or introduce himself to the students. He just arrives, opens the textbook, and reads for the duration of the class. I am able to pay attention for the first five minutes and then I zone out. The syllabus contains a list of topics that will be covered and the date of the final exam but there are no homework assignments or other exams.

When I arrive at my second class for the day, I again find a note on the door. It says that the weather is too sunny to have class and that the professor can be found at the nearest beer garden. A reading is recommended to substitute for the lecture. Anyone who wishes to discuss the reading with the professor should meet him at the aforementioned beer garden.

"I don't see what the problem is, *Schatz*." Fritz says while frying up a pan of potatoes later on that evening. The smell and sound of sizzling butter fills the kitchen.

"Well, the first week of classes is over, and I've only actually had one class. And in that class, the professor didn't take attendance or hold any class discussion, and there isn't going to be any homework, except to study for the final exam. So I may as well not have gone to class this week at all. That smells great, by the way."

"Thank you. Of course you may as well not have gone to class this week. Going to class is a waste of your time. I fail to see the problem."

"The problem is, what's the point?"

"The point of what?"

"The point of going to the Humboldt University if going to class is a waste of time?"

"*Schatz,* are you saying that you *want* classes to be a lot of work?" Fritz asks me as he adds bacon bits to the potatoes. They crackle in the hot butter.

"How else will they know if I'm learning anything?"

"They won't. And who cares?"

"I care. And the professors should care too."

"They care if you pass the exam at the end of the term."

"Just because you can pass an exam, that doesn't mean you've actually learned anything."

"Well, they're not going to force you to learn anything, *Schatz.* That's up to you."

"Why shouldn't they force me to learn anything?"

"Because if they tried to force you, then you wouldn't want to do it, would you?"

"Well, if they forced me, I'd have to. It's just like riding the *S-Bahn* and *U-Bahn.* Why can't they just have a turnstile to make me pay?"

"Are you saying you *want* to be forced?"

"Yes, that's what I'm saying. I want to be forced."

"Then you're not actually being forced, are you? The sheer nature of the word 'force' implies being made to do something that you don't want to do."

"Well, part of achieving anything is working hard, even if you don't really feel like it."

"What you're asking is that the Humboldt professors coerce you into attending classes and doing a lot of work.....even when you don't really feel like it."

"Well, we all have our moments when we don't feel like doing something. But that doesn't mean we don't want to do it."

"I hate to break this to you, *Schatz*, but nobody is going to force you to work hard here, or go to class, or do homework if you don't feel like it; and I can also assure you that the professors are not going to work hard either, or take attendance, or assign homework, if they don't feel like it."

"Hmm ..."

"It's called *Akademische Freiheit*."

"What?"

"Academic freedom. German higher education is famous for it, actually."

"That sounds all well and good, but I'd prefer to be forced."

Fritz shakes his head.

Chapter Eighteen

Thor

By far the highlight of my first week of work and school is Friday, because that's when I finally summon up the nerve to call Thor.

"Hallo, hallo!" he answers the phone, very debonair.

As soon as I hear the sound of Thor's voice, my cheeks turn hot. His voice is deep and silky.

"Um, hi," I answer, my voice high-pitched and un-cool in contrast. "It's Kat Vespucci."

There is a slight pause and then Thor speaks, "Kat who?"

My heart sinks. "Kat Vespucci, the girl you called last week?"

Silence.

"We met in Quasimodo a few weeks ago. Well, we didn't really meet. I just kind of gave you my number." I'm such an idiot! Of course he doesn't remember me!

There is silence on the other end of the line.

"I, um, have brown hair? An American accent?"

No response.

"I was with two friends, a guy and a girl. I handed you a pack of matches, made you look cool in front of all your friends?"

"Sorry, I don't remember anyone like that."

"Made myself look like an idiot in front of all of your friends?"

"Oh yes, Kat! Why didn't you say so? Of course I remember you."

I giggle nervously, not exactly sure if it is a joke or not.

"I'm sorry," Thor apologizes. "I had to get you back for not calling me back until now."

He has a point.

"It's nice to finally touch base with you."

"Yes, sorry about the lag-time," I explain. "I've been very busy."

"Me too, me too—but never too busy to get to know someone interesting. Tell me, Kat. Who are you?"

I have to think a minute, because since the moment Thor has picked up the phone, I have not been able to think. "Well, I'm in college. I'm completing my senior year here in Berlin."

"At Humboldt?"

"Yes. I'm interning too. At the *Bundestag*."

"That's cool. How'd you land that gig?"

"Oh, it's this whole foreign exchange program called *HAA*. I applied for it back in the States."

"I take classes at Humboldt too," adds Thor.

"Yeah?"

"Yeah, what are you studying?"

"I'm taking courses on German politics and culture."

"Me too."

"Wow, I wonder if we're in any of the same classes."

"Hard to say. Mine keep getting cancelled."

"Wow! Mine too. Isn't that weird?"

"Well, that's the *Akademische Freiheit* for you. Leaves me time to pursue my music while I'm here."

"That's true. You really are an incredible guitar player."

"Thank you. I bet you say that to all the incredible guitar players."

I wonder if he can tell I am blushing. There is a few-seconds pause between us.

"So I think we should meet up sometime and get to know each other face to face," Thor suggests.

"Okay," I agree, my stomach doing somersaults. "When?"

"I don't know. I'll have to check my schedule"

"If you want to get back to me, that's okay."

"No. No. Just let me check …"

I hold my breath.

"Okay, I checked my schedule. I'm free right now."

"I beg your pardon?"

"I'm free right now. What are you doing right now?"

"Um, I just got home from work and I'm … I don't know … just sitting here … talking to you."

"Perfect! What do you say we meet at *Friedrichstrasse Bahnhof* in half an hour?"

"Half an hour?"

"Perfect."

"Wait a minute. In order to meet you at *Friedrichstrasse Bahnhof* in half an hour, I'd have to leave … right now, and I'm not—"

"That's what I want!" Thor interrupts me.

"What's what you want?"

"Your attention—from this moment on."

I stop. He is bold. "Why from this moment on?"

"Because there are no guarantees in life … except for this moment."

I pause to let the statement sink in. "Meet you at *Friedrichstrasse Bahnhof* in half an hour."

"Great! See you there."

I gently hang up the receiver and then tear into my bedroom. I whisk off my work clothes and hop into a pair of jeans. Then I whisk off the jeans and hop into a khaki skirt. Then I remember that it is cold outside and whisk the jeans back on. I dart out to the bathroom, but Fritz is in there dying his hair.

"Fritz!" I pound on the door. "I've got to get in there!"

"Oh, *Shatz*, I'm glad you're here. I can't decide whether to bleach my whole head or just half. What do you think?"

"Fritz, I need to get in there. This moment!"

"Whoa, whoa! What's the rush?"

"I'm meeting Thor at *Friedrichstrasse Bahnhof* in thirty minutes."

"I see," Fritz steps out of the bathroom, naked except for tight little underpants and half of his head sizzling in peroxide.

I slide past him, clumsily run my toothbrush across my teeth, cough from the fumes, apply some lip-gloss, and spray on some perfume. Then I grab my purse from my room and sashay out the door.

As I close the apartment door, Fritz pokes his head out from the bathroom. "Don't let him rape or pillage you on the first date."

"What kind of thing is that to say?"

"Sorry, bad Viking joke."

Waiting for Thor at the *Friedrichstrasse Bahnhof,* each second feels like ten minutes. Am I in the right place? I wish I had brought his phone number so that I could call him. Then I start to wonder if I will even recognize him when I see him. We had met such a long time ago. Plus, it is hard for me to imagine that the beautiful guitarist that had mystified me that night at Quasimodo, who had been so far beyond my reach, was coming to meet *me.* Just me. At *Friedrichstrasse Bahnhof.* Any moment now. From this moment on. What if it isn't real? Maybe I should leave.

Thor arrives twenty minutes late. I recognize him instantly. He is pushing through the crowd, wearing the same brown, suede jacket with the upturned collar. His hair is stylishly messy, like I remember it, and he is flaunting that wide, toothy grin with the long dimples that make me want to stab a Swiss Army knife into my adrenaline glands to stop them from over pumping. Thor's dimples, I decide, are an act of God.

When Thor finally reaches me, he puts a hand on my waist and gives me a kiss on each cheek. The scent of cologne I've never smelled before wafts to my nose. My skin tightens. I pray that my face is not tomato red.

"Hi," he says, smiling.

"Hi," I say, smiling.

"Let's go."

"Okay."

Thor grabs my hand and leads me through the crowd and out of the train station. "Sorry I'm late."

"It's okay."

Thor gives my hand a squeeze. He leads me to a little café by the university, but it is closed.

"Well, that's a shame."

I have another suggestion. The *Friedrichstrasse Bahnhof* is right next to the river *Spree*. There is a covered bridge that crosses the river, and under the bridge on the opposite side is a little locale called the ABC Jazz Club. I have passed it a few times on my way to school and work but never gone in. It strikes me as the kind of place where a Swedish guitarist with a suede jacket, an upturned collar, a toothy grin, and big dimples would like to hang out.

"Ever been to the ABC Jazz Club?"

"No, let's check it out."

The club is small and musty. There are no windows, and the walls are made of dark brick. Every time a train arrives or leaves from *Friedrichstrasse Bahnhof*, the whole place shakes like hell. There are posters of Dizzie Gillespie, Miles Davis, and other jazz greats on the walls. To the left of the door is a small stage, elevated about one foot off the floor. Opposite the stage is a narrow bar where a waitress is beginning to set up for the night. There is no one else inside.

"The music doesn't start for another two hours," she tells us.

"Are you open for drinks?" Thor asks.

"If you want," answers the waitress.

"What do you think?" I ask Thor.

"I think it's cool," replies Thor.

"Okay, then let's stay."

The waitress comes out from behind the bar with two cocktail menus. "Would you like to sit at a table or a cuddling couch?"

I blush. "A table will be fine." In the corner of my eye, I catch Thor giving the waitress a wink. He pulls out a stool for me at one of the high tables. I climb on and we order two *Hefeweizen*.

When the beers arrive in tall, curvy glasses, with a lemon slice perched on each rim, we make a toast to our first official meeting. Thor takes a good, long look at me.

"I'm glad you're not blonde," he says, after a few uncomfortable seconds.

"What?" I laugh.

"I'm glad you're not blonde," he repeats. "In Sweden, everyone is blonde."

"In America, everyone wants to be blonde. Brown is such a boring color."

"Your hair is great," Thor says.

That's funny. He's the one with great hair.

"You'll have to excuse me," continues Thor. "I'm terrible at dating."

That's funny. I'm the one who's terrible at dating. "Is this a date?" I ask.

"I don't know. I just broke up with my girlfriend of six years. In fact, I've never really been on a date in my life."

That's funny. I just broke up with my boyfriend of five years.

I've never really been on a date in my life. "I know how you feel."

"You do?"

"Oh, yes. What happened?" I ask.

"Well, you see, we'd been dating since we were kids, and after awhile we didn't know anymore where one of us ended and the other one began."

Thor is my soul mate.

"We just decided one day that we should spend some time apart. That's why I came to Berlin for the semester."

"I completely understand."

"You do?"

"Yeah. Same thing happened to me."

"You just broke up with your girlfriend of six years?"

"Boyfriend … five years."

"Oh, man! I'm sorry."

"Yeah, well—"

"It's really hard, I know."

"Yeah."

"When you love someone but you just can't be with them anymore."

"Is she seeing someone else?"

"Yeah. Is he?"

"Yeah. Do you still love her?"

"Yeah. You?"

"Yeah."

Thor looks down into his glass for a minute. Then he raises it. "Here's to moving on."

"To moving on."

We drink. I notice Thor's hands, cradling his glass. I remember that I noticed his hands at Quasimodo. He has beautiful hands.

"You seem to be in pretty good shape," I observe. "Do you play any sports?"

"I run a little bit," replies Thor. "Sometimes I enter races. Usually just 5 Ks or 10 Ks."

"I'm impressed."

"When I was in the Navy, though, I ran a marathon. That was fun."

"You were in the Navy?"

"Yeah. Had to. In Sweden, Naval service is compulsory for all men."

"Are you serious?"

"Of course."

"That's so funny. I can't picture you in the Navy."

Thor tells a few stories about his time in the Navy and we order another round of drinks. I laugh a lot. Thor is a good storyteller. I can't help but picture him in his suede jacket with the upturned collar and a white sailor's cap.

"Enough about me," he finally says. "I want to hear more about you."

"What do you want to know?"

"Let's get politics out of the way. What do you think of your president?"

"Ugh!"

"Me too."

"No, not *ugh* the president, *ugh* the question."

"Do you not want to talk about it?"

"Not really."

"Why not?"

"It seems like all the young people here always want to talk about politics, and I'm just not used to it, that's all."

"Do you think I'll be angry if you support your president?"

"Maybe."

"Well, do you?"

"Kind of."

"What do you mean, kind of?"

"Well, I didn't vote for him, but—"

"There you go. We can still be friends."

"—but I do support his decision to retaliate against the embassy bombing."

"War monger, are you?"

"No, but I mean, it's important that we do something to ensure that a terrorist attack like that never happens again."

"Well, I think everybody agrees that something must be done. But to demand the support of the world in military strikes without giving those involved a choice on how and when things will be done is rather unfair, don't you think? We are all sovereign countries that deserve to be consulted, not bossed around."

"Hmm ..."

"Then again ... I mean, we're looking at it from different perspectives. If it had been my country ... I mean, it wasn't Sweden that was attacked. Maybe I would feel differently if Nobel Hall was bombed on prize day with thousands of people inside. I can understand that America would want revenge, but you can't just ... I mean, because you're hot and I don't want to ruin my chances with you, I will just say that America would attract more international support with honey than with vinegar."

I am blushing again. I hide my face in a long sip from my glass.

Thor takes a long sip from his glass. "The retaliation to the embassy bombing is just one of the issues that I have with your government. How do you feel about your environmental policy?"

"Environmental policy?"

"Yes, let's just start with CO_2 emissions."

"Um," I hesitate, waiting for him to say something else. Thor's not going to let me off the hook on this one. "I think we should do more to stop CO_2 emissions," I continue.

"You see, there we agree. So why didn't America sign the Global CO_2 Convention?"

"Um ..." I wrack my brain for something to say on this topic—anything. "Maybe we just weren't ready?"

Thor laughs when I say this. "I get it. Not your favorite topic. I can kind of see your position. I mean the Convention did have its flaws. That doesn't mean we had to trash the whole thing, though. Whatever. Next issue ... the death penalty."

"Death penalty?"

"Yes, America is the only developed country still executing people. Why?"

"What about China?"

"I rest my case."

"Don't you think the perpetrators of the embassy bombing should get the death penalty?"

"No."

"Why not?"

"Because it can't be reversed."

"Neither can the embassy bombing."

"So an eye for an eye, then?"

"Yes. I guess. In this case."

"With that philosophy you can justify all kinds of shady activity."

"Shady activity?" I say, surprised at his choice of words. "On our part?"

"Yes, lots of it."

"Like what?"

"Well, the United States is known to have committed torture, assassinations, various crimes against humanity, everything the CIA has done over the past thirty years—"

"Crimes against humanity?" I interrupt. I cannot believe his choice of words. "What do you mean?"

"Well, it could be argued that—"

"What crimes against humanity has the United States ever committed?" I ask incredulously.

"Earth to Kat Vespucci!" Thor teases. "Let's see. For starters, extermination of the Native Americans. Then there was the whole slavery thing. More recently, Japanese internment camps during World War II."

I scrunch my brow as he speaks.

"You're the only country that's ever dropped a nuclear bomb

on anybody; then there was the Massacre at Mai Lai, the Bay of Pigs invasion ..."

My face contorts in horror.

Thor stops. "Look, every country has its black marks. Sweden had its conquering days that weren't very pleasant for those on the receiving end. All I'm saying is that we have to recognize these things and face up to them, so that we can prevent them from happening again."

I am silent. It is a big concept for me to handle. Never, in my wildest dreams, have I considered the United States to be on the committing side of crimes against humanity. The United States is the good guy, the liberator, the giver of chocolate to children in defeated countries.

"Actually," Thor continues, "some people consider the United States' support of Israel to be a crime against humanity in itself."

My spine straightens when Thor says this. Having been raised on *The Diary of Anne Frank*, *Schindler's List*, and *Seinfeld* reruns, this issue is starting to strike a nerve with me.

"Look, Thor. I don't know anything about the Israeli/ Palestinian conflict, or the United States' involvement there. What I do know is that since I have been in Europe, I have gotten the distinct impression that if we didn't support Israel, nobody would."

"You might be right about that," admits Thor and downs the rest of his beer.

The waitress comes by and asks me if I want another one. It is then that I notice that I have not eaten dinner and that I am starting to feel a strong buzz. "Maybe we could split the third," I suggest.

"Sure thing." Thor orders one more *Hefeweizen*. He gives me a few-seconds reprieve and then starts in on the next topic of conversation.

"That's enough politics for today. Let's hit my next favorite topic."

"Good," I am ready for a subject change.

"How do you feel about sex?"

"I beg your pardon?"

"Sex."

"What?"

"Intercourse? Coitus? The Slippery Salsa?"

"Whoa, whoa, whoa!" I sputter. My hand moves to the crucifix around my neck. "Do I have to answer that?"

"I'm just trying to get to know you, that's all."

I do want Thor to get to know me. "Sex is okay," I acquiesce.

"Just okay?"

"Well, I don't really know, because I've never experienced it in its *pure* form."

"What's its *pure* form?"

"You know, within a marriage—"

Thor rolls his eyes.

"—the way God intends it."

"Do you think God really intends sex to be only within a marriage?"

I blink at him. "Yes."

"I don't think he does."

"You don't?"

"Nope."

"Well, in the Bible, it clearly states—"

"Bible schmible."

"Bible schmible? How could you say such a thing?" I am very surprised. "Don't you believe in God?"

"Not really."

I am even more surprised. I have never met an atheist before. I think for a moment. "But you just said that you don't believe that God intends sex to be only within a marriage."

"That's right. I don't believe that he does."

"While at the same time, you don't really believe in *him?*"

"Exactly."

"I see. So let me get this straight. The God that you don't really believe in has nothing against pre-marital sex."

"Exactly! I'd go so far as to say that he encourages it."

"Encourages it? That's crazy!"

"Think about it. If God is God, he invented sex, right? He invented everything. He could have come up with any number of ways for human beings to procreate that didn't involve orgasm. Thumb wrestling. Footsies. But instead, he came up with this incredible ritual involving inhuman amounts of pleasure. Pretty creative, if you ask me. And he didn't invest all that time and energy for people to abstain from it until they're twenty-seven, or thirty-two, or whenever it is that we are getting married these days. He's given humanity a gift that, half the time, we refuse to open!"

"Interesting argument."

"Imagine how he feels. It would be like if you threw the party of the universe and no one came. Imagine how pissed off you would be!"

"You're not convincing me."

"I mean, okay, so you had Adam and Eve, right? The first people on the earth back in the Garden of Eden. Didn't he say to them: 'Be fruitful and multiply?' They weren't married."

"Yes, they were."

"No, they weren't."

"How do you know they weren't?"

"Do you recall a wedding in Genesis?"

"They didn't have to have a wedding. They were the only two people on earth."

"Exactly, so there was no one there who could have performed the ceremony, even if they had wanted to get married."

"You know, for someone who doesn't believe in God, you know a lot about Scripture."

"Well, I live in the Western Hemisphere. I've heard these stories."

"But you don't believe in Adam and Eve?"

"Of course not. Don't be silly."

I laugh. "Okay. So just so I understand you, what you're saying is, God, who doesn't exist, gave humans the gift of sex, to enjoy whenever they want, when he didn't create them in the Garden of Eden."

"That's exactly what I'm saying."

"Well," I ponder the statement for a moment. "I'll drink to that."

"Cheers." Thor is grinning like a cat in a herring factory.

"Cheers." I continue pondering. The beer is starting to make me feel bold. "So I guess you have a lot of pre-marital sex then."

"Used to," replies Thor. "But then my girlfriend and I broke up, and that was the end of that. She is the only one I've 'known,' you know, in the Biblical sense. But that's okay."

"Me too."

"I'm a little bit scared to take that step with someone else, you know? Don't know if I'm up for it."

"Me too."

"No pun intended."

"What?"

About this time the band is set up and begins to play, but neither of us notices.

"So let me ask you something else, Kat."

"Yeah?"

"When you and your ex-boyfriend slept together, did you have huge guilt issues?"

"Of course I did," my hand touches my crucifix again.

"So why'd you still do it?"

"Um. I don't know why. Part of the reason is that it just feels pretty damn good."

Thor smiles.

"But then there was another part of me that felt that that's just what you do when you've been with somebody for a long time. You know what I mean?"

"Did you feel like you had to sleep with your boyfriend to keep him interested in the relationship?"

I think about it for a moment. "I never really thought about it like that, but now that you mention it, I know some girls whose boyfriends did break up with them because they wouldn't have sex. Maybe I had that in the back of my mind, I don't know."

"Interesting."

"Is it not that way in Sweden?"

"No, in Sweden it's different."

I am intrigued. "How so?"

"Well, Sweden was the birthplace of the sexual revolution, for starters. Things are a lot 'freer' there. Everybody just kind of has sex without thinking much about it."

"Sweden was the birthplace of the sexual revolution?"

"Yeah. That's one of our big contributions to society. That and dynamite."

"Wow. Explosive."

"Now that you mention it, though, there was some pressure growing up to have anal sex."

"*What?*" I choke on my beer.

"I knew a couple of girls who felt like they had to have anal sex with their boyfriends in order to keep their relationships together."

I can't believe what I am hearing. "I'm sorry, what did you just say?"

"What?" Thor looks at me curiously.

"What you're talking about right now."

"You mean anal sex?"

"Yes, but ... *stop saying it!*" I look at him with bulging eyes.

"Does the topic of anal sex make you uncomfortable?" Thor asks.

Well, that's a stupid question. "Yes! It makes me very uncomfortable."

"Why?"

"I don't know. Just think about it!" I writhe in pain just thinking about it.

Thor looks at me with his toothy, grin. "So you're saying you've never had anal sex?"

My jaw drops. "Of course I've never had ... I can't believe you're asking me that! I can't believe I'm having this conversation!"

Thor continues grinning from ear to ear. "I bet your friends have anal sex."

"They most certainly do not!"

"You mean to tell me that Americans do not have anal sex?"

"That's what I'm telling you."

"How do you know?"

"I just know."

"Maybe they do, they just don't talk about it."

"Can we change the subject?"

"I mean, how do you know your friends aren't having anal sex if nobody talks about it?"

"I would know if my friends were having anal sex."

"Would you?"

I panic. Would I? It suddenly occurs to me that I have no idea whether or not my friends are having anal sex. I certainly have never asked any of them, and even if I were to ask them, would they tell me the truth? I can just see it now ... *Dana, you wouldn't have anal sex without telling me, would you?*

I burst into laughter. I have just finished my third beer on an empty stomach, and I am feeling extremely affected.

"What's so funny?" asks Thor.

"Can you picture me going up to my friends and asking them if they are having anal sex?"

"No," Thor grins. "Especially not after your reaction when I asked you."

I am laughing a deep, belly laugh now. "'You wouldn't have anal sex without ... without ...'" I am laughing too hard to finish my sentences. Thor is highly amused. "'Without telling me, would you?'" My whole face is hot. Tears squeeze out of the corners of my eyes.

When I finally get myself together, I face Thor, who is taking a deep look at me. "You're really cute, you know that?" he tells me.

My heart skips a beat and I look bashfully at the table. The waitress comes over and asks if we want another round of *Hefeweizen*.

"I'm done," I answer.

"You hungry?" Thor asks me.

"I could eat a horse," I say.

"Let's go."

We pay our tab and bounce out of the ABC Jazz Club onto the street. The chilly night air stiffens my spine as we step out of the cozy music den. The tantalizing smell of *Döner Kebaps* wafts through the air from the stands along the river. We buy two juicy, lamb-filled pitas with dill sauce and no onions and sit down together on a bench overlooking the *Spree*.

"These are so good!" I comment as I eat, trying not to get the sauce all over my face. "I wonder why we don't have these in the States."

"Not enough Turks," answers Thor.

"I guess not."

We are silent for a few minutes as we chew, steam rising from the warm lamb pockets.

"I like the *Spree* at night," I finally speak.

"Me too," agrees Thor.

"There's something peaceful about water in darkness." Our shoulders are touching. It suddenly occurs to me that the date might soon be over, and I feel sad.

"What time is it?" asks Thor.

I look at my watch, "Almost 11:00 PM."

"That late?"

"Yeah."

"Well, do you want me to take you home?"

I hesitate, looking at my feet. "No," I answer.

He smiles.

"But there aren't many places we can go this late at night," I add.

"I know a place."

"What kind of place?" I ask.

"I have a feeling it's just your kind of place," Thor answers.

I look at him quizzically.

He gets up and grabs me by the hand. "C'mon!"

"This better not be your place!" I tease.

"Don't worry," Thor winks. "At least don't worry yet." Thor hails a cab and we hop in. "*Zosch in der Oranianburgerstrasse,*" he tells the cab driver.

Fifteen minutes later, Thor and I step out of the cab on a seemingly abandoned street in front of a sleepy, little café. It looks like an ordinary café, with coffee, sandwiches, and boring art on the walls, only the café has no name, and there are no patrons inside.

"You think this is my kind of place?" I ask Thor. Thor gives me a reassuring smile. We go inside and he leads me down a small, winding staircase. At the bottom of the stairs are two restrooms and a large, wooden door. Thor pushes open the door and we stumble into a basement bursting with people and sound. It is a crowded speakeasy with a stone floor, and a low, stone ceiling, held up by thick, stone pillars. It smells like skunked beer, mold, and sweat. There is a wooden bar serving one kind of beer, the local *Berliner Pilsner*, which flows in an endless stream from the tap. There is a Dixieland Jazz Band belting out lively tunes from a small stage in the corner. Thor says something to me but I can't hear him over the noise.

"What?" I shout and cup my hand to my ear.

"Never mind!" shouts Thor and gives me another wink. He takes my hand and leads me into the crowd. The room is too full for dancing, but we find a spot on the wall where we can lean and enjoy the music. There is a constant stream of beer glasses being passed overhead to patrons too far from the bar to get them themselves. Thor and I are dripped on several times, but we don't care. The band keeps everybody cheerful and upbeat, and I feel alive in the group. The crowd hoots, claps, and stomps along with the music.

"Thank you for bringing me here," I say to Thor.

"What?" he shouts.

"Never mind!" I shout back. He puts his arm around my shoulder and we bob together as the trumpet, tuba, banjo, and bass take turns leading the crowd.

Sometime around 3:00 AM, the beer runs dry, the band gets tired, and everyone goes home. Thor and I find ourselves standing alone on the street in front of the café. I still feel the music pulsing through my veins.

"Do you want me to take you home?" Thor asks me.

"No," I say. "But there aren't many places we can go at this hour."

"I know a place," says Thor.

"Is it your place?"

"Well," says Thor, "it's not exactly my place. I mean … I don't own it."

"Let's go," I suggest.

Thor takes me to his place. It is a studio apartment in a nineteenth-century, courtyard-style complex in the section of the city called *Kreuzberg*. When we get inside, I take off my shoes and sit down on the couch. Thor pours a big glass of water from the kitchen faucet for us to share. He offers me a peppermint candy and takes one for himself. As I get comfortable on the couch, I spy his guitar on the floor by his bed.

"Ooooh, play me something!"

"Okay," says Thor, and he sets the glass of water down on the bedside table.

"Do you know any Springsteen?"

Thor laughs as he tunes the guitar. "I've got something way better than Springsteen."

"Impossible."

Thor begins to strum an instrumental version of "Crash," by the Dave Matthews Band. My skin tightens the moment his fingers begin plucking the strings. I listen to him mesmerized, amazed by the flow of the melody from his hands to my ears. Every cell in my body belongs to him.

When the song is winding down, I ask him not to stop. He switches to "Wonderful Tonight," by Eric Clapton. I am completely under his spell. When the song is over, Thor puts his guitar back into its case and kneels down by the couch next to my head. I look at him with half-closed eyes.

"Ja tycker om dej," he says to me.

"Hmmm?"

"Ingenting," he whispers.

"Is that Swedish?" I ask him.

"Ja."

A smile forms on my lips. "Say something else to me in Swedish."

He thinks for a minute. *"Du är otrooligt vackert."*

"What does that mean?" I ask.

"I'll never tell," he replies.

I smile. We look at each other. His dimples are smiling at me too, which makes it hard to breathe.

"I'd really like to kiss you right now," he says, "but I'm afraid of ruining this perfect moment."

I want him to kiss me so bad I am in pain. "This moment sucks," I say. "Please ruin it."

Thor kisses me. The touch of his lips makes me float. His breath is musk and peppermint. His lips and tongue are silk against mine. I run my hands through the hair on the sides and back of his head. Thor pulls away and touches the tip of his nose to mine. He opens his eyes to half-mast.

"This is terrible," he whispers, a little out of breath.

"What's terrible?" I whisper.

"When I'm kissing you, all I want to do is look at you. And when I'm looking at you, all I want to do is kiss you."

"Do both," I say. Thor smiles, and we do both, until we both fall asleep.

When I wake up in the morning, Thor is buzzing around the apartment. He's got eggs sizzling on the stove and he is going back and forth to his computer sending and receiving instant messages.

"Good morning!" he calls from behind a pan of scrambled eggs.

"Good morning," I reply, looking around to get my bearings. I am in Thor's bed, in my underwear; the rest of my clothes are crumpled on the floor next to the bed.

"Did you sleep well?" he asks, sliding the eggs onto a plate.

"Okay, I guess."

"I slept fantastic!"

I lift myself out of bed, wrap the blanket around me, and join Thor at the breakfast table. "You're in a very good mood," I observe.

"I *am* in a good mood. I feel fantastic! I feel ... inspired, you know? Like I could take on the world."

"That's great," I reply, a little surprised.

"And it's all because of you," he says, pointing his fork at me.

"Wow," I say, not knowing what else to say.

"Last night was amazing! I haven't had that much fun with someone since, well ... I feel alive."

"It was fun, wasn't it," I respond.

"Oh, by the way, I put a pair of sweats and a T-shirt in the bathroom for you to wear home."

"You don't have to do that. I'm fine in my clothes from last night."

"It's no trouble. You'll feel better in some fresh clothes. Plus, this way you'll have to return them and I know I'll get to see you again." I am touched. Thor is the man of my dreams.

Just as we are finishing breakfast, the phone rings and Thor excuses himself to answer it. I get up and go to the bathroom to freshen up. I take the toothpaste on the sink and brush my teeth with my index finger. Then I change into Thor's T-shirt and sweats. The T-shirt says, "Stockholm 10 K–1ˢᵗ place." I am proud of him.

When I emerge from the bathroom, Thor is still on the phone. He is speaking Swedish very softly. I sit back down at the breakfast table and wait for him to finish.

When Thor finally comes back over to me, I have gathered my things. I am wearing his sweats with my heels from last night.

"Classy," Thor teases.

We walk outside together and he waits with me for a cab. When one arrives, he gives me a big hug good-bye and a kiss on each cheek. He tells me he'll call me soon, and I climb into the cab. When the cab pulls away, Thor stands on the corner, waving to me, until I am out of sight. It is cute, but it makes me think of someone who is saying good-bye for a long time. I close my eyes, not wanting to watch him disappear. Plus I haven't slept very long, and I am tired.

Chapter Nineteen

Peter Fechter

My taxi pulls up to the *Plattenbau* on *Coppistrasse* a little after noon; my eyes feel heavy, I haven't brushed my hair, I stink of cigarette smoke, and my clothes from the night before are draped over my arm. Before stepping out, I say a quick prayer requesting not to run into anyone that I know. My prayer is answered as I run into, not *any*one, but *every*one I know. All of Group Four is assembled on the steps of the *Plattenbau,* waiting to embark on our second guided tour of Berlin.

"Are we all here?" calls Herr Stern as I climb out of the taxi, throw my clothes behind a shrub, and slink sheepishly into the group. He smacks his hands together. "Let's go!"

"I was worried you had forgotten," says Pete, moving over to me in the crowd.

"I did forget."

"I love the heels and sweatpants look," Pete teases me.

I glare at him.

The first stop on our guided tour is the former headquarters of the *Staatssicherheitsdienst* (State Secret Police) or *Stasi*, which is right around the corner from the *Plattenbau* on a side street of the *Karl Marx Allee*. When we arrive at the complex, Herr Stern informs us that it was from here that East Germany had launched the most oppressive and over-ambitious surveillance network on its own citizens of any country in the twentieth century. From a toilet breaking to the planning of an escape attempt, if anything at all happened within the borders of East Germany, the *Stasi* knew about it.

Herr Stern explains how the *Stasi* spied on everyone and made records of everything.

"They had entirely too much time on their hands," he says. "If a person was under observation, his phone could be tapped, his conversations taped, his every move followed, photographed, and filmed. Subjects were bribed and blackmailed, and when the *Stasi* couldn't get the information they wanted, they bribed and blackmailed people who knew the subject. The army of unofficial informers was over one hundred thousand strong. Everyone was a potential snitch. No one could be trusted. Everything you did or said could potentially be used against you."

"Sounds like McCarthyism times one hundred," says Billy.

"What was the *Stasi* looking for?" I ask.

"Internal wreckers. Enemies of the state. Threats from within."

"Did they find any?"

"Oh yes, Frau Vespucci. Whether real or imagined, the *Stasi* found their enemies. In millions. There are six million files in this building alone."

"Whoa!'

"One of them is my own," Herr Stern confides.

"No!" we gasp. "Why?"

"Were you an internal wrecker?"

"An enemy of the state?"

"A threat from within?"

189

"Have you read it?"

"What does it say?"

We are all wide-eyed and staring at Herr Stern.

"I have not read my file," Herr Stern answers. "I do not wish to know its contents. Friends of mine who have asked to see their files have been ruined by what they have learned. Details as ridiculous as trips to the bathroom and jogs through the park were recorded. Back then, I took entirely too many trips to the bathroom and too few jogs through the park and have no desire to relive them."

We snicker a bit.

"The files also contain information about drinking habits, spending habits, sexual behavior, and personal relationships," Herr Stern continues. "The most disturbing part is that it was all-too-often family members who provided the information to the *Stasi*."

"Why?"

"Yeah, why would people rat on their family?"

"In exchange for government favors, like a bigger apartment, to be moved up on the waiting list to buy a car, or not to be thrown in jail. Often it was for money. More than one of my close friends has gotten divorced based on information they found in their *Stasi* file."

"Unbelievable!" I start to think about all of the dumb things I have done and said in my lifetime and I am overly thankful that there is, to my knowledge, no comprehensive file documenting all of them.

"I'm going to be more careful from now on," says Pete. This place is right around the corner from where we live.

Herr Stern hears what Pete says and chuckles. "The *Stasi* ceased to exist when the East German regime fell. But if there is one thing I learned growing up in East Germany, Herr Bittner, it is that things are often not what they seem. Better safe than sorry," he says and gives Pete a wink.

"Is that what those green pipes were used for, Herr Stern,

when they were still in use?" I ask, remembering my previous conversation with Herr Fromme.

"Who says they're not in use anymore?" he answers, raises his eyebrow at me, and walks away.

I shudder.

The second stop on today's tour is the Berlin Wall Memorial on *Bernauerstrasse*. Herr Stern informs us that the Berlin Wall is preserved in two locations, and this one is the more somber of the two. The Wall on *Bernauerstrasse* depicts the Wall exactly as it had been before the first brick was removed in November of 1989: a ten-foot-high, concrete barricade surrounded by barbed wire, watch towers, machine guns, heat sensors, and land mines. To the East, we find ourselves looking again upon the thirty-yard stretch of "No Man's Land," or "Death Strip," preserved as it was when it was. It is a barren patch of land void of growth and life, as if Mother Nature herself had arranged a boycott.

I walk up to the Wall and touch the concrete surface. Up until this point, it has existed to me only in pictures. Now I am standing an arm's length away from it. At over twice my height, I feel intimidated by the sheer size of the Wall.

Herr Stern explains that construction of the Wall began without warning on the night of August 13, 1961 and was completed in such haste that it intersected streets and houses that stood in its path. Therefore, people who wanted to flee the Soviet sector in the Wall's early years needed only to enter one of the buildings and jump out of a window that faced the other side. Eventually, the buildings on the border were evacuated and filled with cement.

"As the years went on," Herr Stern continues, "people went to greater and greater lengths to escape East Berlin … hiding in furniture, slamming through checkpoints in cars, digging tunnels, crafting homemade SCUBA gear, constructing makeshift parachutes, etc. As the escapees became shrewder and shrewder, the East German government went to greater and greater lengths to halt the flow of fugitives, eventually issuing the order to the border guards to shoot and to kill. Guards accused of missing on purpose were court-martialed and persecuted by the government. In the end, approximately two hundred people died trying to flee the Soviet Sector.

"One of the saddest stories on record," continues Herr Stern, "was the escape attempt of a young man named Peter Fechter. A teenager, he and a friend tried to jump the Wall. The friend made it, but Peter got shot by one of the border guards and fell back into the Death Strip." Herr Stern points to the sterile strip of land close to where we are standing. "The wounds were not fatal; however, he could not pick himself up and get back to the other side. He screamed for help, but the border patrol threatened the same fate to anyone who set foot inside the Death Strip to help him. People threw bandages to him, but he wasn't able to stop his own bleeding. In the end, hundreds of people watched from both sides of the Wall as he bled to death, his cries for help getting weaker and weaker."

"Jesus Christ," I gasp. "How could East Germany justify something as heinous as this Wall?"

Herr Stern explains, "The official explanation given by the East German government was that the Wall was built to protect the East Germans from fascist Western powers that were trying to force their way in. The official name of the Wall given by the East German government was the Anti-Fascist Protection Wall."

"Why anti-fascist?"

"Well, as one of the groups of people who had been persecuted by the Nazis, the Communists were angered to find that many of the officials who had committed crimes during World War II and the Holocaust were allowed to assume positions in the new post-war West German government."

"Oh."

"That, and the fact that the Communists relied on this idea of the 'enemy within,' as we discussed before, to instill fear and rally support for their policies."

Sasha pipes in: "In fact, throughout the Cold War, the

American CIA and West German intelligence had launched an active campaign of spying behind the Wall, including an underground surveillance tunnel."

"This is a good point," agrees Herr Stern, "there were indeed *some* foreign enemies trying to force their way in. But mostly this wall was to keep the East German citizens in, as was the case with Peter Fechter. There's a memorial to him in the museum at Checkpoint Charlie, which is where we are heading next."

I have never really been a museum girl, but the museum at Checkpoint Charlie takes my breath away. It is a memorial of the Wall and all aspects of it. The museum displays everything from maps to videos to equipment used in escape attempts. One very dynamic display is of a Trabbi car, smaller than a Volkswagen Beetle, whose engine was rearranged to accommodate a human body. It is an actual car that was used by a man to smuggle his girlfriend over to West Berlin. There is a dummy in the car demonstrating just how the woman had fit in. It doesn't seem possible to me that a person could contort her body into that position, but actually, it had worked.

There is a whole gallery of art inspired by the Wall. Some of it is sad. Some of it is hopeful. Some of it is heart wrenching. One painting particularly moves me; it is of a baby being held up from behind the Wall by an anonymous pair of hands for his mother to see on the other side. All we see of the woman is her back and head with long, black hair. The tilt of her head and rigidity in her posture reveals suffering. My eyes moisten.

I also tear up watching a video of the Wall opening on November 9, 1989. Seeing East and West Germans dancing together on the Wall in the biggest celebration that the border had ever seen, holding hands, singing songs, pouring champagne all over each other, is very emotional.

Billy comes up behind me and watches for a while. "And to think some countries are building new walls," he says, shaking his head.

By far the most riveting exhibit in the museum for us is the picture of Pete's parents holding hands on the street just outside of where we now stand. Pete's dad looks beautiful in the wig and dress that Pete's mother had smuggled over for him. Pete's mother is standing proudly beside him, clutching the arm of her hard-won, husband-to-be in drag. I look very closely at Pete's father in the picture, concentrating on his face. With the make-up, there is a slight resemblance to my mother, but no more than many other German women I have seen. *Could you be my mother's lost brother?* I ask the picture. Pete's father's face stares back at me, a twinkle of adventure in his painted eyes as if to say, *You wouldn't know your uncle if you saw him.*

I *wouldn't* know him, would I? And neither would my mother. I step away from the picture and burst into tears.

"Are you okay?" Pete asks me, very surprised.

"Your dad is very pretty," I say as Pete puts his arm around my shoulder.

"Thanks. I'll tell him you said that."

"Did you ever ask him about the stained-glass necklace?"

"Yeah. He doesn't have one."

"Oh. Too bad."

To end the tour, Herr Stern takes us eastward to the most uplifting dedication to the Wall that Berlin has to offer. Right next to *Ostbahnhof*, Berlin's eastern train station, a section of the wall about three kilometers long has been preserved as an art gallery. Known as the East Side Gallery, this section of the Wall is painted with hundreds of murals dedicated to politics, peace, and reconciliation. Though it has the same dimensions as the concrete obstruction that we saw on *Bernauerstrasse*, standing here, decorated with doves, handprints, olive branches, and political cartoons, this piece of Wall evokes virility and the triumph of the human spirit. Something heinous and offensive, with some paint and creativity, has been turned into something beautiful and hopeful. It is an absolute masterpiece.

I turn to Billy and say, "It is as if the Ghost of East German

Past is hovering in the air, whispering that freedom triumphs over tyranny in the end."

"Very deep, Kat," he teases me.

As the tour concludes and we students begin walking separately to the *S-Bahn* across the street at *Ostbahnhof,* Herr Stern catches up with me.

"Frau Vespucci, I have been meaning to ask you, have you been able to locate your family member?"

"No," I answer, "but thank you for asking. I looked in the *Telefonbuch Berlin,* like you suggested, but there are seventy-five entries under the name, Otto Bittner."

"Hmm, I guess it is a rather common name."

We pause for a moment.

"Herr Stern, I've been meaning to ask you," I remember. "How's your daughter doing in China?"

"Oh, thank you for asking, Frau Vespucci. She's doing well now. She had a rough start at the beginning. Quite extreme culture shock, but I think she's adjusted all right now."

"Really? Is it very different over there?"

"Quite, Frau Vespucci. Quite different indeed."

"Wow. I can't even imagine."

"Maybe someday you won't have to, eh?" he says with an encouraging wink.

"Like I said, I can't even imagine."

On the *S-Bahn* ride home, I have too many images running through my head to even consider traveling to China—Pete's parents standing in front of Checkpoint Charlie after the escape, the picture of Peter Fechter bleeding to death in the Death Strip, the woman crammed into the engine of a Trabbi, and my high-heeled feet at the end of my sweatpants. I wonder if Thor is thinking about me. I try to stop thinking about Thor, but I cannot. A Swedish guitarist. Smart. Worldly. Fashionable. Athletic. Eloquent. Good kisser. Yup, I decide. He is the man of my dreams. So why am I biting my fingernails?

I promise myself that I am not going to let this get to me. As hard as I can I will try to pretend that nothing is wrong. I take a deep breath, relax my forehead muscles, put my hands at my sides, and clear my mind of everything but the quiet rhythm of the train. I find that clearing my head is not easy, and I have to really concentrate in order not to concentrate on anything. In fact, I am trying *so* hard not to let it bother me that Pete asks me what is wrong.

"Nothing is wrong," I lie. "Why do you ask?"

"You look like an overly-caffeinated monk trying to meditate."

"Oh," I reply, giving up.

"Thinking about last night?" Pete asks. I blush and give him nothing more than an embarrassed smile. "C'mon," he insists.

"C'mon what?" I ask, my cheeks turning pink.

"Tell me ... you know, where did he take you? What did you do?"

"We went to the ABC Jazz Club. Listened to some music."

"How was the music?"

"I don't know," I laugh. "I can't remember."

"What were you two doing that you can't remember?"

"Nothing. Just talking."

"So, was it good?"

"Was what good?"

"The talking."

"Yeah, it was good."

"So why do you seem so antsy?"

Chapter Twenty

Herr Kaufmann

On the following Monday, I have the long-awaited pleasure of meeting my *Bundestag* Representative, Herr Kaufmann. It is a non-Julia week, so I am sitting at the big desk, writing e-mails to all of my friends back home. There is no assignment for me today, so I am instructed to be a dear and keep myself busy until further notice. I shift uncomfortably in the suit I am wearing and kick my shoes off under the desk. I wish I wasn't wearing pantyhose. As a *HAA* student, I am required to dress professionally and feign diligence while not performing the numerous and important tasks that weren't assigned to me. Suddenly, there is a knock on the door.

"*Kommen Sie herein!*" I call.

Greta pokes her head around the door. "Frau Vespucci, I have someone here who wants to meet you."

"Certainly," I respond.

"Signorina Vespucci!" calls the boisterous voice of my

Bundestag representative as he tangos past Frau Schindler into my office. Herr Kaufmann is a ball of energy in a pressed navy suit with tan skin, a tight smile, impeccably combed light brown hair, and deep wrinkles around his eyes and mouth from years of laughing. He is the exact same height as Frau Schindler. I immediately minimize the window on my desktop and stand up to meet Herr Kaufmann.

"*Guten Morgen, Herr Kaufmann!*"

"Good morning to you, Signorina Vespucci."

"It is a pleasure to finally meet you, sir."

"The pleasure is all mine, young lady." Herr Kaufmann shakes my hand vigorously. "I should actually say *buenos dias* to you, Signorina Vespucci, should I not?"

"You can if you want to, Herr Kaufmann, but I don't speak Spanish."

"Is *buenos dias* Spanish? I thought it was Italian."

"She's right," confirms Greta. "*Buenos dias* is Spanish."

"Tell me then, Signorina Vespucci, how do you say *Guten Morgen* in Italian?"

"Um ..." I remember the film, *Life is Beautiful.* "I think it's 'buongiorno,' Herr Kaufmann."

"Aha! I knew it! Didn't I tell you, Frau Schindler? Didn't I tell you that she speaks Italian?"

"You certainly did, Herr Kaufmann," says Frau Schindler.

"That's very kind of you to say, sir," I say, "But, actually, I don't speak Italian."

"Nonsense! Of course you do. Your last name is Vespucci, isn't it?"

"That's true, sir, it is. But I don't speak Italian. It was my grandparents who came over from Italy. My father was born in America and didn't grow up speaking Italian, and neither did I."

"Don't be silly. You wouldn't go around calling yourself Signorina Vespucci if you didn't speak Italian, now would you?"

I don't go around calling myself Signorina Vespucci, but it isn't my place to argue.

"Frau Schindler, you were correct. Signorina Vespucci is a lovely young lady."

"Yes, Herr Kaufmann. She certainly is."

"She will be an excellent new Monica Lewinsky for me!"

I look at Greta with a shocked expression, not sure if I have heard my boss correctly.

"Oh, Herr Kaufmann, you are too much!" laughs Greta. Herr Kaufmann is grinning so wide that I think his smile might just fly off of his face.

"A joke, Signorina Vespucci! A joke. Life is too short to be serious!"

"I see," I answer, not sure if I find the joke funny or not.

"Frau Schindler!" Herr Kaufmann snaps.

"Yes, sir?"

"Make sure you give our little Signorina Vespucci lots of work to do."

"I sure will, Herr Kaufmann."

"In fact, I think I'll retire when her internship is over. She can take over for me. Do you think you are ready for that, Signorina Vespucci?"

"Yes, sir! Absolutely," I answer, not knowing what else to say.

"Sehr gut!" bellows Herr Kaufmann, and heads for the door. Before exiting, he turns around and asks, "Signorina Vespucci, tell me. How do you say *sehr gut* in Italian?"

"Um ... that's *molto bene*," I remember from a frozen pizza TV commercial.

"Amazing, Frau Schindler!" Herr Kaufmann exclaims. "I told you she spoke fluent Italian!"

"Yes, Herr Kaufmann, you certainly did."

"Well, I will let you get back to work, young lady."

"Thank you, sir."

"Welcome to the *Bundestag!*"

"Thank you, sir." And with that, he is gone. Greta follows him out. I am left with the feeling that a whirlwind has just swept through my office. I am, however, grateful that he has not taken up too much of my time, because I have a busy day ahead of me. As soon as I have finished e-mailing my family, I go to Google and type in "Israel/Palestine." Then I type in "United States, Shah, Iran." Next, I type in "Massacre of Mai Lai." After reading several articles on that, I type in "Bay of Pigs Invasion." Overall, I am absolutely shocked at what I find. With each article I read, I am infected with the desire to learn more. I repeat the exercise, typing in Japanese internment camps during WWII, CIA assassination attempts, United States relations with Saudi Arabia, torture. What I discover is a cornucopia of dexterous deals, clandestine cover-ups, and overt offenses that I never knew about—and I know that I have only scratched the surface.

Conflicting emotions begin crashing around in my head. How could I not have known about all this? Thank God I'm learning about it now. I feel stupid and enlightened at the same time. Part of me wants to shut down the computer and forget these articles. The other part wants to never stop reading. I feel like a teenager who has just discovered that both of her parents have been having affairs behind the façade of a happy marriage. Knowing that, I don't love them any less. But damn!

I think about the people who brought me to this realization: the German man outside of the embassy, Lambert, Thor, and everybody else—all foreigners. It took a handful of foreigners to get me to discover all this stuff about America. And I never would have met them if I had stayed in America. The irony is overwhelming.

Wait, why hasn't Thor called me?

Suddenly, Greta knocks on the door and pokes her head into my office.

"*Schatz!* What on earth are you still doing here?"

"What? Um … I don't know. Do you need me to do something?"

"Are you crazy? It's after five o'clock! Go home before anyone sees you here this late. They'll accuse me of working you to death."

"Oh, um, okay. Sorry," I reply. "I lost track of time."

"Seriously, darling. Pack up immediately and go home, if you know what I mean."

"Okay, I will."

CHAPTER TWENTY-ONE

Billy

Later that week I make plans with Billy and Janika to go to the movies at *Potsdamer Platz*. I still haven't heard from Thor. As I am leaving the *Plattenbau*, I think about giving him a call to see if he wants to join us, but I don't have the nerve.

"There's something different about you," Janika informs me over gelato after the movie.

"What do you mean?" I ask.

"You've got this look in your eyes, like you're here but you're not."

"She's right. It's kind of a cloudy look," adds Billy.

"Cloudy. That's exactly how I feel."

"Why don't you just call him," suggests Janika.

"I did. He hasn't called me back."

"I've never seen you act like this," remarks Billy. "I mean, you had one incredible date with Thor, and ever since, you've been … miserable."

"Not miserable—"

"No?"

"Just really, really forlorn."

"But why?" asks Janika.

"Because, you guys … he was perfect. If I had chosen him out of a catalog, I could not have picked a better match for me. We have everything in common, he's sexy, he's smart, and he smells good. When he's chewing on a mint, his breath smells minty. My heart wobbles at the mere thought of seeing him again."

"Well, that sounds great," declares Janika.

"Yes, it is great, which is why this is quite possibly the worst thing that has ever happened to me."

"Why?" asks Janika.

"Because I have tasted my ultimate fantasy."

"And?"

"And now there is nowhere to go but down."

"Don't you think you're being a little melodramatic about this?" suggests Billy.

"It's like gelato," I explain, taking a long lick of my cone. "Before I came to Europe, I was perfectly content eating Dairy Queen soft-serve ice cream. But gelato is a whole new league of ice cream. All the flavors. The fillings. The nuts, the fruits, the multiple scoops. The zing that lingers on your tongue. It blows all other ice creams out of the parlor. Now that I've tasted it, I can't go back." I look passionately at my waffle cone. "But imagine if someone had the power to take it all away, Billy. Any lick now could be your last. How would you go on, knowing that the best ice cream you ever tasted was out there, but you couldn't have it anymore?"

Billy clutches his cone and moves it away from me. "You're not taking this away from me."

I lean toward him, "But what if I could?"

"You're scaring me."

"Kat," says Janika. "You've only had one date with Thor. Don't you think it's a little early to be planning your break-up?"

"Let's hope so," I answer.

On our walk home from the *S-Bahn* to the *Plattenbau* through the Private Pathway, Billy, Janika, and I pass a young German man with trendy, spiked hair. We hardly notice him walking toward us until he is directly across from us and he mumbles loud enough for us to hear, *"Scheiss Amis!"*

"What did he say?" Billy asks Janika and me as the kid passes.

"I think he said 'Shit Americans,'" I repeat.

"That's the first time I have ever been mistaken for an American," Janika informs us.

"She's Estonian, you asshole!" Billy yells after the kid. "*Scheiss punk!*"

When I arrive home, there is a note stuck to my door from Fritz. It says, "Thor called." My heart leaps out of my chest. "Thor, Thor, Thor! I can't believe he called." I am giddy. "What should I do, Fritz?"

"I think you should call him back," Fritz suggests, walking out of his room. I am so distracted that I barely notice Fritz's shock of peroxide bleached hair.

I take the phone from the hallway into my room. I dial Thor's number and nearly explode waiting for him to pick up. All my excitement, fear, anxiety, and exhilaration comes to a head when Thor picks up the phone and explains to me somberly that he is very sorry, but there will be no second date. "Over the weekend, I got back together with my ex-girlfriend in Sweden."

My heart cracks.

"Given my feelings for you, it is inappropriate for us to see each other again." His voice is stilted and awkward, like someone told him to say that.

"Are you," I gulp, "sure?"

"Yes. I am sorry."

When I hang up the phone, I lean against the wall and slide to the floor. I bury my head in my hands and tremble as the pent up anxiety trickles out through my eyes and nose. I don't bother to get a tissue or a towel; I just let the tears and snot drip down through my fingers and onto my jeans.

As I am crying, it dawns on me that there's a lot more to cry about than Thor. My head is suddenly invaded by lots of thoughts that have been bothering me since I arrived in Germany, things that I have been trying not to let bother me. They crash over me like a wave and the tears keep flowing. It is my family so far away; it is the embassy bombing; it's terrorism in general; it's the people shot to death at the Berlin Wall, the Massacre at Mai Lai, and Lambert's *America Sucks* T-shirt. It's the thought of Matt kissing Katie.

Suddenly, I have the feeling of being on a ship with no rudder, trying to steer, but only getting pushed around by the current. I want off of the ship, but there is no land in sight. I want to go home where good and evil are easy to define, and my morals, as they were taught to me, apply. I want to go home, and I want a hug from Matt, and I can't have either.

Feeling the urge to call Matt increasing, I decide to go for a jog. It is sometimes the only thing that can clear my head when I'm really feeling down. It's cold outside, so I pull on a few layers of sweat clothes, a windbreaker, a baseball cap, and a scarf. I also grab a flashlight. Not wanting to jog down the Private Pathway at night, I set off for the first time in the opposite direction, which leads me down the well-lit street in front of the *Plattenbau*. My jog starts off at a light pace and my attention reduces to the sound of my sneakers thumping on the pavement. The air stings my nose and lungs when I start to breathe heavier, and puffs of white breath burst out into the air in front of me. The road takes me along the length of the never-ending building, and once I reach what I thought was the end, there is another *Plattenbau*. I jog the length of the next *Plattenbau* and by now I have already gotten a good workout. At the end of this never-ending building is not another *Plattenbau*, but a cluster of trees. The street lights end here. I stop jogging.

It is hard to tell in the dark, but it looks to me like I am at the edge of a small woods. I turn on my flashlight and notice a narrow, but well-worn, path leading into the trees. It doesn't look like the kind of place where a young foreign female should be jogging alone at night, but then, it also looks like there is a clearing at the end of the path. A field of some sort. There is dim light coming from the clearing. Maybe it's another sports venue like the soccer field near our *Plattenbau*. I decide to check it out. I say a quick prayer as I head off down the path.

The trail is longer than I expect. After about a minute and a half of jogging, hearing only the thumping of my feet and the panting of my breath, I reach the clearing. It is indeed a field, but not a sports arena of any kind. The field is overgrown with grass half as tall as me. I scan the area and see a crumbling watchtower at the far end, illuminated by one flickering spotlight. The windows in the tower are broken. Tangled coils of barbed wire stretch out in both directions from the tower but lead to nowhere. The smell of rust hits my nose. The skin on the back of my neck tightens. My already fast heartbeat accelerates. My frozen hand reaches inadvertently for my crucifix, but the necklace is buried under my scarf.

Suddenly, I want out of this place. I turn to jog away, but I stumble on a low stump in the middle of the path. My feet trip on each other, and I crash down onto the ground, breaking my fall with my palms. My flashlight skids out in front of me along the frosty ground.

After standing up and brushing myself off, I reach down to get my flashlight. It is on the ground a few feet away, shining in the direction of the stump. Seeing the stump in the light, I realize that it is not a stump at all, but a low plaque, placed in the middle of the path. I pick up the flashlight, shine it on the face of the plaque, and gasp.

It says: "You are now entering the ruins of a former Gestapo work camp. Thirty thousand people labored and suffered here at the hands of the National Socialists from 1942 to 1945. Here, on this spot, three thousand of them left their lives."

I look up at the field again, the watchtower, the barbed wire. There is a light mist in the air lit dimly by the spotlight. My eye catches a puff of my own breath floating ghostlike past my face. My muscles spark, and I take off running as fast as I can. When I arrive back at the *Plattenbau*, I am panicked and wheezing.

"Oh my God, *Schatz!* Are you alright?" Fritz asks me, when he sees me.

"Well, I'll live," I answer him. "But I need to be alone," and I disappear into my room.

CHAPTER TWENTY-TWO

The Spitzenkandidat

When I wake up the next morning, everything around me seems weird and wrong. When I get out of bed, I hate the world. I feel groggy, and I slip in the shower while holding the button down with my foot. The fall jars my whole body. "Owwwww," I wince, rubbing my throbbing hip.

The pipes look uglier than ever as I limp my way down the Private Pathway to the *S-Bahn*. When no one is looking, I stop and eye one of the green, overhead serpents. What a useless eyesore! I feel an anger rise up inside me. I pick up a rock and hurl it toward the pipe, yelling, "What the hell are you? You're nothing but a heinous, hollow, hunk of metal!" I chuck a few more stones at the pipe, sending piercing clangs through the morning air, but it doesn't seem to have much effect on the pipe itself. Hmph! I give it the finger and continue walking down the Private Pathway.

At the end of the path, a Vietnamese man jumps out of the bushes and tries to sell me illegal cigarettes.

"Smoking is a filthy habit!" I scream at the man.

On the *S-Bahn* platform, I have nothing but disdain for the four garbage cans that sit there quietly as I wait for the train. Still not quite sure what goes into which bin, I squint my eyes and try to use telepathy to meld the four containers into one. It is just starting to work as my train arrives, and I am annoyed at the speed and efficiency of the German public transportation system. When I arrive at the office, Greta informs me that Herr Bourne has asked to see me.

I walk over to his office.

"What do you want?" he barks as I knock on his door.

"I'm here to see you," I answer him.

"Well, come in then," he orders through the door, "but you'd better have a good reason for interrupting me like this!"

I come in and sit down in the chair in front of his desk. Herr Bourne picks up the phone and puts the receiver to his ear.

"As you can see, I am clearly in the middle of something," he explains while dialing. "There is only one reason for interrupting me like this, Frau Vespucci," Herr Bourne elaborates.

"What's that?"

"And that is only if you have a very good reason."

The other person's voice mail picks up and Herr Bourne slams down the receiver.

"Well?"

"Well, what?"

"What's your reason for interrupting me like this?"

"I don't know, sir. You're the one that asked me to come and see you. You tell me what the reason is."

"Frau Vespucci!" Herr Bourne scolds me. "Who is the boss around here and who is the intern? I'll thank you not to tell me what to do, unless, of course you've been promoted to Chancellor without my knowledge."

"Um ..."

"Well?"

"Well, what?"

"Have you been promoted to Chancellor without my knowledge?"

"Not to my knowledge, sir."

"Very well, then, *I* am the one in charge here, and *I* will tell you why you are here and not the other way around. Is that clear?"

"Crystal, sir."

"What?"

"It's very clear."

"Good. Now, Frau Vespucci, as you can see, I am a very busy man. But I do need your help on something."

"Okay."

"As you know, I am Herr Kaufmann's assistant legal analyst and research coordinator. I am working on this project ... right now we are quite busy trying to pass a new Immigration Law through the *Bundestag*. The law would allow for stricter regulations and greater tracking measures on all foreigners entering Germany. Are you following me, Frau Vespucci?"

"Yes, sir," I answer, though I have no idea what he is talking about.

"Do you know what I'm talking about?"

"Yes, sir, a new Immigration Law. Trying to pass it through the *Bundestag*."

"Okay," Herr Bourne eyes me over the steel rims of his tinted glasses. "The problem is that the opposition is fighting us at every turn. They claim that such a law would create too much hassle at airports and border crossings and give ordinary Germans the feeling that they are living in a police state. Which is ridiculous. But now, because of the American Embassy bombing, we know that Germany has been an operating base for terrorists, and we must do something about it. Now is the time to push ahead with our case. And here's where you come in."

"Yes, sir?" I say, because I have been wondering where I come in.

"I want to use the U.S. Immigration Code as an example."

"Hmmm." I don't really know much about the U.S. Immigration Code.

"Do you know anything about the U.S. Immigration Code, Frau Vespucci?"

"Oh, yes sir," I lie.

"What I want from you is a report on the U.S. Immigration Code. Have you ever written a report before, Frau Vespucci?"

"Yes, sir. Of course."

"Very good. I want you to explain to me how the laws in the U.S. Immigration Code are changing and how the rights and lives of ordinary citizens are being affected as a result. What law school did you go to, by the way?"

"I never went to law school, sir. I am a senior at Rutgers University."

"Very good. Your law degree will come in very handy here. What I want is an in-depth legal analysis. I want you to take a scalpel, Frau Vespucci, and dissect the U.S. Immigration Code. Then, I want you to compare it line by line to Germany's Immigration Code. Did you study foreign law in law school or just domestic law?"

"I never went to law school, sir. I'm an undergraduate Liberal Arts student."

"Very good. Very good. Then you should have all the background you need. Have you ever written a legal analysis for an actual lawyer before, or just for your law professors?"

"I've never written a legal analysis before," I explain, "for an actual or a fake lawyer."

"Very good. Very good. I expect it on my desk by the end of your term. If you need help along the way, please feel free to ask me questions anytime."

"I have one question, sir."

"Not now, Frau Vespucci. As you can see, I am a very busy man."

"But—"

"Run along, young lady. You've got a lot of work ahead of you." He already has the phone to his ear and has pressed redial.

"—you just said I could ask you questions anytime."

"That's right. Anytime that's convenient for me. If I meant all the other times too, I would have said *every time*."

"I see."

I go back to my office and take a long look out the window. There is an icy rain falling outside, and it makes the streets and buildings around me look varnished. I shudder and sit down at Julia's desk. Instead of taking a scalpel and dissecting the U.S. Immigration Code and then comparing it line by line to Germany's legal code, I open up a blank Word document and type *I want to go home*. For a few minutes, I stare at what I have typed and don't move. Then, Greta knocks on my door again.

"Come in," I call, minimizing the window on my desktop.

"*Schatz!* There you are," Greta exclaims. "Herr Kaufmann has an important favor to ask of you."

"He does?"

"Yes. Run along and see him right away. He's waiting for you in his office."

"Okay." I follow Greta out.

In his office, Herr Kaufmann is entertaining fifty constituents from his voting district in the central-western part of Germany, near the Rheine river.

"Here she is! Miss America!" trumpets Herr Kaufmann as I enter the room. Fifty heads turn and look at me. "I present to you, Katarina Vespucci, my brilliant intern and language genius!"

"How many languages do you speak, exactly, Frau Vespucci?" calls one of the starry-eyed guests.

"She speaks English, German, and Italian fluently," boasts Herr Kaufmann.

"That's not really—"

"How did you learn so many languages fluently, Frau Vespucci?" asks another impressed constituent.

"Frau Vespucci is a smorgasbord of European fillings baked in a savory American crust," explains Herr Kaufmann.

"A what?"

"I think her name speaks for itself, does it not?"

"It does," agree the awe-inspired constituents.

"Friends!" calls Herr Kaufmann. "Frau Vespucci has a surprise for all of you!"

I do?

"She does?"

"Yes! Since you came all the way from the *Rheinland* to see us, Frau Vespucci is going to give you all a personal tour of the *Reichstag* Building."

I am?

"She is?"

"Yes. I am confident you will agree that Frau Vespucci's intelligence is surpassed only by her loveliness!"

"Ohhhh!" the crowd mumbles. "Yes, we are sure we will agree."

"Frau Vespucci! *C'est parti!*" orders Herr Kaufmann.

"Herr Kaufmann," interrupts a starry-eyed constituent, "'*C'est parti*' is French."

"It is? Frau Vespucci!" calls Herr Kaufmann. "How do you say '*c'est parti*' in Italian?"

"*Andiamo,*" I recall from a car commercial.

"Genius!" declares Herr Kaufmann. "I told you she was fluent in Italian."

"Yes, yes, you did," agree the constituents, nodding their approval as Herr Kaufmann herds them out of his office.

"Constituents! You are in good hands," he calls and then shuts the door behind us.

This is going to be interesting. I turn and face my impromptu audience. What on earth am I going to do now? Guess I'll start with somewhere I know.

"I thought I would begin the tour by showing you the *Bundestag* cafeteria," I begin the tour. The constituents follow as I lead the way. "This is where the leaders of your country dine—"

"Don't they have an executive dining room?" interrupts one starry-eyed constituent.

"—when they're not dining in the executive dining room," I quickly add.

"Ohhhh," coo the constituents. I glance quickly at the menu on the wall. It announces that lunch today in the *Bundestag* cafeteria will be pig knuckle with sauerkraut, a traditional Berlin specialty.

"The *Bundestag* cafeteria is known for its local specialties, such as pig knuckle with sauerkraut," I inform the group.

"Ohhhh," coo the constituents. "Will we be touring the executive dining room too?" asks a curious, starry-eyed constituent.

"I'm afraid that the executive dining room is not accessible today," I lie, because I have no idea if or where the executive dining room is.

"Why not?"

"Well, you see," I explain, "the CDU *Spitzenkandidat* is hosting a conference in there today. As the front-runner of the party, he—"

"A conference in the executive dining room?"

"—a lunch conference—"

"Can we go after lunch if we hang around?"

"—an all-day lunch conference—"

"What's it about?"

"—a confidential all-day lunch conference," I add, "of a strictly private and secret nature."

"Ohhhh," coo the constituents.

"Will you tell us what it's about if we guess?" asks a hopeful constituent.

"No," I inform him. "The executive dining room is not allowing visitors today, I'm very sorry."

"We see," explains the group.

"He's a lovely man," says one starry-eyed constituent.

"Who is?" I ask.

"The *Spitzenkandidat*."

"Oh yes, of course," I answer, realizing that I don't even know who the *Spitzenkandidat* is.

"Will we get to meet him on the tour?" asks a starry-eyed constituent.

"Who?" I ask.

"Herr Stehmeyer."

"W—"

"The *Spitzenkandidat*."

"Oh, you mean Herr Stehmeyer?"

"Yes."

"I'm sorry," I apologize. "Because of the confidential all-day lunch conference, which is of a private and secret nature, the *Spitzenkandidat* will not be greeting any visitors today. In fact, he will not be leaving the executive dining room at all."

"There he is!" calls one starry-eyed constituent.

"There who is?"

"Herr Stehmeyer!"

Sure enough, down at the far end of the cafeteria is the *Spitzenkandidat*, just getting up from a table, talking candidly and openly with passersby and a gaggle of aides.

"May we go say hello, Frau Vespucci?" ask the starry-eyed constituents.

This ought to be good. "Okay, let's go say hello." But by the time we can make our way down to the far end of the cafeteria, Herr Stehmeyer has already exited the room.

"May we follow him, Frau Vespucci?" ask the starry-eyed constituents.

This ought to be good. "Okay, let's follow him." The fifty starry-eyed constituents make their way out into the hallway, just in time to see the *Spitzenkandidat* swipe his ID badge and disappear behind a very secret and confidential looking door.

"May we follow him, Frau Vespucci?" ask the starry-eyed constituents.

"I'm very sorry," I explain, "but I don't believe I have access to this very secret and confidential looking door."

"Why don't you try swiping *your* ID badge?" suggests a starry-eyed constituent.

This ought to be good. I walk up to the very secret and confidential looking door and swipe my ID badge. It opens. "Right this way," I announce as I lead the constituents through the very secret and confidential looking door. I wonder if I am going to lose my internship over this.

Once inside, I look around. We are in a windowless tunnel with a downward slope. It looks to me like a secret passage underneath the *Bundestag*. It is illuminated by dim lights, mounted in the floor, giving the tunnel a somber, morgue kind of feel.

"This is a secret tunnel that goes underneath the *Bundestag*," I explain. "It is illuminated by dim lights mounted in the floor to give it a somber, morgue kind of feel."

"Ohhhh," coo the constituents. I am relieved to find that the *Spitzenkandidat* is nowhere to be found. I wonder where this tunnel leads.

"Frau Vespucci, where does this tunnel lead?" inquires a starry-eyed constituent.

"That's what I'm going to show you," I explain.

I lead the starry-eyed constituents down the tunnel, which eventually bottoms out and begins a slow ascent back up. After a good walk, we finally come to a door at the end of the tunnel. I swipe my ID badge, and the door opens. The constituents follow me through it. Once through the door, we find ourselves in an empty hallway with nothing but an elevator and a spiral staircase. Both lead only to the third floor. I guess the third floor is our only choice from here. I hope it doesn't lead directly into the *Spitzenkandidat*'s office.

"Meet you on the third floor," I instruct as some of the constituents join me in the elevator, some head for the stairs, and some wait for the next elevator. When the elevator reaches the third floor, the constituents and I step out of the elevator and directly into the plenary chamber of the German *Bundestag.* Luckily, the house is not in session. As soon as the constituents realize where we are, they let out a chorus of "ooooohs" and "ahhhhhs."

"Your laws are made right here," I announce proudly. The "ooooohs" and "ahhhhhs" continue. I take the opportunity to inform my audience about the color of the seats in the plenary chamber, "*Bundestag* blue," and to point out the symbolic one-ton steel eagle that is dangling over everybody's heads. I don't elaborate on the eagle, however, because I have no idea what it symbolizes.

"What does the eagle symbolize, Frau Vespucci?" asks a starry-eyed constituent.

"It symbolizes something heavy," I explain. "In the air."

"Something strong?" suggests another starry-eyed constituent.

"Yes."

"Strong like steel?" asks another starry-eyed constituent.

"Exactly, strong like steel."

"But it is held up by such delicate cables?" points out another starry-eyed constituent.

"Yes, the cables are very thin," I confirm.

"Do the cables symbolize democracy?" asks another starry-eyed constituent.

"Yes, the cables symbolize the delicate hand of democracy, holding up your strong republic."

"Ooooooh!" coo the constituents. "What powerful symbolism."

From there, I know exactly where to go, and I take my group of fifty starry-eyed constituents into the parliamentarian corridor with the Russian writing.

"This is graffiti that the Russians left on the original walls of the *Reichstag* Building when they sacked it in spring of 1945."

There are "ooooohs," and "aaaaahs," all around.

"I wonder what it says," wonders one starry-eyed constituent.

"This one says, 'This is the day of victory over Fascism,'" I explain.

"You can read Russian, too?" blurts a starry-eyed constituent.

"No," I explain. "A Russian friend of mine transla—"

"What does this one say?" asks another starry-eyed constituent.

"This one says, 'I came from Vladivostok to obliterate Berlin.'"

"Amazing! She really is a language genius!"

"What about this one?"

"This one says, 'Igor was here, 1945.'"

"It does not say that."

"It does."

After the parliamentarian corridor, I lead the group further up the spiral staircase to the roof. There I let them stroll through the glass dome and I point out other sites that I know, like the Brandenburg Gate, the site of the book burning on *Bebelplatz*, the East Side Gallery, the Checkpoint Charlie Museum, and the *Plattenbau* on *Coppistrasse*. It is especially cool being under the glass dome with the icy rain pouring down all around. After I have run out of things that I can remember from my tour of the *Reichstag* Building, I start to make stuff up, like about how the architect that designed the building had been a fan of American baseball and had designed the slope of seats in the plenary chamber to match the exact dimensions of the box seats in Yankee Stadium.

"Ooooo!" coo the constituents. "Baseball is a confusing sport."

With that, I decide to take my leave of the starry-eyed constituents before I am exposed. I explain that I have to get back to an important project for Herr Bourne, and I instruct them to take the public elevator out. One by one, each starry-eyed constituent shakes my hand, and thanks me vigorously for the tour and for my expertise.

"How do you say thank you in Russian?" one of them asks.

"Spasiba."

"Amazing!" exults the group. "A language genius!"

As soon as I can, I steal back to the comfort of Julia's office. I sit down, kick off my shoes under the desk, and sit cross-legged on the chair. I re-open my Word document and complete the assignment that I had been working on that morning.

I want to go home, I continue typing. *I want to go home; I want to go home; I want to go home.*

CHAPTER TWENTY-THREE

The Soviet Heroes

It is, overall, a mopey week for me, and I make no plans for the weekend, which means that when the weekend comes, I have nothing to do, which is the worst when you are feeling mopey.

"I don't understand what's wrong," says Fritz, not really paying attention, when I try to explain it to him.

"Nothing is wrong."

"So what's the problem?"

"I've got nothing to do ... and on top of that, there's nothing I feel like doing. Nothing *is* the problem."

"If nothing is wrong, then why are you so down?"

"Oh, forget it. I'm going to see if Pete's home. Maybe he can cheer me up."

Pete is home, but he can't cheer me up because he is naked when I ring the doorbell. The reason Pete is naked is because Jenny is over and she's naked too.

"Jenny?" I ask as Pete explains with nothing but a blanket around his waist and a guilty grin on his face.

"Yeah," he admits. "Haven't I mentioned that?"

"No, you haven't."

"Should I have?"

"I don't know."

"It's not serious. It's just something we … uh … do … from time to time."

"Hi, Kat!" Jenny calls out from behind Pete's partially closed bedroom room.

"Hi, Jenny. Sorry to bother you two."

Suddenly Lambert appears behind me in the hallway. "Hi, Kat. Hi, Pete. Is the ignorant bastard here?"

"You mean Nat? Yeah, I think so. Nat!" Pete yells in the direction of Nat's room. "Lambert is here for you."

Nat comes out of his room, dressed to go out. "I was wondering where you were, you flaming gay liberal pansy. Do you have the directions to the bar?"

"Yes," says Lambert.

"See you guys later," Nat says to me and Pete.

"Later."

Nat and Lambert leave together.

"They're getting along well," I say to Pete.

"Yeah, ever since their big falling out they've been inseparable."

"Hmm."

"Indeed."

"Anyway, I'll let you and Jenny get back to … each other."

I decide to go up to the tenth floor to see what Janika is up to. There, I find her and Billy having tea.

"Please. Come in," says Janika. "Join us,"

"Thanks," I say. "I would like that a lot."

"Are you still being all mopey?" Billy asks me.

"Yeah. Still wallowing, I guess." Janika puts a cup of steaming tea in front of me. The smell of mint wafts up to my nose and reminds me of Thor.

"Look on the bright side," says Billy. "At least now you don't have to have anal sex with Thor."

I miss-swallow a sip of tea as he says that and start coughing. "Thanks, Billy. That makes me feel a lot better."

"Anytime," Billy gives me a hearty smile.

"It's actually not Thor that's bringing me down."

"No?"

"No. I think, in my mind, Thor was supposed to be my rebound that was going to cure the rejection from Matt. But then my rebound rejected me, and ended up being another log on the big rejection fire."

"The big rejection fire?" mocks Billy. "Now you've crossed over from mopey to morbid."

I shrug my shoulders.

"Let's turn your big rejection fire into a big resilience fire. A big resilience campfire!"

"Hmm …"

"Everybody loves campfires. Janika, sing '*Kumbaya*' with me."

"What?"

"Were you allowed to sing '*Kumbaya*' in the Soviet Union? It's kind of religious, you know, with the whole 'Oh, Lord' part and all."

"I don't think I know what you're talking about, Billy."

Billy sings: "*Someone's sleeping, Lord, Kumbaya. Oh, Lord, Kumbaya.*"

Janika and I stare at Billy.

"Are you finished now?" I ask.

"Sorry," Billy snickers.

I have to admit, he's pretty funny. "So what are you guys up to today?" I ask.

"We were talking about heading over to the Soviet Memorial in Treptower Park. Do you want to come?"

I think it over for a minute. The Soviet Memorial in Treptower Park could be interesting. It's certainly better than nothing. "Okay, I'll join you guys. When are you leaving?"

"We're just waiting for Irina and Sasha. They should be here soon."

"Great," I say. "I'll just go grab a coat."

That afternoon, Irina, Janika, Sasha, Billy, and I head off together to explore the Soviet Memorial in Treptower Park. It is only two *S-Bahn* stops away from us in Eastern Berlin. When we get out at Treptower Park, we have to walk a ways through neatly trimmed grass and trees before we come to the memorial. The air is crisp, but there is no precipitation, so it is actually a nice day. I take a few deep breaths and let the fresh air enter my lungs. I am glad to be out of the *Plattenbau*.

"What does the Soviet Memorial commemorate?" I ask Sasha as we walk.

"The Battle of Berlin."

"Oh. I don't know anything about it, to tell you the truth, except that when it was won, the Russians sacked the *Reichstag*."

"Well, it's good you came along with us then. A good portion of the battle was fought right here where this park is. If you can imagine, over three hundred thousand Soviets died taking over the city."

"Jesus!" I exclaim. "Three hundred thousand people died in the Battle of Berlin?"

"Three hundred thousand *Soviets* died in the Battle of Berlin."

I ponder that number. I know that Giants Stadium in the Meadowlands holds about eighty thousand people. I picture it packed on Super Bowl Sunday—that's not even one third of the people, or Soviets, that died in one battle of World War II. "When was the Battle of Berlin?" I ask Sasha.

"April to May, 1945."

Sasha's figures on casualties remind me of the Gestapo work

camp that I stumbled across earlier in the week. I shiver. Never have I been so hounded by history as I have since I arrived in Berlin. Never have I felt so close to history as I have since I arrived in Berlin. You can't escape it here. I think about how indifferent I am to history in New Jersey. Except for on the Fourth of July, I never think at all about the American Revolution. I know that Morristown and Trenton and the Delaware River played important roles somehow, but don't ask me for details. The only time I think about the American Civil War is when I hear "The Night They Drove Old Dixie Down" by the Band on the radio. To me, these are events tucked away in the same file of my brain as dinosaurs and the Crusades.

But the history of Berlin is recent and alive; it calls out from corners, cracks, and cobblestones; windows, walls, and watchtowers; pathways, parks, and plaques; bullet holes and bombed-out buildings. You'd have to be a very closed-off person to remain indifferent to the things that happened here—some of them during my own lifetime.

Approaching the Soviet Memorial, we pass through a stone archway carved with wreathes and the Soviet hammer and sickle. Along the top of the arch runs the inscription: *"Ruhm und Ehre den Helden der Sowjetarmee."*

"Glory and Honor to the Heroes of the Soviet Army," Billy translates as we walk wide-eyed under the archway. "Have you ever seen the hammer and sickle displayed like that before?" he asks.

"No," I shake my head. "Only in pictures." We pause for a moment. "Have you ever thought of the Soviets as the heroes?" I whisper to Billy.

"No," he shakes his head.

Coming into the memorial, the first thing we see is a large, white statue of a woman kneeling with a head of braids bowed to the ground. She holds herself up with her right hand and clutches her chest with her left hand.

"That's Mother Russia," explains Sasha as we behold the sculpture.

Stretching out in front of Mother Russia is a vast field and flowerbed that marks the grave of five thousand Soviet soldiers. Lining the field on the left and right sides are large marble tombs depicting scenes from the Battle of Berlin. Each block of stone features a quote from Joseph Stalin, praising the bravery and sacrifice of the soldiers in the good fight against tyranny and oppression.

"It's funny seeing quotes from Stalin about fighting tyranny and oppression," whispers Billy as we stroll past the marbles.

"Yeah," I laugh. "How about that?"

The memorial comes to a head at the end of the field where a small hill gives rise to an eleven-meter bronze statue of a formulaic Russian soldier clutching an infant in his arms. He is crushing a swastika at his feet with an oversized sword. The soldier has a fierce look on his larger-than-life face, which stares eastward, into the distance, beyond Mother Russia. This figure strikes me as both terrifying and triumphant. Most of all, it is big.

"The man symbolizes a conglomeration of all the men buried in this field," explains Sasha to Billy and me. "He's the ideal Soviet soldier. The child he has saved symbolizes the future."

We climb the steps up the hill to the pedestal underneath the statue. There is a crypt inside the pedestal lined with a colorful mosaic depicting ordinary Soviet citizens paying their respects to the dead. There is a thick book in the center of the vault, which lists all the names of the known fallen soldiers. I take a few minutes to admire the mosaic. Then I turn around and gaze down at the memorial ... the tombs, the mass grave in the middle, and Mother Russia on the opposite end. I am overwhelmed with the feeling of sorrow for the lives lost. Impulsively, I take hold of my cross, close my eyes, and start to pray.

"What are you doing?" asks Sasha as he notices me.

"Oh ... um ... just ... um ... saying a prayer."

"You don't have to pray for them," he informs me.

I open my eyes and look at Sasha. Then I look around at the whole scene. There is not a single trace of religious symbolism, yet I can't help but want to pray.

"I know I don't have to," I reply, "I just—"

"Just thank them."

Chapter Twenty-four

Bob Wilkens

I do thank the Soviet soldiers who died fighting Nazi tyranny, and when I leave the cemetery, I don't feel so bad about Berlin, about Germany, about anything in my life. There's nothing like being faced with three hundred thousand deaths to make you appreciate being alive. It doesn't even bother me that on the *S-Bahn* ride home from Treptower Park, a cold drizzle begins to fall.

"You knew the nice weather wouldn't last," says Irina.

"You know Berlin," I answer. "Four seasons a day."

When I arrive home, there is a note on my apartment door. It is from Pete.

"No hecklers in the rain," it reads. "Meet us on the soccer field?"

I throw on some old clothes and meet my friends on the field. Needing a release, I lope up and down the field, dribbling, passing, calling for the ball, and clapping in encouragement of my teammates. Drops of sweat, rain, and mud run down our faces. About half way through the game, Jenny slide tackles Istvan and sends them both careening down onto the wet ground. When Erald sees this, he slide tackles Anne, sending them both careening down onto the wet ground. Anne grabs hold of Pete in mid-fall and pulls him down onto the muddy field with them. Jenny jumps on my back and the two of us tumble down on top of Pete, Erald, and Anne. I extend my leg and trip Istvan as he skips by to plunge a handful of mud onto Jenny's head. Erald rips out a handful of grass and tosses it at Istvan. The scene turns into a raucous pile of dirt-slinging, turf-hurling, grime-drenched international interns. As I launch mud balls into my friends' faces, and take a few in the face myself, I can't help but think of the war of *Watt* on the day of the Embassy bombing. The only difference is that this sludge fest is ending in smiles and laughter instead of tears.

The next week, I am given yet another reason to smile. My father tries to call me at work, but doesn't get through Julia's firewall because he doesn't introduce himself properly.

"I can't believe you hung up on my father!" I snap at Julia from my intern table in the corner. "What the heck is wrong with you?"

"Well, if he had announced himself as your father when I first answered the phone, then I would have known who he was and given the phone to you," Julia explains.

"It is not your job to teach my family and friends German phone etiquette," I stand up from my table and am about to really let Julia have it when the phone rings again.

"Yes, Dr. Vespucci, she's right here," answers Julia and then hands the receiver to me.

"Sleep with one eye open," I whisper to my office mate as I take the receiver.

"What's that, Kat?"

"Nothing, Dad. Hi. How are you?"

"Fine. Just fine. Listen, your mother and I were wondering—"

"Hi, dear," my mom speaks into the phone.

"Your mother is on the line too."

"Hi, Mom."

"Your mother and I were wondering if you'd given any thought to what you were going to do after graduation."

"After you've returned from Germany in May."

"Huh," I think. "I hadn't really thought about it."

"Well, as you know, with the current state of the economy, the job market is pretty tough."

"Huh," I think. "I hadn't really thought about it."

"Yes, the economy is in the toilet, but your father has a patient who's in the pharmaceutical business."

"Yes," my father adds. "I have a patient who is in the pharmaceutical business."

"I see."

"You remember Bob Wilkens, dear?"

"No."

"Yes, you do, dear, he was at our twenty-fifth wedding anniversary party."

"The one with the idiopathic hypoglycemia."

"Well, Bob is looking for some bright and perky young sales reps, so your father suggested he contact you."

"Finished a whole plate of prosciutto by himself."

"Oh, yes. I remember him. What pharmaceutical company does he work for?"

"Yes, that's the one. Your father and I told him all about your qualifications and your experience, and he's interested in interviewing you."

"Raritan Pharmaceuticals."

"Huh," I say. "I don't know if pharmaceutical sales are really—"

"Starting salary for the position is around fifty thousand dollars a year, plus commission," adds my father.

"Wow! Would I be able to use my German in the job?"

"Which is pretty good for an entry-level position, considering the economy is in the toilet," adds my mother.

"No. Probably not. Eventually you'd get a company car."

"What kind of traveling would I be doing?"

"You really need to start putting money away into a retirement plan, Kat."

"It would be mostly local travel, dear ... within New Jersey ... so you wouldn't have to pump your own gas."

"Retirement plan? I don't know, Mom and Dad. It doesn't really sound—"

"Tell her about the company car."

"Does it matter that I have no background whatsoever in pharmaceuticals?"

"I just told her about the car."

"Fifty thousand dollars a year, Katarina, dear. Think of all the trouble you could get into with that money! Sorry, I didn't hear you tell her about the car, you have to speak up."

"Does it matter that I have no background in sales?"

"I told her eventually she'd get a company car."

"There will be training for the position, dear. Don't worry about that. And they'll probably give you a gas card too, with gas prices rising up the wazoo."

"Well, I guess it wouldn't hurt to interview with him."

"That's my girl! I'm sure you'll get along great with Mr. Wilkens."

"Despite his idiopathic hypoglycemia."

"We'll have him get in touch with you soon. His name is Mr. Wilkens. Bob Wilkens."

"You met him at our twenty-fifth wedding anniversary party."

"Prosciutto. Yes, I remember. Thanks Mom and Dad."

"You're welcome, dear."

"We love you."

"Love you, too."

230

I hang up the phone, feeling a little strange. I haven't even thought about having to get a job after returning home from Germany. Start saving for my retirement plan? *What?* They're right, though. This is my senior year. I won't be returning to Rutgers at all. I'll be graduating and then I'll have to get a job. I wince at the thought. I just started my job here, and it isn't exactly floating my boat.

I realize I have to get started on my legal analysis of the U.S. Immigration Code, so I skip out of the office and head to the *Bundestag* library to check out some political journals. It is a good excuse to put some distance between Julia and me.

In the *Bundestag* library, I run into Billy, who has been given the assignment to write an in-depth political analysis on whether or not the expansion of the European Union will make it a stronger or weaker political body.

"Have you ever written an in-depth political analysis before?" I ask Billy.

"Please," he answers. "I'm a psyche major."

"I know how you feel." While we are both sifting through piles of *Foreign Policy Magazine, Economist, Der Spiegel,* and *International Politics Journal,* I tell Billy about my conversation with my parents about Bob Wilkens and the pharmaceutical sales job.

"Do you really want to go back to America when this year is over?" Billy asks me.

"Of course," I answer, surprised at his question.

"Will you get to use your German at all in the position?"

"No."

"Will they send you anywhere cool?"

"No. But I will get a company car."

"How's the money?"

"Good."

""Well, that's good," says Billy. "If I were me, and I am, I wouldn't take it."

"What? Why not?"

"C'mon, do you really think you could get passionate about pharmaceuticals?"

"Probably not," I laugh. "What are you going to do when this is all over?"

"I don't know ... I might try to stay here."

"What do you mean, stay here?"

"I mean not go home."

"Are you serious?"

"Sure."

"But, you can't just ... not go home."

"Why not?"

"What about graduation?"

"They can mail my diploma."

"What would you do?"

"Whatever I could."

Silence.

"That's crazy," I respond after a few more minutes of flipping through magazines.

"What's so crazy about it?"

"I don't know. I don't see how you could just ... not go back."

"See it."

"For me, I mean ... I just never considered that."

Billy finds an article that is of interest to him and is now reading intensely.

"So ... will the expansion of the European Union make it a stronger or weaker political body?" I ask him.

"Beat's me. Your guess is as good as mine."

When I arrive home from work later on, Fritz is standing over a pot of boiling water, trying to steam a letter open.

"What are you doing?" I ask him.

"I'm trying to get this letter open without actually opening it."

"Why don't you want to open it?"

"Because I don't want the person whose letter it is to know that I'm trying to read it."

"Oh, is it for Carmelita?"

"No, it's for you."

"What? Fritz, give me that!" I march over to him and snatch the letter from his grasp.

"See, I knew you wouldn't let me read it."

"This is from Matt!" I exclaim. "Omigod! I can't believe it!" My adrenaline glands jump into production. I take the letter into my room and take a few deep breaths before opening it. *I'M SORRY!* it says in big letters on the back of the envelope. I peel the moistened seal open with shaky hands.

The first thing that falls out is a young picture of Matt. It was taken on Christmas morning in front of his family's Christmas tree. He looks about six years old and he is wearing *Dukes of Hazards* pajamas. He is opening a present and looking into the camera with adorable, oversized eyes. I totally melt when I see his image, so little and innocent. Damn him! He knows how cute he is. And he knows that I am still every bit in love with him as ever. I turn the picture around and read the back. "Here's begging," it says. I like where this is going.

Accompanying the photo is a groveling letter apologizing for all of his mistakes, explaining how he had been scared at the thought of me leaving the country and how I am the only one he really loves. He asks me to forgive him and to wait for him and to take him back as soon as I return to the States.

"Telephone for you," Fritz says, poking his head into my bedroom.

I take the call. It is Bob Wilkens, inviting me to participate in the Raritan Pharmaceutical Co. sales training in New Brunswick, New Jersey, next May.

"Yes," I tell him, still staring at Matt's letter. "Definitely, yes."

"Great," Bob Wilkens replies. "We'll be delighted to have you on our team."

"It will be nice to be part of your team, sir."

"We'll be looking forward to your return to New Jersey in May."

"Me too, Mr. Wilkens," I tell him. "Me too."

CHAPTER TWENTY-FIVE

St. Nicholaus

With my job after Germany settled and my love affairs finally in order, it is smooth sailing in Berlin for once. A sense of normalcy sets in, and it is extraordinary to me to see just how ordinary my life in the neo-Communist, ex-workers Paradise has become. I have accepted the walk down the Private Pathway and the Private Pathway Tunnel as an enjoyable part of my morning and afternoon routines. I have accepted the pipes as a unique and interesting part of the landscape of *Lichtenberg*. I have adjusted to the weather, accepting umbrellas, raincoats, and warm sweaters as everyday parts of my wardrobe. Though the weather no longer bothers me, I readily complain about it with Frau Schindler every Monday, Wednesday, and Friday morning over three strong cups of coffee. On weeks when Julia is in the office, I spend most of my time in the *Bundestag* library conducting my research. On weeks when Julia is out of the office, I sit at her desk with my feet up like I own the place.

Occasionally, Herr Kaufmann takes me along to a committee meeting or a conference. The most interesting one so far has been a discussion in the Foreign Ministry with Russian officials concerning compensation of descendents of Russian slave laborers during Nazi rule. I am amazed to learn that, more than half a century after the end of World War II, discussions like this are still going on. It makes me wonder. Has the United States ever compensated the families of slaves? Native Americans? If so, it never made it into my history classes.

On Tuesdays and Thursdays I attend classes and it no longer bothers me when they are cancelled or moved to a *Biergarten*. Regularly after classes I meet Billy and Janika at *Potsdamerplatz* for half-price movies and gelato. After work, we foreign students typically meet each other over tall, curvy glasses of *Hefeweizen*. On weekends, a group of us usually go dancing at one of the many techno clubs in Eastern Berlin. In fact, we hardly ever venture all the way over to the West, unless it is for work.

On Wednesday nights, we try whenever we can to hear live music. Sometimes we even go back to Quasimodo, but Thor is never there. It's better that way, now that I'm back together with Matt and he's back together with whatever-her-name-is in Sweden. Not that I'm looking to run into Thor, but I have tried to go back to *Zosch* a few times where we heard the Dixieland band on our date together, but I just can't find where it was. I'm starting to wonder if it was ever really there at all.

One of the highlights of the week for me is the day that a bunch of us foreigners get together to play soccer. We have to vary the times to foil the hecklers, but we can usually coordinate it once a week. Other times, we all go to Café Avalon, watch DVDs on somebody's laptop, or drink beer on one of the balconies and wave at the TV tower. I spend almost all of my time with people from the program and rarely find myself alone.

And every once in awhile, not so often anymore, but every now and then something strange happens ... something surprises me, like today when I notice that it is a holiday and I hadn't noticed at all.

Now, I've never really been one to remember dates, but I had been looking forward to November ninth this year because it is the anniversary of the fall of the Berlin Wall. What better place to celebrate Wall Fall Day than Berlin, where it all took place. I had been looking forward to attending the cookouts and concerts, parades and parties, festivities and fireworks that I would expect to take place on this wonderful day. This is the day when East and West Berliners alike had joined hands, danced together on top of the Wall, and poured champagne over each other in an explosive celebration of the moment that tyranny had cracked in East Germany—as we had seen in the museum at Checkpoint Charlie. I had wanted to share in this German experience and feel the excitement that was sure to be in the air on the day of one of the most amazing events of my lifetime. Which is why I am dismayed when, around seven o'clock this evening, I look at my calendar and realize that I have totally missed it.

"Why didn't we celebrate Wall Fall Day today?" I ask Fritz as I boil up some sausages for us to share.

"I don't know," Fritz shrugs. "Why would we?"

"Well, maybe because it's a holiday?"

"It's not a holiday."

"Of course it's a holiday. It's Wall Fall Day."

"The Chancellor made a speech. I saw some articles about it in the paper. What more do you want?"

"I want a celebration! November ninth is a great day in German history."

Fritz gives me a strange look that I don't know how to interpret.

"What's the look for? Am I over-boiling the sausages?"

"*Schatz*, November ninth also happens to be the anniversary of *Kristallnacht*."

"What?"

"The beginning of the Holocaust. The night the Nazis ravaged the country, burning Jewish businesses and synagogues."

"Oh," I exhale heavily, my gaze hitting the floor.

"So it's not exactly a day we like to celebrate."

"I see," I reply, the wind gone from my sails. "I'm sorry." I turn back to the stove and concentrate on the sausages. After a few minutes, something else dawns on me.

"We didn't celebrate the Day of German Unity either. October third. Why not that one?"

"What's to celebrate?"

"It's the day that East Germany officially unified with West Germany. It's the day that Germany became a whole country again."

"There were speeches and articles, *Schatz*, as always. You just missed them."

"Speeches and articles? That's how you commemorate the day of your reunification? I didn't even see any German flags hanging around."

"You know we don't fly our flag."

"Except at soccer games."

"Yes, soccer is the only occasion where we show national pride."

"But October third is your national holiday. Surely you can fly your flag on your national holiday. I mean it's like our Fourth of July."

"No, it's not. Nothing is like your Fourth of July."

"What do you mean?"

"I've heard about your Fourth of July. A friend of mine was in New York on the Fourth of July once, and he said he was afraid to leave his hotel. It was like you were preparing to go to war. A flag on every lamppost. People singing patriotic songs. Wearing red, white, and blue T-shirts. You Americans are insane."

"Insane to be patriotic?" I ask.

"Patriotism leads to nationalism."

"So."

"Nationalism leads to war."

"Not always."

"I hardly expect you to agree. You're a patriotic American. You've probably got your USA T-shirt folded up in your drawer, and you parade around the apartment in it singing the 'Star Spangled Banner' when I'm not home."

"Don't be ridiculous. All I'm saying is, I don't see anything wrong with flying your country's flag on your national holiday, that's all. And I do not have a USA T-shirt."

"By the way, there was some mail for you today." Fritz hands me a package that has just arrived from the States. I open it. It is a present from Dana, my best friend in the States.

"What is it?" Fritz asks.

"It's a USA T-shirt," I answer. There is a little note inside from Dana that says, "Wear it proudly!"

Another cultural surprise hits me on December sixth. It is late at night, or rather, early in the morning, and I am having trouble sleeping. The reason I am having trouble sleeping is because someone is repeatedly ringing the doorbell. Fritz and I arise from our beds and stumble to the door to see what the matter is. When we open the door, we are greeted by a very drunk Milena from the Czech Republic, Marika from the Slovak Republic, and Dominik from the Slovak Republic, who is in Group One. Dominik is dressed as St. Nicholaus, Milena is wearing white wings and a halo, and Marika is wearing red horns, a red tail and carries an aluminum foil pitchfork. They are inebriated and adorable, and they stream into our apartment singing in tongues, presumably Czech and Slovak, and banging pots and pans. But this visit is not all fun and games. St. Nicholaus approaches Fritz and me, and the mood suddenly becomes serious.

"Have you been good this year?" he asks us. Marika hisses and threatens us with her pitchfork.

"Yes, yes, very good," Fritz and I reply. Milena cheers and dances around us. All three of them shower us with candy, chocolate, glitter, confetti, and shots of vodka from St. Nicholaus' sack.

"Now sing us a song," demand the holiday intruders.

Fritz and I attempt to sing "Silent Night," but I keep messing him up because I only know the lyrics in English. We start laughing, and Marika becomes angry and threatens us again with her pitchfork. Instead Fritz and I try singing it in a round, he in German, me in English. Eventually, St. Nicholaus is satisfied and he cuts us off.

"We have many other *HAA* girls and boys to visit tonight."

Marika insists that Fritz and I do another shot before they leave, while Milena does another one herself.

"Children! Always be good," Dominik commands, and tosses another handful of candy from his sack of goodies. "Until next year!"

And then faster than Fritz can say "Happy St. Nicholaus Day!" the trio jingles out of the apartment. Fritz and I are left alone in our pajamas—and a big mess of confetti.

CHAPTER TWENTY-SIX

Matt

With that jolly, midnight surprise, the holidays are upon us. In the blink of an eye, the streets of Berlin are decorated with holly leaves and lamps that look like candles. Booths pop up on street corners selling hot apple cider and *Glühwein*, a hot, spiced wine that makes you feel like you are glowing. Both *Alexanderplatz* and the *K'udamm* are transformed into sprawling Christmas markets, the best of East and West, selling all kinds of goodies, such as gingerbread hearts, marmalade dumplings drenched in vanilla sauce, cuckoo clocks, and brightly painted nutcrackers. Walking the streets of Berlin during the month of December, I start to wonder if the Germans themselves hadn't invented Christmas.

On the Sunday before Christmas, I go with Janika to hear Bach's Christmas *Oratorio*, performed in the Kaiser Wilhelm Memorial Church. With the smells of the Christmas market outside, and the sounds of violins, cellos, and jingle bells bouncing about the ruins of the church, I am overcome with the spirit of Christmas. On Christmas Eve, Billy and I go to Mass at the famous Catholic *Marienkirche* at *Alexanderplatz.* The first thing that impresses me about the church is its age. A cornerstone at the main entrance tells that it was built in the year 1270.

I point it out to Billy. "That's five hundred years before America was even a country."

"Huh."

Upon entering the church, I am blown away by its sheer size. The huge barrel-vault leading up to the main altar gives the impression that it can encompass all of God's creation at once. The steeple at the front of the church seems to stretch up to heaven itself. During Mass, I have a hard time focusing on the sermon, because I am marveling at the paintings and statues in gold and marble. The sweet smell of incense tickles my nose. The organ sounding throughout the service is so powerful that it evokes the voice of the Almighty himself. The scene here is a far cry from my Spartan little church at home with its simple wooden construction, double row of pews, and humble panel of stained glass windows.

While the experience is rather surreal for me, one thing comforts me greatly. The format of the Mass is exactly the same as it is in America. And on top of that, the experience is evoking the exact same feelings of guilt in me that I always feel on Christmas and Easter, typically because of the fact that I haven't been to church since the last Christmas or Easter. It is a shameful, embarrassing feeling, and it is familiar and comforting, making me feel not so far away from home at this special time.

Something else makes me feel not so far away from home at this special time, and that is Matt's arrival two days after Christmas. He has decided not to wait for me to come home, but to visit me in Germany for a week and a half and spend New Year's here. When I pick him up at Berlin Tegel Airport, I leap into his arms and wrap both of my legs around his waist in a bear hug that I never want to release. After about a minute of intense hugging, he pries me loose, and plants a kiss on my face. That is the kiss I've been missing! It feels like sliding my feet into my favorite pair of slippers after being forced to wear wooden clogs for the past four months. His lips are soft and familiar and fabulous. It's almost hard to kiss him back because I'm smiling so wide. I am Matt's girlfriend again, and having him here with me in Germany is the best Christmas present I could have asked for.

His visit comes at the perfect time because I have the week off from work and school. It is Matt's first time visiting Europe, his first time out of the country and the tri-state area actually, and I am exhilarated to show him around the country that I have grown to appreciate. Walking hand in hand with him around the sights of Berlin, I feel comforted, satisfied, and at peace.

During the first two days of Matt's visit, we frolic around Berlin. I show him all the sights: the *Plattenbau, Alexanderplatz, Unter den Linden*, the book burning memorial, Humboldt University, the Brandenburg Gate, the *Reichstag* Building, the Berlin Wall, the Museum at Checkpoint Charlie, and the Soviet Memorial in Treptower Park. I also show him how to admire the green pipes from the balcony, how not to pay while riding the *S-Bahn*, how to separate trash into plastic, glass, paper, and "the rest," and most importantly, how to negotiate the water-saving shower. We conclude that it really is much better when done in pairs.

Matt seems to be enjoying Germany very much and compliments me frequently on my ability to understand the cryptic things that are being said around us, and especially my ability to contribute to conversations in this foreign tongue, going so far as to ask and answer questions on a variety of topics. He confesses to me later, though, that the one thing he is really looking forward to is the delicious, pure, legendary German beer that he has been hearing about his whole life. As soon as he says this, we head straight for the nearest beer garden and order a round of *Hefeweizen*.

"What the hell is this crap?" Matt demands to know after forcing down his first swallow of delicious, pure, legendary German beer. His face is contorted in an expression of pain.

"It's beer," I stare at him in amazement. "What do you think it is?"

"It's warm."

"It's not warm," I explain. "It's room temperature."

"It's disgusting."

"It's not disgusting," I explain. "It's good, German beer. If you drink it too cold it destroys the taste."

"I can hardly taste it anyway with all this foam on top."

"Oh, that's called the crown," I explain. "Beer is supposed to have a crown in Germany. It shows that the beer is fresh and was poured properly."

"Poured properly is without foam," Matt corrects me. With that, Matt takes his thumb and wipes it down the side of his nose. Then he sticks his thumb into the beer and stirs until the foam dissolves.

"Why on earth did you do *that?*" I demand to know.

"Nose grease helps the foam go away," he explains.

"That," I reply, "is disgusting."

As Matt stirs his beer with his greasy thumb, he fishes out the lemon.

"And this lemon needs to go too."

"The lemon adds freshness and zing to the beer," I explain.

"If I want freshness and zing, I'll order lemonade."

"Take another sip, honey. You just need to get used to it."

Matt looks at me skeptically.

"Anyway, I want to make a toast," I raise my glass. "To you in Germany. To us. Together again. I'm so glad you're here."

"To us," Matt replies and raises his glass to mine. After the toast, we both take hearty swigs. When I put my glass back down on the table, I'm smiling wide. Matt looks like he's trying not to vomit. He pushes his *Hefeweizen* away from him and waves the waitress over to our table. I want to die in embarrassment as he orders a cold Budweiser.

"Maybe you just don't like *Hefeweizen*," I try to console him. "There are lots of other brews you can try."

Unfortunately, Matt has the same reaction when I introduce him to German *Schwarzbier* and to the local *Berliner Pilsner*.

"It's okay, honey. You don't have to love everything about Germany."

For New Year's Eve, Herr Stern has organized a party at the Humboldt University where the whole group can ring in the New Year together. From Humboldt, it is only a stone's throw to the Brandenburg Gate, where half of Germany will gather together and wait for the final countdown to the New Year.

I am really excited about spending the New Year with Matt and all of my friends. The evening starts early, with dinner in Janika's apartment on the tenth floor. Janika makes a meal of Russian-style crepes for me, Matt, Billy, Irina, and Marek. Marek has brought a bottle of Polish vodka to kick off the celebration early. Matt watches Janika intently as she flips the crepes in the pan without using a spatula. I've seen him try to do that with eggs many times, but he just doesn't have the same finesse.

"Your friend Janika's cool," Matt tells me during a moment when no one is listening.

"I like her too," I answer. "She's Estonian."

"You keep saying that, but I don't get that impression."

"What do you mean?"

"Well, I don't know her that well, but she doesn't seem like the type."

"To be Estonian?"

"Yeah. Stoners are usually all mellow and can't open their eyes all the way."

I blink for a few seconds. "I said she's Estonian."

"A what? It sounds like you're saying *a stoner*."

"*Est-on-i-an!* From the country, Estonia."

"Est-where, who, what?"

I stare at Matt, not knowing what to say.

"So, you don't mean she smokes a lot of herb?"

"I mean that she is from a very small country on the Baltic Sea—called Estonia."

"The *what* sea?"

"You obviously haven't looked at a map of Europe, have you?"

"No. Why would I? Since when are you Christopher Columbus?"

"You don't have to be a goddamn explorer to—"

At my curse, all conversation in the room stops. Everyone looks at me and Matt. I am suddenly self-conscious about having this argument with him in front of the others, and I swallow the rest of the sentence. I take a deep breath and whisper to Matt, "I have a map in my apartment, honey. I'll show you later where Estonia is."

After dinner, the whole group meets in front of the *Plattenbau* to walk together to the *S-Bahn*. Marek's Polish vodka has taken effect a long time ago, and we are all in a fantastic mood. That is, until Matt spies Lambert wearing his *America Sucks* T-shirt under his open jacket.

"What *the fuck* is that?" Matt exclaims loudly enough for everyone in the group to hear. I look at Matt and then at Lambert very nervously.

"A T-shirt," Lambert replies, "What does it look like?"

"What exactly are you trying to say with that T-shirt?" Matt snarls at Lambert.

"*Va te faire foutre,*" Lambert replies.

"Lambert!" says Nat, who isn't far behind. "Matt is Kat's guest. Don't talk to him like that."

"Sorry," says Lambert. "Would it be better if I said it in English? Fuck off!"

"Knock it off," says Nat. "This isn't the time or the place."

"I'm sorry, but it was your charming countryman here that started it."

"What is he trying to say with that T-shirt?" Matt asks me, still unable to believe his eyes.

"He doesn't mean it. He's just trying to rattle your cage," I explain. "Don't pay any attention to him."

"I certainly do mean it," Lambert corrects me.

"I'm going to kill him," Matt informs me.

"Please don't kill him," I say to Matt. "At least not tonight."

"Look, Lambert. Could you please just change the T-shirt?" Nat asks in an attempt at reconciliation.

"Yes," I agree, "tonight is supposed to be a happy occasion."

"That's right!" Lambert raises his voice. "Tonight is supposed to be a happy occasion. And what about all the civilians killed in your retaliatory bombings? Where's their New Year's party?"

"You fucking French asshole!" Matt yells, stepping up to Lambert.

"I'm Belgian, you fucking American *connard du jour!*"

Matt gives Lambert an abrupt shove on both shoulders. I hop behind Matt, trying to hold him back. "You should be on your knees thanking us for those air strikes! I got buddies out there getting shot down so assholes like you have the freedom to run your fucking mouths." Matt gets right into Lambert's face and it looks like he might clock him. Pete steps in between the two of them.

"Forget about it!" Pete tells Matt.

I am starting to feel frantic and out of control of the situation.

"Out there?" Lambert shouts. "You probably don't even know where *out there* is, you ignorant prick. Can you even locate the Middle East on a map?"

"That's it!" Matt pushes Pete out of the way and lunges at Lambert. I scream. The two tumble to the ground and Matt lands on top of Lambert, pinning him to the ground with both hands. "You shut your fucking mouth, or I'm going to shut it for you!"

"What the hell is wrong with you, Matt?" yells Pete. "He's half your size!"

All of the guys rush to Matt and push him off of Lambert.

Matt scurries back onto his feet and away from them, flushed and out of breath.

Janika and Irina rush to Lambert's side and help him up from the ground. "Are you okay?" they ask. He is shaking his head to clear it. "Do you want us to call the police?"

"No!" yells Matt, in between huffs. "No need to call the police. It's okay. It's over. I made my point."

"I think *I* made *my* point, you psychotic asshole!" shouts Lambert as the girls dust him off and lead him back into the *Plattenbau*.

I pull Matt to the side. "You're an ass! What the hell is wrong with you?"

Matt closes his eyes and takes a few deep breaths. "If I see him again, I will kill him."

By now everyone has disbursed and it is just Matt and me standing alone in front of the *Plattenbau*.

"How could you do that to my friend? Are you crazy?"

"That guy is not your friend," Matt corrects me.

"Yes, he is!" I correct him.

"He goes against everything that we are."

"Oh, and you're a real model human being right now!" I yell. "Not everyone thinks like you. Get over it!"

Matt looks like he's really going to let me have it, but he hesitates. He starts to say something else, but stops again. "I'm sorry," he finally says.

"Yeah, I'm sorry too," I say. "Sorry you ruined New Year's for us."

"Look, it won't be so bad, just the two of us. Let's just go to the Brandenburg Gate and watch the countdown. Just you and me."

Matt and I end up spending the New Year wading through the crowds in front of the Brandenburg Gate, being bumped, shoved and spilled on by thousands of drunk, rowdy Europeans. I don't even feel like giving him a kiss at the stroke of midnight.

CHAPTER TWENTY-SEVEN

Julia

With New Year's Eve now over, Matt's visit is as well. Before I know it, I am saying good-bye to him at the entrance to the Departures Terminal at Tegel Airport, feeling very sad for a few different reasons. I pretend that I am sad he is leaving, but mostly I am sad he came.

Matt is crouching on the ground, taking off his shoes to go through the security check. He stands up, sneakers in hand, and gives me a bear hug.

"You're not going to forget about me after I leave, are you?" he asks.

"I could never forget about you," I answer.

"Well, I'll be thinking about you."

" … "

"You know, Kat, you really impressed me this week."

"I did?"

"I mean I've just never seen you acting this smart before."

"What do you mean?"

"Don't get me wrong. It's good. But this side of you, this worldly woman thing you've got going on. I've just never seen it before."

"Maybe I just never had a chance to show it before."

"It makes sense, since you're living out of the country now and all."

"Yes, it does."

"I mean, it's cool and all. Very different." Matt closes his eyes for a minute and sighs. He opens them and gives me a very concentrated look.

"What's the look for?"

"Um, so, this is a stupid question, I know, but I guess you're going to stay for the whole year, then?"

"Yes," I say. "It's only four more months."

"Just promise me one thing."

"What's that?"

"Promise me you'll be the same old Kat when you come back in May."

"What? That's ridiculous."

"I know, I just … I would really like everything to be like it was," he says.

"You'd better go," I say, looking away toward the departures screen. "You'll miss your plane."

I know that my relationship with Matt is over, and I should probably tell him that right now, but he seems so pathetic and helpless standing there that I can't bring myself to deliver the *coup de grâce*. I smile a little at the thought of that expression. Lambert taught it to me.

When I look back at Matt, he has tears in his eyes. "Okay, it's time for me to go," he says and picks up his bags.

Seeing him about to leave for good sends a pang through my heart, and my eyes well up too. Matt kisses me sweetly on the forehead.

"I love you," he says.

"You too."

He disappears into the security check.

The next thing I know, I am sitting again at the table in Julia's office trying to write a legal analysis of the U.S. Immigration Code. Though I have, by now, read dozens of articles on it, I still don't know anything about Germany's Immigration Code with which to compare it. So, instead of pounding the keys just yet, I decide to take another trip over to the *Bundestag* library. I spend a few hours there collecting documents, have lunch with Billy, and when I return to the office, I find that the door is locked.

That's strange. Through the small window along side of the door, I can see that the light is on. I knock, but there is no answer. Maybe Julia went out to lunch and forgot that I am here today.

I go across the atrium to Greta's office to see if there is a spare key. There is. I bring the spare key back to Julia's office, and just before I am about to use it, I think I hear the sound of someone bumping into something. I knock again but receive no reply. I put the spare key into the lock, turn the handle, open the door, and walk in to find Julia and the *Spitzenkandidat* performing the Slippery Salsa on the desk.

The air smells of sweat and perfume. Julia is on her back, her head tossing, her blouse unbuttoned, her chest struggling against her red satin push-up bra, her skirt pushed up around her stomach, and her legs, in thigh-high stockings, suctioned around the *Spitzenkandidat's* waist. The *Spitzenkandidat* is standing over her with a look of intense concentration on his face, his pants around his ankles, his hands on Julia's hips, and his hips rocking in and out of her. Julia and the *Spitzenkandidat* are so wrapped up in each other that they don't even notice I have barged into the room until I verbally announce myself.

"Holy *crap!* Julia! Herr Stehmeyer!"

The momentum in the room comes to a screeching halt.

Julia scrambles for Herr Stehmeyer's jacket to cover herself. "How the hell did you get in here?"

"I used the spare key."

"What spare key?" Julia demands to know.

"This one," I hold the spare key up for Julia to see.

"Thank you, Frau Vespucci, for the demonstration. Now would you kindly get the *hell* out of my office?"

I don't think it is the best time to remind Julia that it is also my office, so I kindly get the *hell* out of Julia's office. My mind is whirling. Julia is having an affair with the *Spitzenkandidat*. He's married! Not to Julia. What a scandal this will turn out to be! What should I do? Should I try to keep it a secret? This could ruin Herr Stehmeyer's marriage, his reputation, his career. What would the party say if it found out? What would the country say if it found out? What would the world say if it found out?

No, I must not tell a soul about this. I must keep it to myself and never let a word of what I have witnessed pass my lips. It is just too big. I must repress it deep in the back of my memory, keep it under lock and key, no amount of bribery, blackmail, convincing, or coercion will ever get me to reveal what I have seen. I will take it to my grave and never tell another living soul as long as I live.

"Why keep it a secret?" asks Billy, after I have related the story to him in full detail. "I mean, what has she ever done for you?"

"You have a point," I admit.

"I mean, she's never been nice to you. You don't owe her any favors."

"You are absolutely right," I agree.

"True, this could ruin his marriage, his reputation, his career, but it's not your fault he can't keep it in his pants."

"And how!"

"I mean, Julia will never forgive you, but she should have thought of that before hanging up on all of your friends for not introducing themselves properly when calling you in the office."

"I couldn't agree more."

253

"Besides, how are you supposed to take a scalpel and dissect the U.S. Immigration Code when your co-workers are constantly fornicating on your desk?"

"It's her desk too … But you're right, Billy!" I come to my senses. "You've never been more right in your life. What Julia and the *Spitzenkandidat* are doing is wrong. Why should I keep it a secret? The party deserves to know what kind of leaders they have. The country deserves to know what kind of leaders they have. The world deserves to know what kind of leaders Germany has!" With that, I storm out of Billy's office and march directly over to Greta's office to report the event to her.

"Explain to me again, darling, why you suspect that Julia and the *Spitzenkandidat* are having an affair."

"Because I saw them—"

"Well, you can't really be sure, darling, can you, unless you've actually seen them—"

"—with my own two eyes."

"—with your own two eyes."

" … "

" … "

Greta drums her fingers nervously on her desk. She stares pensively at the wall.

"You're sure they weren't just talking, darling?"

"Yes, I am sure."

"Because the only way to truly be sure is if you—"

"Saw them. I know. I did."

"—in the act."

Greta continues to drum her fingers nervously on the desk.

"Oh, bother, this again?" she finally speaks.

"I beg your pardon?"

"I suppose the secret's out again," Greta repeats.

"You mean you know about this?"

"I told her not during working hours," Greta shakes her head.

"And you didn't say anything?" I ask, confused.

254

"Didn't say anything to whom, darling?"

"To the party."

"The whole party knows about it, darling. The whole country even. Heck, probably even the whole world knows. No, actually. The whole world doesn't care about German politics. But they would if they did, if you know what I mean, darling."

"The whole country knows about Julia and the *Spitzenkandidat?*"

"Yes, last year they were caught late at night under the eagle in the plenary hall."

"But, he's married!" I sputter.

"Yes, he is. His second wife would have cared. But his current one doesn't."

"And he didn't lose his job?"

"What does it have to do with his job, darling?" Greta wants to know.

That's a good question, I think to myself. Actually, it doesn't have anything to do with his job. "It has everything to do with his job!" I declare.

"Oh, it's just one of those things in life, if you know what I mean, darling."

"What's just one of those things in life?"

"People having sex—"

"What does that mean?"

"—if you know what I mean."

I stare wide-eyed at Greta.

"By the way, darling, how's your legal analysis coming along?"

"Fine." I am startled by the question. "My legal analysis is coming along fine."

"That's a doll."

"I guess I'll just be getting back to that then."

"Yes, run along, darling. You let me know if there is anything else I can help you with."

"Okay … I will," and I leave Greta's office.

When I get back to Julia's office, the door is unlocked. Julia is sitting at her computer typing away on some unknown project. I walk in and sit down at my end table.

"Did you have a nice lunch?" Julia asks me as if nothing has happened.

"Charming," I answer her without so much as a glance in her direction. I have no time for Julia. Instead, I flip open the laptop, hit the Power button, open Word, click Blank Document, and attack the keyboard with reckless abandon.

"The world we live in is not the safe haven that we would like it to be," I type. "Recent terrorist attacks around the globe have shown the world's most powerful countries that they need to take steps to improve their security. This analysis will show that there are obvious holes in the Immigration Codes of the United States of America and the Federal Republic of Germany, and it will attempt to explain how stricter laws that are being proposed will impact the security of both countries as well as the ordinary lives of citizens."

Legal analysis, I laugh to myself as I type. I hope Herr Bourne likes this when I hand it in in four months, because I have no idea whatsoever what I'm doing.

CHAPTER TWENTY-EIGHT

Sally Bowles

To my astonishment, the next few months pass by quickly. While I wouldn't exactly say that spring has sprung in Berlin, it is perhaps starting to yawn and open its eyes. The days are getting longer, the rain is not as chilling, and the wind is not as hostile as it was throughout the winter. I, myself, am feeling quite cheerful. Final exams are coming up, and I am hardly studying for them at all. No one is. The beauty of *HAA* is that the academic portion of the program is evaluated on a pass/fail basis, which means that if you pass, you get the credits, and the grade never shows up on your U.S. college transcript. All we need to pass are Cs. And good thing too, because the lack of any sort of expectation in Germany to show one's academic progress, the so-called "Academic Freedom," has really limited my ability to learn anything. In fact, I haven't been to class since Christmas.

Without the stress of classes or exams on my shoulders, I am free to focus on my legal analysis at work. Eventually, I learn to stop asking Greta for other tasks to do around the office after being sent several times to fetch coffeecakes for her afternoon break. On one of the days I don't ask her for something else to do, she comes knocking on Julia's and my office door.

"Hard at work, darlings, as always?" she asks, peeking her head into our space. I am working from the laptop at the table in the corner and Julia is pretending to be engrossed in whatever it is she is doing at her desk.

"Yes, as always," I say.

"Kat, darling, I want to ask you … if you don't have plans for this evening, I have more theatre tickets to give away."

"Oh? What is the play?"

"It's *Cabaret.* Have you heard of it?"

"Yes, I have. Isn't that an American musical?"

"Yes, darling, it is. It is an American musical, but it's set in Berlin. It's really very genius they way they've done it. They've translated the dialogue into German, but they sing the songs in the original English. Very historical, this play. Set in Weimar Berlin before World War II. An excellent production, darling, really. It's getting rave reviews. It's a shame I can't go myself."

"And, where is it playing?" I ask, without needing to.

"Um, at *Alexanderplatz*, darling, you know—"

"Over there," I say, pointing toward the East.

"Yes, ahem, over there."

"Well, I don't actually have any plans for this evening. But I couldn't take these tickets—"

"Don't be silly, darling, of course you can."

"—without giving Julia the chance to take them herself. What do you think, Julia, would you like to go see a free play this evening at *Alexanderplatz*?"

Julia shoots daggers at me with her eyes. "Why, that is very kind of you, Kat, but actually, I have already seen that play. You take the tickets."

"Oh, really? You saw it already? Did you like the music?"

Julia hesitates. "Yes."

"What was that main song in it? I can't remember." Julia sends another volley of visual daggers in my direction. "Surely you remember that song. Anyone that has seen the play would remember it."

Julia huffs sharply. "I saw it a long time ago."

"C'mon, even I know that song, and I haven't even seen the play. It starts, *'What good is sitting alone in your room? Come to the Cabaret,'* " I sing.

"Yes, I get it. That is the song."

"But I just can't remember how it goes from there…oh, wait, *'Life is a Cabaret, old chap! Come to the Cabaret!'*"

"*Um Gottes Willen*, I don't know the song! Just take the damn tickets." The veins in Julia's forehead look like they're about to burst.

"I think 'Cabaret,' is the name of the song."

Julia turns to her computer screen and types something furiously. She stares at the screen for a moment and then says, "The song is called *'Willkommen.'*"

"Congratulations, you can use Google."

"That's right, darlings," says Greta, looking nervously at the two of us. "*'Willkommen.'* So will you take the tickets, Kat?"

"Yes, Greta, I would love to go see a free play this evening at *Alexanderplatz*. Thank you."

"That's a doll. You'll have a lovely time … over there. It's too bad Julia has already seen it, if you know what I mean. It really is a wonderful production." Greta hands me the two tickets and walks out.

"You're missing out," I say to Julia, after Greta has left. "It's really not so bad … over there."

"I said to you, Kat Vespucci, that I have already seen the play."

"Sure you have."

Greta is not lying. It really is a wonderful production. Fritz joins me at the theatre at *Alexanderplatz* after work and we watch the play together. It is the story of Sally Bowles, renowned performer at the burlesque Kit Kat Klub in Berlin that the Nazis eventually shut down. The play has music, history, comedy, suspense, dancing, and more music. Fritz is very excited, because a family friend of his is the actress who plays Ms. Bowles. I am particularly impressed with her myself. She is large for a woman, but limber and agile. She is also a bit old for Ms. Bowles, but she delivers her performance with remarkable authority, knowing when to sing and when to scream, when to float and when to stomp, when to whimper and when to wail. She steals the show from the Emcee, and I can hardly take my eyes off her throughout the play.

When the lights come on at intermission, I take the opportunity to look up the actress in the Playbill. "Her name is Bittner!" I remark to Fritz. "Anna Bittner."

"No, it's not," Fritz corrects me.

"Yes, it is," I show him her name in the Playbill. "See, Sally Bowles played by Anna Bittner."

"That's just a stage name."

"Oh, well. Right. You know her. So what's her real name?"

"Otto."

"I'm sorry?"

"Otto."

"Otto?"

"Yes."

"Her name is Otto Bittner?"

"Yes."

"Why would her name be Otto Bittner?"

"Because her sex reassignment surgery is not yet complete. Although I'm not quite sure she wants to go all the way through with it. She's kind of in a good spot now."

"What?"

"Best of both worlds, really."

"What the heck are you talking about?"

"There are a lot of advantages to being a woman up top and

a man down below. You wouldn't think of it at first, but there really are."

"Wait a minute, Fritz, what you're saying to me is that Sally Bowles is being played by a man."

"You should try not to pigeon-hole people so much, *Schatz.*"

"A man, who has gone half-way through a sex change operation."

"You say potato, I say woman in a man's body."

"And the man's body is called Otto Bittner."

"Yes, her real name is Otto. Anna is just her stage name."

My heart starts beating faster and my stomach sinks to the floor.

"How well do you know Otto, Fritz?"

"Pretty well, I'd say. She's a friend of my parents."

"Um, do you know his family?"

"I've never met any of Otto's family. And neither has she. She grew up in an orphanage. Got into theatre at an early age. I've always just called her 'Uncle Otto.'"

"Uncle Otto." I puzzle for a moment. I don't know how to respond to Fritz at this point. I lean back in my chair and sit dumbfounded until the second act begins.

When the play gets rolling again, I ask the person next to me to borrow his binoculars. Otto is wearing a black bobbed wig and heavy stage make-up, so I can't say whether he resembles my mother or not. Focusing in, it appears that his chin and cheeks are smooth, but he definitely has an enlarged Adam's apple for a woman. Then I focus in on Otto's chest. Those are bonafide breasts under that bustier, and not just a padded bra. I can't bring myself to zoom in on Otto's crotch.

The play concludes in a loud and emotional musical number, *"Im cabaret, au cabaret, to cabaret!"* sings the cast, and the house erupts in applause.

"Do you want me to introduce you to her?" Fritz asks me as

the audience gives a standing ovation. "I can get us backstage," he shouts in my ear over the roaring applause.

"What? Why?" I stammer, still too dumbfounded to think properly about what I should do.

"You were gaping at her the whole show. I'm sure she would love to meet a fan."

The cast is taking bow after bow, and the audience is calling out Sally's name. Otto is beaming and bowing and blowing kisses at the audience.

"C'mon!" Fritz grabs my hand and leads me away from our seats toward the back of the auditorium. He leads me around a corner and down a hallway to a door that is being blocked by an attendant.

"Fritz here for Otto," Fritz says to the attendant.

"Right this way, sir," the man opens the door and lets us through.

Backstage is a flurry of activity. Actors, costumes, props, guests, and flowers are zooming in every direction. Suddenly, Otto appears from behind the curtain. He is even larger in person than he was on stage. He is wearing his can-can dress from the last scene, fishnet stockings, and black high heels, but he has removed his wig to reveal shortish, whitish hair matted down on his head. When he sees Fritz, he smiles a large lip-sticked smile and bats his long artificial lashes.

"Fritz, my sweet bee!" he says in a baritone voice that contrasts drastically with the light and wispy voice of Sally Bowles. "How wonderful to see you!"

"Uncle Otto!" says Fritz. "You were fabulous, as usual!" The two embrace and kiss each other on both cheeks.

"Oh, you flatter, bee. Don't stop!" The two explode in laughter.

"I'd like you to meet my roommate, Kat Vespucci," says Fritz, pushing me directly in front of Otto.

"Hello," I croak.

"She couldn't take her eyes off you the whole show," Fritz adds.

"The girl has taste, what can I say?" Otto bellows. He embraces me in his big arms and squeezes all of the wind out of me. I have to turn my head to avoid smashing my face into his breasts.

"Um, I enjoyed the show very much," I say after the hug, trying to gather my composure. "You are very talented."

"*Schatz,* give her your Playbill to sign," Fritz urges me.

I shakily hand Otto my Playbill. When he takes it, it dwarfs in his large hand. He writes something on it and hands it back to me.

"Well, sweet bees, you've been too good to me. Thank you for coming. I must be running along now. My public awaits. Those fools!" Otto cackles at his own joke.

"Okay," says Fritz. "I'll see you sometime at *Mutschmann's.*"

"Yes, sweet bee, looking forward to it. Nice to meet you, Kat, honey."

"Nice to meet you too, Uncle Otto." I wave good-bye to him and watch him disappear into his dressing room. I look down at my Playbill. He signed it, *Kat, Thanks for the support and compliments. Great girls think alike. —Otto*

Why didn't he sign it Anna?" I ask Fritz.

"She doesn't actually go by Anna. She just has them put that in the Playbill so as not to confuse the audience. Among her friends, she goes by Otto. It's important to her to hold onto some of her masculinity as she undergoes 'the change.'"

"Are you sure that this person is your Uncle Otto?" Pete asks me later in the evening over beers and pipes on his balcony. It's much warmer out now. During our balcony talks, our breath no longer hangs in the Berlin air, except for when Pete exhales his cigarette.

"Well, he's definitely someone's Uncle Otto. Whether he's *my* Uncle Otto or not, well, that remains to be seen. Incidentally, he's half-way to becoming Aunt Otto."

"You've got to meet him again and ask him if he has the stained-glass necklace."

"Oh my God, Pete, meet him again?"

Pete nods. "Yes, why not?"

"Because he's ... he's ..."

"He's ... what?"

"Meet him again?"

"Yes."

"Shit. You're right. Shit. I've got to meet him again."

"You met him once, and you survived. You'll do fine."

"You know, your last name is Bittner too. Maybe you're related to him."

"There are thousands of Bittners in Berlin, Kat. But even still, it would be cool to meet him. Are you going to tell your mother?"

"God, no! Let's just wait and see if he has the necklace."

"Well, sweet bee, I've had a lot of jewelry in my time, but I've never had a necklace like that!" Uncle Otto says in bass tones, squinting hard at the picture of my mother, my uncle, and my grandparents in front of the factory in Dresden. Uncle Otto, Fritz, Pete, and I are sitting around a small café table on the *Ku'damm*, sipping cappuccino and discussing family history. Uncle Otto is wearing a long, curly blonde wig, light make-up, a low-cut V-neck sweater, a tight denim skirt, and open-toed high-heels revealing red, pedicured toenails.

Sitting next to Uncle Otto, Fritz looks masculine. "*Schatz,* you should have told me earlier in the year that you were looking for your long lost Uncle Otto," he says. "I would have introduced you to her right away."

"Look at how cute I was," says Otto, holding the picture up for Fritz to see. "And look, this picture proves that I'm a natural blond!"

Pete shoots me an amused glance.

"Look at the two of you gorgeous little treasures!" Otto reaches out with both hands and pinches both Pete's and my cheeks. "My new niece and nephew, Kat and Pete." Otto is beaming. "You know I haven't any family. Did Fritz tell you? I was an orphan. And now I have such beautiful family all around me!"

"How were you orphaned?" Pete asks.

"I haven't a clue in the world, sweet bee. All I know is I was. Not a clue in the world what happened to my biological parents. I was dropped off as an infant on the church doorstep, and that's where the nuns found me. And the rest is history."

"How did the nuns know your name was Otto Bittner?" Pete asks.

"Oh, they didn't, bee. That's the name they gave me."

"Well, then it's unlikely that we're actually related."

"Actually related? Oh no, don't be silly. Of course we're not actually related. I'm not related to Fritz either, but that doesn't stop us from being family. Come here, you two little treasures." Otto stands up, reaches out his long arms, and wraps them around both Pete and me. Both of our faces press against Otto's bosom. Pete's pale cheeks turn crimson. "It's so good to finally meet you two!" Otto coos, rocking the two of us back and forth.

Chapter Twenty-nine

Herr Bourne

And with that, it is the end of the semester. Before I know it, I'm shopping with Uncle Otto for an outfit for the homecoming party that my parents have told me they are throwing for me when I get back.

"What did I do without you, Uncle Otto?" I say as the two of us browse through an underground, second-hand, thrift store, called *die Garage*, in a converted warehouse in the section of the city called *Kreuzberg*. There are no price tags in *die Garage*. You take a basket when you go in, put what you want to buy in the basket, and they weigh it when you check out. You pay for your clothes by the kilogram. Otto is a regular here.

"I don't know, sweet bee, but no one should have let you out of the country with those baggy clothes of yours." Today, Otto is wearing a sleeveless, low-cut, short, purple, spandex dress that looks like it required a shoehorn for him to get on. He's got a short, black wig on, reminiscent of his character, Sally Bowles.

"I agree that this top is very sexy," I say, while modeling a black leather tube top that he has picked out for me, "but I can hardly breathe in this!"

"You know what they say: *'Wer schön sein will muss leiden.'*"

"Are you sure suffering is a necessary part of beauty?"

"Oh, absolutely, my child. You don't think these size fourteens squeeze naturally into these pointy-toed heels, do you?"

"I suppose not."

"But they sure do make my ass look good, wouldn't you agree?" Otto leans over and points his rear end toward the mirror that we are both looking into.

"Absolutely."

Otto admires his posterior for a moment and then returns his attention to me. "That *Nichtsnutz, Arschloch, Scheisskopf* ex-boyfriend of yours is going to pop his trousers when he sees you in this top!"

"You think?"

"Not that I hope you ever run into that *Arsch mit Ohren* again! Are you sure you have to invite him to the party?"

"Ha, ha. 'Ass with ears.' I like that. He's not directly invited to the party. He'll get the invitation through his parents. I'll be surprised if he shows."

"I just can't believe him. I can't *believe* that *Vollidiot* cheated on you. And then broke up with you. And then came here. And then attacked your friend. And then, worst of all, ordered Budweiser!"

"I know. What's really hard to believe is that it took me this long to get rid of him once and for all."

"Well, better late than never, sweet bee. All I have to say is it's a good thing you and I didn't know each other when he was here, because I would have torn him a new asshole. And I don't mean that in a good way."

"Wow. Uncle Otto, yes, since you put it that way, I guess it is good that you and I didn't meet sooner."

"C'mon, sweet bee. Enough deliberating. I am buying you that tube top. And then we're getting gelato."

Come Monday, I am sitting in Herr Stern's office, having our final meeting. He hands me a letter with my exam grades and transcript. On my exams, I got straight Cs—*score!* They are the lowest grades I've ever gotten in my life. On my transcript, it says, *Bestanden.*

"These aren't really great grades, Frau Vespucci. But you passed. Congratulations!"

"Thank you, Herr Stern." He also hands me an official letter stating that I have completed all requirements of the program.

"Frau Vespucci, I want to ask you, how's your search for your family member going?"

"Why, funny you should ask, Herr Stern. Yes, in fact, I did find Otto Bittner."

"You did?" Herr Stern smacks his hands together. "How wonderful! You must be so pleased."

"Oh yes."

"How did you find him?"

"Well, it was an accident at first. But then it turns out that my German roommate, Fritz, knows him quite well, so he was able to introduce us properly."

"Imagine that! What wonderful news, Frau Vespucci. Your family back home must be so pleased!"

"Thank you, sir. Um, I haven't actually told my family back home yet. I'm still, um, getting to know Otto, so it's a little early in the relationship to introduce him to my parents."

Herr Stern crinkles his brow.

"I'm just waiting for the right time to break the news to them. Right. Well. Would you look at the time? Greta will be expecting me soon in the office."

"Well, I trust you know what's best, Frau Vespucci. However and whenever you break the news to your family back home about Otto, I'm sure they will be quite surprised."

"Quite."

Back in the office, I put the final touches on my legal analysis of the U.S. Immigration Code. After a final proofread, I save it for the last time and click print. As I watch the pages pulse out of the printer on Julia's desk, I can't help but feel proud of myself. Never before have I written something so significant, so immediate, so *long*, in German. I hope that Herr Bourne will be pleased with my efforts.

"It's amazing, Frau Vespucci!" comments Herr Bourne after taking a few minutes to read over my legal analysis. He appears to be so impressed that he can hardly speak.

"Thank you, sir," I blush.

"I can't find words to describe it," he comments, flipping through a few more pages.

"It reads as if—" he pauses, trying to find the right words.

"Yes?"

"It almost reads as if you had no idea whatsoever what you were doing."

"I beg your pardon, sir?"

"It reads as if you have absolutely no legal background at all."

"That is correct, sir."

"What is correct?"

"I have absolutely no legal background at all."

"And you call yourself a lawyer?"

"No, sir."

"Where did you get your degree from, Law School for Dummies?"

"Not even, sir. I've never been to law school."

"I mean … listen to this, *'the world we live in is not the safe haven that we would like it to be,'*" Herr Bourne reads aloud. "Where in God's name did you get that from?"

"What do you mean?"

"I mean what's your source?"

"My source?"

"Ideas don't just come out of nowhere, Frau Vespucci."

"That's my idea, sir."

"Oh, *your* idea?"

"Yes, sir."

"You're not only a lawyer now, you're also a policy analyst?"

"No, sir."

"Jumping to your own conclusions about the state of the world."

"That conclusion is based on research, sir."

"Well, now we're getting somewhere. Based on whose research?"

"On my research."

"*Your* research? Now you're trying to pass yourself off as an expert again. Really, Frau Vespucci, I'd really like to see those credentials of yours, because I had no idea we had such an authority in our midst!"

"I'm not trying to pass myself off as an expert, Herr Bourne. I was just giving you my opinion, based on—"

"Your opinion?"

"Yes, my opinion."

"I care even less for your opinion, Frau Vespucci, than I do for your so-called research."

"I'm sorry. I thought you'd want some independent thought."

"You thought! That's exactly what you're *not* supposed to do, Frau Vespucci. Didn't they teach you anything in law school?"

"No, sir, they didn't."

"What, exactly, do you expect me to do with this analysis?"

"I'm not sure I understand what you're asking me, sir. You can do whatever you want with it."

"So when Herr Kaufmann and I bring this in front of the *Bundestag* Immigration Committee next week, and they ask us why we need stronger immigration laws, am I to say, 'Well, you see, *Bundestag* Immigration Committee, recent terrorist attacks around the globe have shown the world's most powerful countries that they need to take steps to improve their security. There are obvious holes in the Immigration Codes of the United States of America and the Federal Republic of Germany, and stricter laws will greatly impact the security of both countries, not to mention the lives of citizens?'"

"Yes, more or less."

"And when they say, 'Wow, that's very profound, Herr Bourne. How do you know?' I will say, 'Frau Vespucci told me so.'"

I squint my eyes at Herr Bourne.

"'She considers herself to be an expert.'"

I am suddenly highly offended. "How am I supposed to know what you should tell the *Bundestag* Immigration Committee?" I retort.

"As my intern, Frau Vespucci, it is your job to tell me what to tell the *Bundestag* Immigration Committee!"

"I don't know who you think I am, Herr Bourne."

"Just who do you think you are, Frau Vespucci?"

"I'm just a student in your office who has spent the past four months working on a project that was way above my head, with no help from you."

"You're just a student in my office who has spent the past four months working on a piece of crap!"

My spine straightens. "I have never been treated so rudely in all of my life."

"We have no time for hurt feelings, young lady. I need you to take back this poor excuse of a legal analysis and turn it into something I can use next week in front of the *Bundestag* Immigration Committee."

I just sit there staring at Herr Bourne in disbelief.

"Quickly, Frau Vespucci," urges Herr Bourne. "We don't have a moment to lose." He holds out the paper for me to take.

"You can take this piece of crap, as you say, and shove it," I answer him. With that, I stand up to walk out of Herr Bourne's office.

"Sit back down, young lady," Herr Bourne scolds. "Or else!"

"Or else what?"

"I'll withhold your pay!"

"I've already been paid the last of my stipend," I remind him. "And I've already got the letter that says I've fulfilled all requirements of this program." I hold up the letter that Herr Stern gave me this morning.

"Then today is your last day in this office!" Herr Bourne orders, the veins popping out of his forehead.

"That is correct, sir."

"What is correct?"

There is a knock on the door.

"What is it?" Herr Bourne shouts. It is Greta.

"There you two are! Come and join us in Herr Kaufmann's office. We're having a little celebration for Kat on her last day in the office."

As Herr Bourne and I stifle our rage and go out and join the festivities, I can't help but think to myself, "I am so ready to be done."

Chapter Thirty

Kat Vespucci

The going-away party in Herr Kaufmann's office is one of many going-away parties that fill up my last week in Berlin. There is a formal wine and cheese party in the *Bundestag* reception hall where we are thanked and bade farewell by our *Bundestag* representatives; there is an informal party for the whole group at the Humboldt University student club where we are thanked and bade farewell by the *HAA* staff; and there is another pizza dinner at the XII Apostles where we students sit in our original four groups and reflect on the experiences of the past year.

"Remember last time we ate here?" Billy teases me after the waiter takes our pizza orders. "You ordered a holy beer by accident, and we all thought you were a fundamentalist Christian?"

"How could I forget?"

"They still think you're a fundamentalist Christian," Billy points to the rest of the group.

"What?" say the students who are listening to Billy.

"*Ya ne panimayu,*" says Sveta to Marek in Russian.

"I didn't understand it either," says Marek, "but Sveta, the gig is up. You speak German now. No more relying on me to translate into broken Russian."

"Hmm. I suppose you have a point. Sorry."

"And Kat, remember how you hid a map of Europe on your lap and tried to pretend like you knew where all of the countries were?" Billy prods.

"You knew about that?" my face turns red.

"You were so dumb back then," Billy cackles.

"Billy, you jerk! I wasn't dumb," I defend myself. "I was just young and naïve."

Billy is laughing. "Bet you still don't know where a lot of the countries are."

"Oh, you're gonna get it!" I threaten. I reach under the table and pinch a handful of pudge above his knee. This tickles him and he squirms under my grasp.

"Where's Lithuania?" Billy asks me, trying to swat my hand away, but I've got a good grip.

"Stop teasing me and I'll let go." I pinch him harder.

"Where's Lithuania?"

"It's in the Baltics," I answer. "Everybody knows that." I squeeze his knee as hard as I can.

Billy lets out a squeal and slaps the table repeatedly.

"Stop teasing me and I'll let go."

"Where in the Baltics? Where in the Baltics?" Billy persists through the discomfort. Tears start to spill out of the sides of his eye.

"Does this hurt or tickle?" I ask him.

"It tickles!"

I dig my fingernails into his flesh.

"Ow, now it hurts! Where in the Baltics?" he shouts.

Everybody else is staring at the two of us. I look to Odelia for help and mouth the words, "Where in Baltics?"

Odelia laughs and points downward with her index finger.

"In the south!" I answer Billy. "Lithuania is the southernmost of the Baltic countries. So there!" With that, I release his leg. Billy's rosy face has turned purple.

"Maybe you're not so dumb after all, Kat Vespucci," Billy says, wiping the tears from the corner of his eyes.

"That's right!" I answer. "Now let's see how you do with a little trivia about your own country!"

"Ask me anything."

"What's the capital of New Jersey?"

"That's easy," Billy scoffs. "Jersey City."

"*Wrong!*" I laugh in his face.

"New York City!" Pete interjects.

"What? Oh, you're gonna get it next! Anybody, anybody?" I ask around the table. "Does anybody know the capital of New Jersey?"

Milena, Marika, Irina, Sasha, and Eva nod that they do not.

"It's Trenton," says Janika.

Everybody looks at Janika.

"That's right! How on earth did you know that, Janika?"

"Well, I looked it up when I first met you. This is embarrassing to admit now, but I didn't know where, or even what, New Jersey was when we first met."

"How do you feel, Billy? Pete?" I tease. "The Estonian knows more about your country than you do."

"She's obviously never been to New Jersey, that's why. If she had, like us, she would have repressed all memory of it," Billy answers.

I seize Billy's knee under the table again, and he bursts out laughing. This is the exact moment that our pizzas arrive. In the horsing around, a waiter's arm gets bumped into a bottle of olive oil, sending it spilling over onto Iosif's lap.

"Oh!" Iosif exclaims, bringing the back of his hand passionately to his forehead. "These jeans are vintage. I just bought them at *die Garage*. I will never wear them again!"

275

"Wait! Don't worry!" I call out. Everyone looks abruptly at me. "Iosif, I can fix this."

"No, you can't Katarina Vespucci. It is hopeless. These vintage jeans are lost."

"Trust me," I say. I grab the salt shaker from the middle of the table and walk over to Iosif. I unscrew the cap and dump all of the white grains onto his lap. When I am done, he has a mini-Mont Blanc. Everyone looks at me as if I am crazy.

"Just wait, Iosif," I say, and pat him on the arm, "There is nothing to worry about." I go back to my seat and begin to eat my pizza, this time pepperoni (two *p's*). Everyone else begins to eat their pizza.

"Five euros says Iosif will never wear those vintage jeans again," says Erald, putting a five euro bill onto the table.

"Ha! I'll take that bet," I say, and put five euros of my own onto the table.

"I'll put five on Erald," says Pete.

"I'll put five on Kat," says Marek.

"Me too," says Istvan.

"Count me in for five on Erald," says Billy.

"You are all on!" I say, adding another five to the pile. After ten determined minutes, I give Iosif the cue. He stands up and brushes the salt onto the restaurant floor. Sure enough, there is no stain left. The salt has absorbed the olive oil and left his vintage jeans clean.

"Ha, ha, *ha!*" I laugh diabolically as I scoop up the money on the table and hand half of it to Marek. "This will teach you to doubt me."

Later that evening, Marek and I use our winnings to treat all of Group Four to one-euro tequila shots at Café Avalon. That's when it hits me that it is our last night in Berlin and I may never see many of these people again.

"I'm not ready to go home!" I cry into Janika's shoulder. At some point, after several shots and a *Berliner Pilsner*, I start to cry and I can't stop.

"Don't worry," Janika tries to calm me down. "You are ready to go home."

"Nooooo," I moan.

"You've got everything set at home," Janika reminds me. "You've got your job waiting for you. And your parents and friends."

"I know," I sob.

"America is waiting for you."

"What's wrong with Kat?" asks Billy.

I pick up my red, wet face, let go of Janika, and suction myself to Billy, burying my face into his soft shoulder.

"I'm going to miss you so much."

Billy laughs and pats me on the back. "I'm going to miss you too."

Pete rolls his eyes.

"What's going to happen to all of this when I go back?" I ask the group.

"What do you mean?"

"As soon as I get on that plane, this will all be just memories."

"Good memories."

"What if I forget how to speak German?"

"You won't forget how to speak German."

"What if I forget where Estonia is?"

"You won't forget where Estonia is. You can always look at that mini-map you bought."

"What if I forget about the Massacre of Mai Lai, the Bay of Pigs, or the U.S. support of the Defenders of Islam during the Cold War?"

"Lambert will remind you of all of that."

"What if I never see you guys again?"

Everyone is silent for a minute.

"We're all going to write," Irina pipes in.

"I'm making a list of everybody's names, phone numbers, and e-mail addresses," says Sveta, handing me a piece of paper and a pen so I can add my name to the list of everybody's names, phone numbers, and e-mail addresses that she is making.

"Do you guys promise to keep in touch?" I let go of Billy and take the pen and paper from Sveta.

"Of course we will."

"Yes."

"Definitely."

"We'll always be friends."

"Oh, come on!" says Pete. Everybody looks at him. "Let's be honest. We'll write each other for a few months and then we'll just move on. Some of us might send Christmas cards for a few years, but let's face it, this is definitely the last time that we'll ever all see each other."

"He's right!" I wail, and hide my face again in Billy's shoulder.

"Actually, I was just kidding," says Pete. "I didn't mean it."

"Yes, you did!" I retort.

"Okay, I did! But I'm sure we'll at least send tasteless forwards and jokes to each other for the rest of our lives. Istvan and Marek will see to that."

"It's true," says Marek. "I've already sent one about a Belgian, a hamster, and a tube of K-Y Jelly."

"You did not!" says Janika.

"Well, not yet. I thought I'd wait until I'd never see any of you again before I actually send it," explains Marek.

"I just can't believe it!" I explain, shaking my head. "I just can't believe the year is over. I can't believe that tomorrow morning we're all getting on separate planes and flying to different corners of the world!"

Again, the group is silent.

"Actually," clarifies Pete. "I'm not going anywhere."

"What do you mean, you're not going anywhere?" I ask.

"I'm not leaving."

"What do you mean, you're not leaving?"

"I mean I'm not going anywhere."

"You said that already."

"Sorry."

"Why aren't you going anywhere?"

"Because I don't want to."

"Well, neither do I," I argue, "but we have to."

"No, we don't."

"But *HAA* is over. We can't just stay here."

"Yes, we can," says Billy.

"What do you mean, we can?"

"We can stay here, if we want to. We just have to find jobs."

"What kind of jobs are you going to find?" I am incredulous.

"There's this company called Berlin Walks. They give English-speaking tours of the city. Pete and I are going down there tomorrow to interview. We think we have a pretty good chance of getting hired. If not, the Irish pubs always need English speakers."

I look at Billy and Pete. "Both of you are staying?"

"Yeah."

"Where are you going to live?"

"We're going to live with Uncle Otto until we find an apartment. She says there are a lot of cheap places in *Kreuzberg*."

"Live with Otto!"

"Yes, she offered. Why not?"

"Just like that?" I ask.

"I'm not ready to go home," explains Billy.

"I am home," explains Pete.

"What about America?" I ask.

"It's not going anywhere," Pete answers.

I feel like my brain is about to bulge out of my skull. Instead of pursuing the conversation any further, I close my eyes and take a deep breath. Then I go over to the jukebox and pick a few songs. "No more talking!" I tell the group. "Only dancing," I command as "Dancing Queen" begins to play.

We dance, take pictures of each other, and drink German

beer until Café Avalon closes at two o'clock in the morning. Dizzy and spinning, we stumble home for the last time to our *Plattenbau* on *Coppistrasse*. As we are tottering down the Private Pathway, I'm not sure, but I think I see the masturbating flasher hovering in the bushes by the entrance to the Private Pathway Tunnel.

Most of the group has safely moved on into the tunnel when he tiptoes out into the lamplight and opens his coat. I can't make out all of him, hidden among the trees, but I stop and do a double take, squinting to make sure that my eyes are not deceiving me this time. Sure enough, there he is ... the emaciated, ashen, white torso and the pink, semi-erect penis, which he pumps in his palm, causing his saggy gray testicles to oscillate betwixt his bony, translucent thighs.

This time, I don't scream and look away. Instead, I make direct eye contact with the flasher. The man is startled. He closes his coat and darts back out of sight.

"Masturbating flasher, wait!" I yell.

The group stops and turns around to look at me. I dive into the bushes after the man and seize him by his collar before he can make his getaway.

"What's going on?" I hear someone murmur.

"Where did Kat go?"

"Um ... she seems to have taken a dive into the bushes."

I pull the masturbating flasher out of the woods by his coat. I am surprised at how easy he is to push around.

"Kat, have you gone crazy?" Pete asks.

I struggle with the man until I have ripped his trench coat off of him. Then I turn him around to face the group.

"There!" I yell. "Isn't that what you want? Now everyone can see!"

The man is frozen stiff, standing there white, frail, and naked, except for his knee-high socks and blue Velcro Pumas.

"Though if I were you," I point to his pelvis, "I wouldn't show that little guy to anyone."

With that, the man blanches even whiter than before. He snatches his coat back from me and scampers down the Private Pathway in the opposite direction.

"What just happened?" asks a voice.

"Kat was talking to some naked guy."

"Did I see what I think I just saw?" responds another voice.

"I must be really drunk," reasons someone else.

"No, I think Kat just exposed the masturbating flasher," explains another voice. "He's a legend around these parts."

"I bet that's the last time he'll be poking around here."

"Let's go home," I say, and we all call it a year.

When we finally get home, I ride the elevator up to my apartment on the seventh floor, stumble down the hall to my room, trip over the luggage that I have piled in front of my bedroom door, and crash down on my bed. Before falling asleep, I grab my alarm clock to set. My plane is leaving at eight o'clock in the morning, so that means that it is only a matter of hours until I have to wake up.

Five o'clock, I figure out through the fog in my head. Phew! That's early! I fumble around with the alarm, struggling to push the right buttons. I finally get it … five o'clock, and let my head sink into my pillow.

The high sun blaring from under my curtains wakes me up the next morning. I feel surprisingly rested for having only gotten two hours of sleep. I sit up, yawn, and rub my eyes. It's surprisingly bright in my room for before sunrise. I look at my clock.

"Omigod!" I hit the alarm button and see that it is set for five o'clock in the afternoon instead of five in the morning.

"Fritz!" I scream, darting out into the hall.

"Yes, *Sleeping Beauty?*" he answers from the kitchen. He is making an omelet for lunch.

"What time is it?"

"Noon."

"My plane left at eight o'clock this morning!" I slide down into a chair at the kitchen table, my head in my hands.

"No, it didn't."

"What do you mean, no, it didn't?"

"Well, I wouldn't exactly call it your plane, since you weren't exactly on it."

I stare at him in disbelief.

"Want some eggs?" he offers.

"What am I going to do?" I look to him for advice.

He looks back at me with a blank expression. "Eggs?"

And then the unthinkable dawns on me. "Maybe this is a sign, Fritz!"

"What?"

"An omen."

"The eggs?"

"Maybe I'm not supposed to go home?"

"I think you're reading a little too far into this."

"No!" I exclaim. "No, I'm not."

"No, you are. They're just normal, ordinary eggs. Not even organic."

"Fritz! Stop it. Didn't you hear me? I'm not supposed to go home."

"You have to go home. Your room has already been assigned to the next *HAA* student."

"I'll stay somewhere else. Pete and Billy are staying with Uncle Otto."

"Oh, well, she'll definitely let you stay there if there's room. But *Schatz*, what's the rush? You can just get a later flight, that's all."

"No, Fritz! I have to stay. You know why?"

"No, I don't."

"Because there are no guarantees in life—except for this moment!"

With that, I dart into my room and put on the clothes that

I have set aside for the plane ride. In an instant I am bounding down the stairs to Pete's apartment. I knock on his door.

Pete almost falls over when he answers the door. "What the hell are you still doing here?"

"Do you think there's room for me too at Uncle Otto's?"

"What?" Pete is shocked.

"I thought I might try giving a few Berlin tours before heading home," I tell him.

Pete grins from ear to ear. He grabs me and gives me the biggest hug of my life. "Kat Vespucci, that is the coolest thing I have ever heard you say."

I give a little giggle at the unexpected embrace.

"What made you decide to stay?" he asks me.

"I don't know Pete. I can't really explain it. It's just … somehow I feel I've discovered something over here that I can't leave yet. There's this whole other world that I never knew existed."

"You just realized now that there is a whole world outside of America that you never knew existed?"

I shrug my shoulders. "Yeah."

"Interesting." Pete is grinning at me like a kid on Christmas morning. "Are you sure it's not just because New Jersey is the armpit of America?"

"You be careful, there!" I retort. "You can take the girl out of Jersey, but you can't take the Jersey out of the girl."

"By the way, did you know that New Jersey is the only state where they only charge you for tolls on the way out because they know you're never coming back?"

"Knock it off, Pete. I'll defend New Jersey till I die."

"I guess it's probably for the best you don't go home. I don't think you meet the minimum hair height requirement anymore."

"Shut up!"

"And I saw you wore out your last Bon Jovi muscle shirt."

"That's it!" I swing playfully at him.

Pete ducks under my arm and lifts me over his shoulder.

Squealing, I squirm to free myself and knock us off balance. The two of us land on the floor, Pete on his back, me straddling his stomach, pretending to perform a WWF arm bar.

"And I heard your father sold your IROC-Z."

"Now you're asking for it!" I tickle his sides.

Pete grabs me by the hips and rolls me off of him, pinning me to the floor this time. I struggle to free myself, but Pete is too heavy for me to budge. So there we are, stuck on the floor, looking at each other.

"What's Matt going to say about this?" he teases me.

"I broke up with Matt. Over e-mail. Uncle Otto made me. We haven't talked since he left Berlin. What about Jenny?"

"Oh, that ran its course. I think she's running off to Budapest with Istvan," Pete explains.

"Oh. I'm sorry."

"It's okay. What about your family?"

"You and Otto are my family," I remind Pete.

"Ewww!" he says, jumping off of me like a flea from a flea collar.

I laugh a big, hearty laugh as I sit up and smooth my hair and clothes. Pete is laughing too, but looks a little bit uncomfortable.

"Well, we still don't know for sure," I try to comfort him, giving him the benefit of the doubt. Pete shoots me a skeptical look out of the corner of his eye. "But better safe than sorry."

"Yes, exactly," he agrees. "My thoughts exactly."

"You're such a guy!"

"It's not my fault you're hot!"

"That's disgusting."

Pete shrugs his shoulders as if he can't help himself.

"Okay, you're hot too."

"That's disgusting."

CHAPTER THIRTY-ONE

Uncle Otto

The next day, I decide to go see Herr Stern to tell him that I have decided to stay in Berlin and to see if maybe he can make some suggestions on how to get a job. It's a clear and very sunny day, and as I ride the *S-Bahn* to the center of town, I notice the glare on the ball of the *Fernsehturm* in the shape of a cross. When I arrive at Herr Stern's office at the Humboldt University, he is sitting at his desk doing paperwork. Sunbeams, streaming in through his window, blind me at first and illuminate dust particles floating in the air.

"Frau Vespucci!" Herr Stern exclaims and smacks his hands together. "To what do I owe the pleasure of your visit this afternoon?"

"Well, Herr Stern—"

"Actually, young lady, shouldn't you be long gone by now?"

"Well, Herr Stern, that's what I have come to talk to you about." As I am sitting there explaining the situation to Herr

Stern, the reflection of something colorful and bright keeps hitting me in the eye, and it is distracting. I can't see what it is, but it is casting beams of red, blue, green, and yellow into my face. I squint at the bookcase behind Herr Stern's desk to see if I can make out where the reflection is coming from. Herr Stern sees where my gaze is focused and turns around himself to stare at the object.

He gives a sigh. "Pretty isn't it?" he says.

"Yes, what is it?" I ask.

Herr Stern turns around and picks up a necklace that is dangling from a little stand on one of the bookshelves.

"I put it out today to let it do its thing in the sunlight." He holds it out for me to see. It is a pewter necklace with a stained-glass pendant in the shape of a diamond. "I was wearing this necklace when the rescue worker found me in the rubble. That's what I'm told anyway. I have no idea who made it or where it came from. But it's all I have, Frau Vespucci. All I have left of my first life."

I stare in utter bewilderment at the necklace in his hands. I look up into Herr Stern's face.

"Uncle Otto," I say, and I burst into tears.

"What is it, Frau Vespucci? What's wrong?"

"Nothing's wrong," I tell him, shaking my head forcefully. Steadying myself on the arm of the chair, I reach down into my purse and take out the picture of my mother and her family before the war, wearing the same necklaces. My hands fumble as I remove the brittle picture from the yellow envelope and lay it on Herr Stern's desk.

"There's a lot more of your first life left than you ever imagined."

THE END

Made in the USA
Lexington, KY
28 December 2009